PRAISE FOR FREYA BARKER

Freya Barker writes a mean romance, I tell you! A REAL romance, with real characters and real conflict.

~*Author M. Lynne Cunning*

I've said it before and I'll say it again and again, Freya Barker is one of the BEST storytellers out there.

~*Turning Pages At MidnightBook Blog*

God, Freya Barker gets me every time I read one of her books. She's a master at creating a beautiful story that you lose yourself in the moment you start reading.

~*Britt Red Hatter Book Blog*

Freya Barker has woven a delicate balance of honest emotions and well-formed characters into a tale that is as unique as it is gripping.

~*Ginger Scott, bestselling young and new adult author and Goodreads Choice Awards finalist*

Such a truly beautiful story! The writing is gorgeous, the scenery is beautiful...

~*Author Tia Louise*

From Dust by Freya Barker is one of those special books. One of those whose plotline and characters remain with you for days after you finished it.

~*Jeri's Book Attic*

No amount of words could describe how this story made me feel, I think this is one I will remember forever, absolutely freaking awesome is not even close to how I felt about it.

~Lilian's Book Blog

Still Air was insightful, eye-opening, and I paused numerous times to think about my relationships with my own children. Anytime a book can evoke a myriad of emotions while teaching life lessons you'll continue to carry with you, it's a 5-star read.

~ Bestselling Author CP Smith

In my opinion, there is nothing better than a Freya Barker book. With her final installment in her Portland, ME series, Still Air, she does not disappoint. From start to finish I was completely captivated by Pam, Dino, and the entire Portland family.

~ Author RB Hilliard

The one thing you can always be sure of with Freya's writing is that it will pull on ALL of your emotions; it's expressive, meaningful, sarcastic, so very true to life, real, hard-hitting and heartbreaking at times and, as is the case with this series especially, the story is at points raw, painful and occasionally fugly BUT it is also sweet, hopeful, uplifting, humorous and heart-warming.

~ Book Loving Pixies

ACKNOWLEDGMENTS

As always I'm grateful to a small army of people who make it possible for me to focus on writing my stories; My agent, Stephanie Phillips of SBR Media, who is the world's best 'pimp'.

My editor, Karen Hrdlicka, and alpha reader and proofreader, Joanne Thompson; without these two amazing women my writing would be a mess!

My publicists, Debra Presley and Drue Hoffman of Buoni Amici Press; these two ladies make everything I do look good!

My amazing formatter, CP Smith; always able to turn my simple words int pieces of art.

My awesome beta team who share their welcome opinions and offer suggestions.

The fabulous blogs and early reviewers who help get the word about my books to you.

And as always you, my readers, you're my constant motivation and I'm so very grateful for each and every one of you.

Lots of love!
Freya

FREYA BARKER

PROTECTION & SECURITY

PASS

SERVICES

LIFE & LIMB

P A S S   S e r i e s

ALSO BY FREYA BARKER

STANDALONES:
WHEN HOPE ENDS

ARROW'S EDGE MC SERIES:
EDGE OF REASON
EDGE OF DARKNESS

PASS SERIES:
HIT & RUN
LIFE & LIMB

ON CALL SERIES:
BURNING FOR AUTUMN
COVERING OLLIE
TRACKING TAHLULA
ABSOLVING BLUE

ROCK POINT SERIES:
KEEPING 6
CABIN 12
HWY 550
10-CODE

Northern Lights Collection:
A CHANGE OF TIDE
A CHANGE OF VIEW
A CHANGE OF PACE

SNAPSHOT SERIES:
SHUTTER SPEED
FREEZE FRAME
IDEAL IMAGE

PORTLAND, ME, SERIES:
FROM DUST
CRUEL WATER
THROUGH FIRE
STILL AIR
LULLAY (A CHRISTMAS NOVELLA)

CEDAR TREE SERIES:
SLIM TO NONE
HUNDRED TO ONE
AGAINST ME
CLEAN LINES
UPPER HAND
LIKE ARROWS
HEAD START

Life & Limb
Copyright © 2020 Freya Barker
All rights reserved.

This book is a work of fiction and any resemblance to any person or persons, living or dead, any event, occurrence, or incident is purely coincidental. The characters and story lines are created and thought up from the author's imagination or are used fictitiously.

ISBN: 9781988733517

Cover Design: Margreet Asselbergs
Cover Image: JW Photography
Cover Models: Katy Mccain & Josh Bitterman
Editing: Karen Hrdlicka
Proofreading: Joanne Thompson
Interior Design by CP smith

LIFE&LIMB

PASS Series

CHAPTER 1

DIMAS

"Have a safe flight."

Her meticulously made-up face shows disappointment at my words. The pouty lips and batting eyelashes; childish on the thirty-something heiress I'd been assigned to for the past few weeks.

"You could still come with me," she purrs, pressing her tits against me.

Fucking hell.

I knew it had been a mistake to go there with a client—or rather, the daughter of a client—but it had been her last night in town. Not an excuse; certainly not one that will fly with my brother, who happens to be my boss as well. He wouldn't give the first shit that she'd been coming on to me for two weeks and I'd resisted her overtures, only to give in to them last night.

What can I say? She's a good-looking woman, and I'm a guy who just came off a month-long assignment in South America with a bunch of crusty archeologists wanting protection on their dig. Not much action to be had in the middle of the Amazon, amid the ruins of some ancient settlement.

I'd barely had a shower and a good night's sleep when I got back and Yanis, my brother, had me signed up for this protection detail.

Mercedes Rockton, daughter of Texas oil magnate, Bruce Rockton, had been in town preparing for an exhibit at a local gallery displaying her art. Although, to call her sculptures art requires a stretch of the imagination I do not possess. The unrecognizable blobs of clay, decorated with painted pink polka dots or purple feathers, looked more like a kindergarten craft project gone awry. Yet, last night at the opening, I heard comments like *primitive realism* and *brilliantly insightful* to describe the mess, only confirming people are nuts.

She was still on a high from what I guess was a successful evening, when I finally took her up on the reiterated invitation. Thank God I had the presence of mind to double-wrap, even though I never even took off my pants.

Still a big mistake…on so many levels. Yanis will surely rip me a new one if he finds out, which is why I'm trying not to piss her off, otherwise, she'll run to Daddy and the shit will hit the fan.

"Mercedes, like I explained last night, and again this morning, I'm flattered, but my work doesn't allow for involvement of any kind." To my great relief, the boarding call for her flight sounds over the public address system. "You should be on your way. Your detail in Dallas will be waiting for you."

Ten minutes later, I'm in my truck on the way to the office.

The company, PASS—stands for Protection And Security Services—is located in a building not too far from the Grand Junction airport, in an industrial area. When I take the turnoff to the office, I notice a ton of emergency vehicles parked outside a warehouse just up the street from us. Driving by, I spot the Mesa County coroner's van with the back doors open. That doesn't look good.

I'm not a fan of some of the local cops and I'm pretty sure the feeling is mutual. The only one in our office who has a decent relationship with them is Bree Graves, who generally functions as our liaison with law enforcement. So instead of stopping to find out what's up, I continue driving to the office to find out from her what's going on.

"Morning," Lena, our office manager, greets me from behind the front desk when I walk in. "Did you hear?"

"The police presence?" I'm sure that's what she's referring to. "I saw, but I don't know what's going on. Noticed the coroner was there, though."

"They found a body in that vacant warehouse with the for lease sign up for the past three months. That's all I know."

"More than I knew," I tell her. "Is Yanis in?"

"Should be shortly. He had an early morning

meeting with a new client."

"Thanks." I rap my knuckles on the desk and move down the hallway to the offices.

My first stop is the small kitchen to grab a much-needed coffee, before heading into the large office Bree, Jake, and I share. Radar, our tech specialist, has a separate space for all his computers and electronic gadgetry. Yanis has the other office and there's a large conference room as well. At the end of the hallway is a locker room, with showers and bathroom, and an exit to the three-bay garage at the back of the building where our surveillance vehicles are parked out of sight.

"Get the oil princess on her flight?" Jake asks when I walk in.

Jake Hutchinson is my brother from another mother and he basically grew up with us. We both enlisted at eighteen and served together on the same unit. I may have mentioned the woman's persistent pursuit.

I avoid looking at him when I respond.

"Yup, got her off okay." I wince at the unintended double entendre. Something that does not go unnoticed by Jake, who snorts.

"Tell me you didn't," Bree, sitting at her desk just down from Jake, scolds.

"Okay. I didn't." I doubt my denial will go very far, so I abruptly change the topic. "What do you know about this body found down the street? What have you heard?"

"Called in around eight this morning. Anonymously.

Cops had to wait for the property manager to get there with a key. Found him right inside the bay door."

"Him?"

"That's about as far as the information flow goes at this time, other than he was in boxer shorts and his face was pulp."

"Hookup gone wrong?"

"In an empty warehouse?" Jake comments.

"People have kinks," Bree suggests with a shrug, eliciting raised eyebrows from both Jake and me. "Well, they do," she adds defensively.

"Is that a fact?" Yanis' voice sounds behind me, and Bree's eyes fly over my shoulder, as a deep flush colors her cheeks.

I feel for her and turn to my brother. "Got a minute?"

He drags his eyes from Bree and nods at me.

"Sure, come in."

I spend the next twenty minutes debriefing my most recent assignment, not including the ten minutes of insanity just inside her hotel room last night. I have to work hard at keeping a straight face when Yanis gives me one of his penetrating stares.

"I'll need a written report by the end of the day for the client," he finally says.

"No problem."

When I get up to head back to my desk, he stops me.

"Don't forget, we're running front of the house security for the Gavin Jenkins' concert at the amphitheater tonight. We're all on the hook for this one."

Only a few times a year, big name stars drop into Grand Junction for a show or concert, but when it happens, regular venue security is usually not sufficient, so we're called in. It's no one's favorite assignment, but it's been a nice sideline that pays well and has kept us afloat in years when things were tight. They no longer are, not since landing a major account with a film production company last year put us firmly on the map. Problem is, we're just about the only game in town with enough manpower to handle jobs like this, even if we need to call in every operative on file.

Over the day, Bree was able to gather odds and ends of information. By the time we were getting ready to head out to the amphitheater, we'd learned the dead guy had been in his thirties or forties, and had received a solid beating. No clothes or other identifying items were found, oddly enough, so it would depend on the post mortem and forensics to get some clarity there. In the meantime, we had a uniformed officer show up asking if any of us had seen anything, which none of us had.

"I've gotta stop at the shelter and give Rosie her backstage passes."

"Rosie likes country?"

I'm surprised; she doesn't look like a country girl to me. Rosie, Jake's wife, is four months pregnant. A feisty redhead, she's always struck me as more of a classic rock chick.

Jake turns to me with an eyebrow raised. "Rosie doesn't like country, per se," he grumbles. "Rosie likes fucking Gavin Jenkins."

I don't even try holding back the chuckle. My friend has been royally fucked since Rosie came into his life. Ruthless operative turned hopeless pussy when it comes to his sweetheart of a woman. It's been fun torturing him this past year or so, but I have to admit, with the news a couple of months ago he and his wife are expecting, I felt a pang of envy.

Rosie's already waiting outside when we pull into the parking lot of the shelter. Beside her a woman I haven't seen before.

A fucking Amazon. Tall—at least taller than Rosie, which really isn't saying much—built like the proverbial brick shithouse, with long sleek dark hair. She looks like *Xena: Warrior Princess*.

"Who is—" I don't even get a chance to finish my question before Jake snaps.

"Willa, and she's Rosie's new friend and employee, so don't even fucking go there."

I immediately raise my hands defensively.

"Just looking. No touching."

Willa

I about shit my pants when Rosie said she'd be able to get us backstage passes.

I fucking love Gavin Jenkins, and not just in an abstract, platonic kind of way. Hell no, I could climb that man like the tree he is.

When Rosie's husband drives up with the highly anticipated passes, I'm about to jump out of my skin. Jake gets out of the SUV and my eyes are focused on his hand holding an envelope, which is why I initially miss the second man getting out on the other side.

Jake plants a hot one on his wife, something I'm learning he does every chance he gets, when I hear a deep voice behind him.

"Don't hold back on our account."

I look up, and up, to meet a pair of green, amused eyes. The man has to be at least six three, towering easily over the rest of us. Talk about a tree, he's built like one. A gorgeous one. Dirty blond hair and slightly russet beard, with a bright, open smile aimed at me.

Christ have mercy. Look at those damn shoulders.

Gavin Jenkins forgotten for the moment, I focus on the size of the hand he holds out.

"Dimas Mazur, I work with Jake."

Damn, even his name is sexy as all get out. It takes me a second but I finally shake his hand, mumbling my name.

"Wilhelmina Smith."

"Dimi," Jake growls a warning I don't understand.

With a little squeeze of my hand he's still holding in his, he let's go with a rumbled chuckle that sounds really good.

"Hey, Rosie, looking radiant as always."

"Dimi." She grins at him like the two are sharing a private joke, which doesn't seem to make Jake any happier.

"We've gotta go," Jake announces curtly before turning to Rosie with a softer tone. "Drive to the back parking lot. One of us is going to be at the stage entrance. We'll let you in from there. I don't want you to deal with crowds in your condition."

"Jake, I'll be fine," she protests.

"You will," he returns. "Since you'll be going in through the stage entrance."

I smile. You'd think I'd be annoyed at the blatant me-Tarzan-you-Jane display, but one look at Jake and everyone can see the man adores his wife. Can't say I've ever been on the receiving end of such devotion, but from the soft look on Rosie's face, I can imagine what it might feel like.

Glancing away when they kiss—again—I catch Dimas grinning at me.

"You get used to it," he assures me and I snort.

This place is crazy.

As instructed, we came in the stage entrance where a woman wearing the same 'security' shirt Jake and his buddy had on, let us through.

The seats are great, right up front, close enough for Rosie to catch a sweaty bandana Gavin flings into the audience toward the end of the show. I snicker when she can't stop saying, "Oh my gosh," for the remainder of the concert.

I'm pretty sure I'm deaf by the time the screaming

dims a little and the same woman who let us in—
Rosie calls her Bree—comes to get us from our seats
to take us backstage.

There's a crowd in the hallway outside the dressing
rooms. Mostly women dressed in a shitload less than
Rosie and I are wearing, which is basically jeans and
a shirt. I've never been one to play dress-up, and I've
learned Rosie isn't either.

My idea of dressing up is wearing a pair of black
or dark-wash jeans with boots and a top a few steps
up from a T-shirt. I rarely wear jewelry or makeup. I
did when I was a teen and back in college, but since
enlisting at twenty-four—right after receiving my
master's degree in social work—I haven't bothered.

Most of my eight years, spent as a clinical social
worker in the armed forces, I was stationed in
Germany at Landstuhl Regional Medical Center.
There was little time to fuss over appearance even if I
cared, and I didn't. Never picked it up again, not even
when I got back Stateside five years ago.

People can take me as I am or don't let the door hit
them in the ass on the way out. That wasn't always
easy working at the VA hospital in town, where office-
appropriate attire was required, which is why one of
the things that makes working at the South Avenue
Shelter so great is the casual atmosphere. Much more
my speed.

I got the job two months ago, when the shelter
officially opened its doors, and haven't looked back.
The place is great, the facilities are amazing, I work

with really nice people, and my boss is awesome. In the very short time I've been here, Rosie has become a good friend.

I hear her little squeal when we're finally guided into the dressing room, where a very sweaty, and mostly annoyed looking Gavin Jenkins is doling out signatures on everything, including a couple of boobs and an ass. There are some things you can't unsee, no matter how hard you try.

Up close the star is fast losing some of his shine, and I find myself more interested in the man standing behind him. His arms crossed over his impressive chest, Dimas Mazur keeps a close eye on overenthusiastic fans who can't keep their hands to themselves.

His face is stern, but when he spots me, he breaks out in a big smile, throwing me a jaunty wink.

I almost forget to have Gavin Jenkins sign my backstage pass.

CHAPTER 2

WILLA

"*L*OOKING A BIT rough."

I look up from my desk to see Ron Midwood hanging against my doorway. Ron is the shelter's intake coordinator. A nice guy, probably a few years younger than my thirty-nine, but not by a whole lot. He asked me out a couple of times and I've declined. Mostly because I'm not interested in anything other than maybe someone to warm my bed on occasion, and it doesn't seem like a smart idea to have that someone be a guy you work with every day.

"I know. My ears are still ringing from that concert Rosie and I went to two days ago, and I haven't been able to sleep properly."

"Don't look at me for sympathy; anyone volunteering to listen to Gavin Jenkins for an entire evening deserves whatever's coming to them."

I grin. Ron is pretty outspoken, one of the things I really like about him.

"Whatever. I went to support Rosie," I lie. I totally

went to ogle the guy, even if I don't much care for his music, but instead of lying awake these past nights fantasizing about the country singer, it was the security guy who turned out to be front and center in my imagination.

"Sure you did," he agrees teasingly, before approaching and dropping a file on my desk. "New customer. Dave Williams, fifty-two, history of alcohol abuse, and has been on the street for approximately three years. He's a vet. Did several tours in Afghanistan. Got hurt his last round and lost vision in one eye."

"Other than that, any known diagnoses?"

"Not according to him."

It's sad, yet we see it so often. Strong people dedicating their life to fighting on the front lines for their country, only to return home and find so much of themselves was left on the battlefield. They have trouble adjusting to civilian life, often too proud to look for help, resorting to alternate ways of coping, and so many of them end up disenfranchised.

"Where is he?"

"Having breakfast in the dining room while we get a bed ready."

I follow Ron to the common dining room where only a few breakfast stragglers are left. He points out the large man sitting at a table by himself, shoveling down a plate piled high with food. I pour myself a coffee—which is made fresh every couple of hours— say good morning to Brad Carey, one of our residents who has volunteered to help in the kitchen, and head over to the solitary man.

His head comes up when I approach and a familiar suspicious look slips over his face. I get this look often.

"Mind if I sit?" I ask while already sitting down. "You good for coffee?" He nods but doesn't take his eyes off me. "I thought I'd come say hello. My name is Willa and I'm the social worker here at the South Avenue Shelter. You're Dave, right?"

He grunts what I assume is affirmatively to his name, but then immediately narrows his bloodshot eyes.

"Don't need no shrink."

His voice sounds growly like Henry Cavill's in this new Netflix series I've gotten hooked on. Unfortunately, Dave isn't exactly blessed with Henry's looks. His nose looks like it's been broken, more than a few times, has mushroomed out of proportion, and has an almost blue hue. I'm sure the alcohol abuse hasn't helped. Dirt is crusted in the strained wrinkles on his face, making him look much older than his years.

"Good thing I'm not a shrink then," I counter with an easy smile. "Think of me as part of the welcoming committee. I try to make new residents welcome. I know Ron has likely already told you about what we can offer you here and what the rules are, so I won't bother with those. What I'd like to add is my office is right down that hall, third door on the right, and unless I'm already in with someone, it's always open." I pull a laminated card out of my pocket and slide it across the table. It's an emergency card I hand out to all new residents. It lists my name, and a direct line to my office. If I don't answer after three rings, the call is automatically forwarded to my cell phone. I ended up getting them laminated because people are more likely to hold on to them that way. "That's my direct line. No one else picks it up or has access to the voicemail. You don't have to come to me—or call— but I hope if you find yourself needing a listening ear, or facing a crisis, you'll use that number or walk through my door."

He pulls the card toward him with a dirty finger, studying it closely before his eyes come back to mine. A slight nod is all the answer I get, but I don't really expect more than that. A lot of these guys have learned not to trust. Such is life on the streets.

"Now, as I know Ron told you, we expect residents to attend one group meeting a week," I tell him as I stand up. "We have three a week: Monday, Wednesday, and Friday at noon. What he probably failed to mention is I bring a couple of dozen donuts from Home Style Bakery for every meeting." That earns me a sardonic raised eyebrow and I shrug. "What can I say? Food is a great motivator." I indicate his eggs. "Well, I'll let you get back to breakfast. Hope to see you around."

With a wave at Brad, I head back to my office, but my ass has barely sat down when a police officer walks in.

"Ms. Smith?"

"That would be me."

Behind him I spot Rosie mouthing, "*I'm sorry,*" from the hallway.

"Can I come in?" he asks with feigned politeness, since he's already inside and closing the door on my boss.

"By all means. Have a seat." I indicate a chair on the other side of my desk. "What can I do for you? Officer…?"

"Officer Bergland," he clips, as if it pains him to share that information.

"Ms. Smith, I have a few questions around an investigation the police are conducting."

"Okay. Depending on what it's about, I'll do my best to answer what I can."

I'm purposely putting that out there, right off the bat. In my profession, we deal with privileged information we are not obliged to share unless consented to by the patient. I'm sure Officer Bergland is well aware of this fact, but still seems annoyed at my statement.

Too fucking bad.

"Are you familiar with one Arthur Hicks?"

"Art? Yes, he's a resident here."

"Resident? Doesn't that imply he lives here?"

I'm getting a little annoyed with the cop's arrogant tone. I'm sure Rosie already informed him Art lives here. I lean forward with my elbows on my desk.

"I'm not implying anything, I'm stating a fact. Art

Hicks is a resident at South Avenue. Why is it you are asking about Art?"

He ignores my question and asks another of me instead.

"Isn't it true, Arthur Hicks has not been seen at the shelter in the past three days?"

I'm trying to remember if I've bumped into him over the past few days, but I don't think I have. In fact, I don't think I've seen him since the group meeting on Monday. Not that it's unusual, often times the guys go out and do their thing during the day, only to return at night. We have a curfew set at eleven, which basically means the doors are locked and whoever is not inside loses out.

The objective is to try to reintegrate these people into a regular life, but only if they choose it. This isn't a prison where we are accountable for every moment of a resident's time.

"Not sure. I know the last time I saw him personally was Monday. I don't know if he was here or not."

"According to the sign-in sheets Ms. Hutchinson showed me, he didn't sleep here after Monday night."

"First of all, it's *Mrs.* Hutchinson," I snap, annoyed. "And if you already knew Art wasn't here, why bother asking me?"

I'm pretty sure I'm not making any friends, but I don't give a flying fuck. This cop is being an ass.

"Do you have any reason to be uncooperative, Ms. Smith?"

"How the hell can I be uncooperative when

you haven't even told me what this is all about?" Frustrated, I find myself raising my voice. I'm sure I can easily be heard from the hallway.

"Two days ago, a body was found with obvious signs of a severe beating. We were able to identify him by fingerprints we had on record for Arthur Hicks."

I gasp. "Art? Oh my God...he's dead?"

Immediately following the shock, my eyes burn with unshed tears. No fucking way in hell am I going to spill even one in front of this asswipe. It's not the first time I've lost a patient, and I'm sure it won't be the last, but Art was one of the young guys, not even forty, and he'd been doing so well. Seemed optimistic about a new job he'd found, had hopes he'd be able to afford renting his own place soon.

"Beaten to death, yes," Bergland confirms. "And it was a card with your name on it, our officers found outside the warehouse where the body was found, that led me here."

"Warehouse?" I'm still trying to compute Art is dead.

"Near the airport."

"Airport? That's on the north side of town, how would he even get there?"

"Since your card was there, we were hoping you could tell us."

I shake my head. "I don't know anything about a warehouse. I hand out those cards to every new resident, whether they stay a night or longer. I gave one to Art as well."

"Ms. Smith, did Arthur mention anything to you? Did he ever mention to you what or who he might be involved with?"

I push back my chair and stand, my hands resting on my desk.

"As I'm sure you're well aware, Officer Bergland, anything Art may or may not have shared with me falls under privileged information."

The officer stands as well, an angry flush on his face.

"The man is dead. It's your choice if you don't want to share, it's mine to bring you in for questioning."

The door behind him swings open and Jake comes in, followed on the heels by the subject of my fantasies.

"You don't have to say another word," Jake barks, and I snap right back.

"It's not like I was going to!"

DIMAS

I look at my boots to hide my grin.

Damn, the woman is magnificent. Those dark eyes flashing like hot glowing coal.

The fifteen-minute drive from the office to the shelter had taken us ten minutes with an irate Jake behind the wheel.

Rosie called Jake the moment Officer Bergland showed up and asked to see her. She'd dealt with the officer last year when she'd been witness to a hit-and-run, and the experience hadn't exactly been a good one. So while she had him wait outside her office, she immediately got on the phone with Jake. All he had to do was say there was trouble at the shelter, and I hustled outside after him.

Rosie had been waiting in the lobby and in a few words filled us in with what she knew, which hadn't been much.

"I'm investigating a homicide," Bergland explains. "Ms. Smith may have information."

"What I just managed to hear from the hallway was you threatening Ms. Smith with a trip to the station, even after she explained the rules of privileged information. Something I'm sure you were already well aware of."

Jake folds his arms over his chest and I take over.

"Badgering seems to be your method of choice, isn't it, Officer Bergland?"

The cop's eyes flit back and forth between us, and wisely deciding he wasn't getting anywhere, he tries to move to the door. Except, I'm in the way.

"I will see you again," he shoots over his shoulder at Willa.

"I can hardly wait," she sneers back at him, not in the slightest intimidated.

Magnificent.

Even as I'm grinning at her, I step aside to let the weasel pass.

"What was that all about?"

Rosie squeezes in beside me and immediately

moves to her friend's side.

"He didn't tell you?"

"Only that he was working on an investigation."

"They found Art dead," she says, emotion coloring her voice.

"Our Art? What? How?"

"All he said was he was found in a warehouse, badly beaten, and they had to identify him by his fingerprints." Rosie gasps softly, and I share a look with Jake. That's the body they found down the street from the office. "Apparently they found my card nearby."

"Your card?" I ask Willa, but Rosie answers for her.

"Willa hands a laminated card to all of our residents. So they can call her if they need someone to listen."

"With your phone number?"

I may have been a little loud with my question, but it's better than the, *"What the hell were you thinking?"* that had been on the tip of my tongue.

"How else are they going to get hold of me if not with my phone number?" she asks sarcastically.

"Please tell me not your personal number?"

She narrows her eyes at me. "I'm not an idiot. I have a separate office line that gets rerouted to my cell after-hours."

"So everyone who comes in here gets a card?" Jake wants to know and successfully draws the woman's attention.

"Everyone," she confirms. "A lot of these guys

struggle but think it looks weak if they ask for help. I want to give them a more anonymous way to talk. A large percentage of our residents are veterans who have seen and experienced more than their share of the lack of humanity. Sometimes it helps to talk to someone who understands with the safety of a phone line between." My snort slips out and her eyes sharply turn on me. "I don't see what's funny."

"Someone who understands?" I ask angrily.

It's a sore point with me, health professionals claiming to know how we feel, what it's like, what we've dealt with over there, but they don't have a fucking clue. Pretty placating words and pats on the head don't do shit to erase the memories of waking up in a sweat in the middle of the night, too scared to take a fucking piss because we can't remember where we are. Or dreading the fucking Fourth of July because with every goddamn firework that goes off, we have to resist hitting the ground when our brain instinctively sends out those signals on hearing a loud bang. Or the flashes of your brothers who'd never come home, blown apart and bleeding all over the goddamn eternal sand. Or your own leg, nothing but a ragged, bloody stump, and someone collecting your foot from the other side of the road before laying it on your chest for transportation. Then spending hours staring at the bottom of your own fucking boot.

Like some fucking diploma gives you an understanding of any of that.

"Dimi," Rosie tries to intervene, but Willa holds

up her hand.

"Yes, I understand some. I'm a veteran myself."

I admit, that takes me aback, and you can call me a sexist pig because I probably am.

"Combat?"

"No," she admits, and I'm about to blow her off when she adds, "but I spent eight years at Landstuhl and whatever was left to pick up from the battlefields came to us to put back together, both physically and mentally. So I've seen my share."

I nod and look down at my boots. She may not feel the need to duck at every exhaust backfiring, but I have no doubt watching torn up bodies come in day after day after day, for eight fucking years, gives you some right to speak to understanding.

"Sorry," I mumble, lifting my eyes to her. There really isn't anything else to say, I jumped to conclusions that were wrong.

"Not to worry," she says with more grace than I would've mustered. "You're not the only one." Then she throws me for a curve when she tilts her head. "Where were you deployed?"

"Iraq."

"How many tours?"

"Two."

Then she blows me away when she asks, pointing at my leg, "Bomb? Grenade?"

"IED."

CHAPTER 3

WILLA

"MOM IS SO stupid."

I glance at my sniffling niece, Brittany, sitting in the passenger seat beside me.

I just whisked her out of my parents' house where she and her mom, my sister, Connie, had been about to launch WWIII over my mother's birthday cake. My mother, who doesn't do well with confrontation on the best of days, had already been near tears when I broke up the mother-daughter war about the purple hair my niece was sporting. Something she apparently managed to do at a sleepover with a friend last night.

We're celebrating Mom's sixty-seventh birthday today, which in our family means that my father— retired army colonel—and my brother in law, Jim— also career military—are out on the Devil's Thumb Golf Course for their first round of the season, while the women stay at home.

Mom and Dad live in Delta, about forty-five minutes from Grand Junction, and my sister and her family are about half an hour the other way in Montrose. Getting together with the whole family is always stressful since we all seem to be from different planets, other than making an occasional appearance for a birthday or holiday. I see Mom more often since I take her to most of her doctors' appointments. Especially during the spring and summer months, when Dad is too busy playing golf with his buddies.

"You're twelve, kiddo," I remind her gently. "I know you don't like hearing it, but since you're going to be stuck with your parents for at least another six years, you're going to have to deal."

"You like my hair, though, right, Willa?"

I glance again, and smile at her.

"It looks good on you, but..." I quickly add with emphasis. "That doesn't negate the fact you apparently went ahead with the purple dye, even after your mother apparently told you not to. That's not smart."

"But she's so stuffy, she doesn't even know what looks good. Last week, she came to school to help with pizza lunch wearing a pencil skirt and high heels. Who does that?"

I have to bite back a grin at my niece's consternation. Britt's not lying; my sister is stuffy. Just like my mother, Connie has morphed into this picture-perfect housewife, who wouldn't dare leave the house without makeup or a fully coordinated outfit. Very much my opposite. I'm the odd duck in the family. Turns out, maybe my niece is too.

"Be that as it may, Britt, but going against something your parents explicitly forbade you to do isn't going to fly without consequences. You're smart enough to know that."

"Dad doesn't care."

The softly uttered comment says more about the sudden purple hair than anything else does.

Jim, her father, is very similar to my dad. Focused on a career that takes him from home long stretches of time, and when he *is* home he barely pays attention to Britt. Heck, Connie had her in ballet for years, and not once had he made an appearance at one of the recitals. That had been the battle over Christmas, when Britt announced she didn't want to dance anymore.

Poor kid just wants to be seen.

"I don't envy you, sweetheart," I tell her, grabbing onto one of her hands. "Twelve is a hard age. Everything around you changes so quickly, and you wanna jump ahead to catch up with everyone. I was the same way. Your grandma used to tell me I was too big for the napkin and too small for the tablecloth."

"What does that even mean?"

I chuckle. "I'm not really sure, but I suspect it's one of those Dutch sayings from her childhood she remembers. Something about no longer really being a child, but not a grown-up yet either." I don't have to see her to know she's rolling her eyes. "Look, all I can tell you is your parents love you and want the best for you. Sometimes it's a safety issue and then it's up to you to trust them. Sometimes it's about you becoming your own person, and then you're gonna need to show them they can trust you to do that responsibly. Dyeing your hair purple may not have been the way to do that."

"Now you're talking like an adult," she pouts, clearly not intending that as a compliment. It still makes me laugh.

"Because I am, smartass." I spot the Sonic drive-thru. "Wanna go grab a milkshake before we head back?"

"Yeah."

She smiles like any twelve-year kid would at the promise of a milkshake, even if her hair is purple.

By the time we get back, Dad and Jim are watching a game on TV, each holding a tumbler of Dad's good scotch, while Mom and Connie are in the kitchen getting dinner ready. Being that I never was one to conform to tradition, I walk over to the wet bar, pour myself a snifter of Dad's Laphroaig, and sit down on the couch next to Jim.

"So, how are the Rockies looking?"

A displeased grunt from my father and a raised eyebrow from my brother-in-law are the only responses I get, not that I expected anything else.

My small act of defiance gets boring, after about five minutes, so I take my glass and head for the kitchen to see if I can lend a hand.

"Wilhelmina…" Mom says in a scolding tone when she sees the tumbler in my hand. "That's your father's favorite scotch."

I open my mouth to make a smart remark when the phone in my pocket starts buzzing. A quick glance at the screen shows Brad Carey as the caller.

"Hey, Brad. What's up?"

I try to keep my voice even, despite the immediate concern I feel.

I've known Brad since last year, when he came into the VA hospital I worked at with a badly infected stump. His right leg was missing from mid-thigh and his prosthesis hadn't been properly fitted.

At the time he'd been living on the street and, as per standard procedure, I was sent in to do a welfare check. We'd seen each other a couple of times since, mostly in passing, until I started at the shelter and found him signing in as one of our first residents.

He's a quiet man, friendly enough, and comes to the group meetings once a week, but he has never shown or spoken about how he ended up on the streets in the first place. He seemed oddly together and therefore out of place, which is why him calling me now has my hair stand on end.

"Need you to do something for me," he says in an almost whisper. "Need you to get in touch with a friend of mine, Dimas Mazur. Only him. Tell him this was not me."

"Sorry?" I was briefly distracted by the name he mentions. "What was not you?"

"Just tell him I need a lawyer," he hisses, before I hear a crash, and then dead air.

Five minutes later I'm in my RAV on my way back

to Grand Junction.

My family had not been pleased. My father, as usual, vocal with his opinion about my patients, who he likes to describe as a bunch of women, implying that somehow makes them weak. Not only insulting my patients but my gender as well, although the latter no longer surprises me.

I ignored him and my brother-in-law, kissed my mother and promised to call her later, ruffled my niece's purple hair with a wink meant just for her, before walking out with a, "later, Sis," for Connie.

I try the shelter number for the third time, but it keeps bumping me to voicemail. I keep trying the number, as well as Rosie's cell, with no results.

A long forty-five minutes later, I pull into the parking lot behind the shelter. We have two supervisors on the weekend and one of them is pacing the hallway on the phone.

"Marcus, what's going on?"

"I can't get hold of Rosie."

"Me neither, she usually visits her mother on the weekends, maybe she left her phone in the car." Wouldn't be the first time. Pregnancy is messing with her mind. "What is going on? I got a call from Brad, and—"

"Cops picked him up," Marcus interrupts. "Brad. They took him out of here in handcuffs. Jason followed them to the police station, but he's not getting any information from them."

"Okay, call Jason, tell him to hang around at the

station until he hears from me. I'm gonna try to sort this out."

Rosie's office, like Ron's and mine, is always locked during the night and on the weekends. We have confidential files that no one but us should have access to. I open Rosie's door and go straight for the planner on her desk where she keeps all her contacts.

It takes me less than a minute to find an entry for 'Dimi.'

DIMAS

My phone rings just as I put down my camera on the passenger seat after taking a damning picture that will prove what our client already suspected; his business partner is secretly meeting with the competition.

Not quite as distasteful as trying to catch a cheating spouse, but definitely equally boring.

I don't recognize the number on my screen.

"Hello."

"Dimas?"

"Speaking."

"This is Willa Smith. I work with Rosie at the—"

"Know who you are, Willa," I interrupt her.

I lean back against the headrest with a pleased grin on my face. My day just got a whole lot more interesting.

"Right. About an hour ago, Brad Carey, one of our residents, called to ask me to contact you. This was right before he was taken away in handcuffs by police."

"He what?" I shoot up straight in my seat, hitting my fucking head on the ceiling of the damn inconspicuous Corolla we keep for stakeouts.

"Was taken in handcuffs by police," she repeats. "Look, I'm on my way—"

"He called you an hour ago and you're just calling me now?" I'm already starting the car and pulling away from the curb outside the restaurant.

"Yes, well I—"

"Where are you now?" I bark, furious she waited so long to contact him.

Shit, Brad isn't going to do well confined. Not after spending five months in a six-by-six cell in a bunker in the hills outside of Fallujah, Iraq, courtesy of a group of militant insurgents.

"On my way to the police station," she snaps, clearly irritated.

"Don't move. I'm on my way." With that I hang up the phone and immediately dial the office where Radar answers.

"Bored already?"

"Get Hank Fredericks on the line. Get him to meet me at the GJPD immediately. Tell him it's for a brother."

Hank Fredericks owns the largest law firm in town and is on retainer with PASS Security. He's also a fellow vet.

"On it," Radar clips, hearing the urgency in my tone.

The rest of my short drive I spend hoping Brad was able to keep it together without freaking. One of the reasons he ended up on the street is because he couldn't hack living in the only places his measly VA disability could afford. I'd offered help, but his pride prevented him from accepting any.

When Rosie opened the shelter a few months ago, I carefully suggested he go talk to her, which he ended up doing, but he would only accept a bed if she let him work it off in the kitchen. He's been the resident cook ever since.

When I pull into the station's parking lot, I see her standing on the step right outside the door. The long, almost black, hair easily recognizable. I can tell when she spots me, her eyes immediately narrow.

"Where is he?" I immediately ask, walking up to her.

"They're holding him in a room for questioning. That's all they'll tell me."

"What exactly did he say to you?"

"He told me to get in touch with you, and only you. He said to tell you it wasn't him and that he needs a lawyer. That's when the line went dead." I'm already walking up to the door when she continues behind me, "For your information, I was at my parents' in Delta and I couldn't get a hold of anyone at the shelter. I even—"

I stop with the door in my hand and turn to face her.

"Go home, Willa."

"He's my responsibility," she says stubbornly.

"Go home," I repeat. "He's my brother. I've got this."

She folds her arms over her chest with a stubborn lift of her chin.

"Please," I force from my lips. "I'll call you later. I promise."

I fucking know how Brad is, and until I have a chance to see for myself he's not curled in a ball drooling on himself, or head-butting anyone who gets too close to him because his demons won this round, I don't want to expose him any more than necessary. His nightmares are his own to share. He'd do the same for me.

"I'll give you my—"

"Saved your number when you called, darlin'," I cut in.

"Is it too much to ask to let me finish one fucking sentence?" she spits, before she turns on her heel and rushes down the stairs, mumbling, "Fucking men."

Hank shows up ten minutes later, and where I was not successful either, he is. After throwing some legal shit at the cop who comes out to speak to him, the tune changes and he's let in to see his client.

An hour and a half later, I'm driving Brad back to the shelter at his request. He said he had dinner to cook, looking none the worse for wear. Thank fuck.

I walk in with him to see if perhaps Willa is there, but I encounter Rosie instead.

"What are you doing here?"

"Radar called Jake, Jake called me, I called Willa, except she already knew. She was here trying to put a meal together for the guys, which meant I had to rush in to spare them that torture." Rosie leans closer. "She tried once before and we almost had a mutiny on our hands."

I spend a few minutes sharing what I know, when I remember I promised to call Willa.

"Do you have her address?"

"Who? Willa?" I recognize the glint in Rosie's eyes, but even without it would be hard to miss the shit-eating grin on her face. "You didn't exactly leave a good impression, Dimi."

"I know."

"Twice in a row."

I sigh deeply. "I fucking know, all right? Just tell me where she lives, so I can do my groveling in person."

She grabs a pen off her desk and scribbles something on a piece of paper before handing it to me. As I'm walking away, she calls after me.

"I like her, Dimi, if you chase her off I'm gonna be pissed."

I wave my hand over my shoulder, but apparently she's not done yet.

"As far as I know, she's single!"

CHAPTER 4

WILLA

OKAY, SO IT'S entirely possible I overreacted a bit.

In hindsight, I get why he's pissed, I probably would be too. I should've found a way to get a hold of him before I hit the road back to Grand Junction, but I'm a doer, not a delegator. Not an excuse, I know. For someone who is supposed to know how to communicate with people, I seem destined to tick this man off.

I stopped in at the shelter to make sure there'd be something to eat for the residents, but Rosie came in shortly after and told me to go home. It's impossible to relax, though. Worry over what was happening to Brad had me restless, so I cleaned. Not that there's much to clean in my place, I don't have much of a life outside of my work, so I tend to keep up with things. I guess it's the one thing my parents instilled in me that took hold: structure.

I have a couple of friends—or rather, glorified

former colleagues—I still see on occasion, and I've become close with Rosie, but mostly I stick to myself. Not that I'm averse to connecting with people, I'm emotionally invested in everyone I deal with at the shelter, I just prefer keeping my private life more simple. On occasion, I'll meet someone I'm attracted to, but I'm always clear from the start I'm not looking for anything beyond the physical.

Growing up in a family where gender roles are still so clearly divided, I don't particularly have faith any long-term relationship I get involved in wouldn't at some point put those boundaries on me. So I don't cook, I don't dress to impress, I swear when I feel like it, and I don't make apologies for being forward. There are guys who appreciate that, but inevitably at some point, the shine of independence wears off and expectations find their way in.

Maybe it's just I haven't met the right guys, although Lord knows I've put in the effort.

I strip my bed and wash my sheets for the second time this week, when I run out of things to do. Other people might bake or can or some such thing when restless, but that requires skills I don't have, so laundry it is.

I've just cracked a beer to settle my nerves, and am switching the load from washer to dryer, when someone knocks at my door.

I bought my house four years ago when I got tired of listening to my neighbors in the apartment complex. A cute, single-level, detached, two-bedroom house—

with a view of the Colorado River from the front windows—since I have no neighbors across the street. It had been a bit run-down but came at a manageable price, so I was able to have some upgrades done two years ago to suit my needs.

In all my years here, no one unexpected has ever knocked on my door. No neighbors, no surprise visitors, not even Jehovah's Witnesses out to gather souls. Which is why it takes me a minute to get moving to the front door. I sneak a peek through the frosted side panel.

Don't ask me how I recognize the man standing on my step, because not much more than a vague outline is visible, but it's enough to have me unlock and open my door.

"Hey," Dimas says, and I'm struck again by how far up I have to look to find his eyes. I'm not short, but this man is *tall*.

"Hey," I echo. "What are you doing here?"

"I promised to update you. Do you mind if I come in?"

Instead of answering, I step aside. I watch him stop in the middle of my living room and scan my open concept space as I close the door. Seeing him in my space is doing weird things to my insides. I feel… exposed. In a much too enticing way.

"Are you gonna stand over there?" he asks, a slight twitch lifting his mouth, and I come unglued from my spot.

"No, of course not," I rush to say, as I dart past him

to the kitchen, putting the island between us like some safety barrier. "So what's happening?"

He wanders over and casually pulls out a stool, taking a seat like he's planning to stay a while.

"I just dropped Brad back off at the shelter."

I press my hand against my chest and blow out a breath.

"Thank God for that. What did they want with him?"

"Well…" he starts, but I quickly interrupt.

"Wait, do you want a beer? I just cracked one myself."

"Sure."

He waits for me to dive into the fridge and slide one in front of him, before picking up my own I'd left on the counter.

"Sorry, go ahead," I mumble.

"It has to do with that Hicks guy they found. Someone told the cops they saw Brad arguing with the guy a few weeks ago at the shelter."

I remember that incident. I intervened. Art got a bee in his bonnet over the portion of food Brad had served him at lunch, claiming he was being shortchanged. Brad had walked into the kitchen but Art followed him. By the time I got back there, they were standing nose-to-nose and it had taken a bit of calming down for each to back off. Not the first time tempers flared over stupid stuff, and I'm sure it won't be the last. I'm used to it.

"That was over food," I blurt out. "Dumb arguments

like that happen all the time. Some of these guys have trouble coexisting with others and can blow up over nothing."

"True enough," he agrees with a smirk. "Except they found Brad has a bit of a reputation with his fists." At my raised eyebrows he continues, "He won a state amateur boxing championship before he left for basic training. Hicks had been beaten severely and Brad had scraped knuckles on his right hand."

"That's ridiculous. So they automatically assume it's him? He has scrapes and cuts all the time, so do half of the other guys at the shelter. Hell, whenever I try my hand in the kitchen I either slice or burn myself." I take an angry swig of my beer, almost choking when it goes down the wrong way.

"Easy, sweetheart."

He reaches over to take the beer from my hand while I try not to cough up a lung. The unexpected endearment is cause for another bout of coughing.

Charming.

"It didn't take long for Hank to point out the same to the cops," Dimas continues.

"Hank?" I manage to rasp.

"Lawyer PASS has on retainer," he explains. "Guess they weren't expecting a reputable lawyer to show up to represent a homeless guy, but I'm sure this isn't the last of it. I'm sure they'd like things tied up neatly with one homeless guy beating another to death and will try to make the pieces fit somehow."

I hear the indignation in his voice and I feel the

same. It pisses me off to think they might focus their energies on Brad, while whoever is responsible for Art's death gets away with it.

"Typical," I snarl, disgusted.

Dimas chuckles. "What makes you so sure Brad is innocent?"

"Easy. The day after that argument I saw him serve Art a double portion. Why would he do that if he somehow was still pissed? The whole thing is preposterous."

"Agreed."

I narrow my eyes. "What about you? How come you're so sure?"

"He and I go way back. Spent a lot of hard time together, but a big part of that is his story to tell."

"I understand."

I do. I may not know exactly what he's referring to but I suspect it has to do with their time overseas, and I certainly respect not wanting to give me what should be personal information.

He puts the beer to his mouth and I find myself fascinated by the movement of his throat below his beard as he drains it all at once. Disappointment follows closely when he sets the empty bottle down on the counter and stands up.

"I should go."

"Okay," I mumble stupidly.

Maybe I should've said something to make him stay, but it's too late now. I indulge myself by staring at the flex of his ass, underneath those fabulously fitting jeans, as I follow him to the door. I barely manage to raise my eyes from their intense focus when he suddenly turns around.

Yikes. Would've been awkward to get caught staring at his junk…and now I can't stop thinking about his junk. Dammit.

Judging by the crinkles around his eyes, he may well have a good idea where my focus and my thoughts were.

"Before I forget, updating you wasn't the only reason I came by. Coulda done that over the phone." I was wondering about that but didn't want to read too much into it. "Been a bit of an ass to you. Twice, so far," he adds with a self-deprecating smirk. "I should probably apologize for that. I'm sure it's hard to believe, but I'm generally an easy guy to get along with."

"Actually, I've been a bit quick on the trigger myself, so you're not the only who should apologize." I look away from his intense gaze. "I have some hot button issues I can be reactive to."

"Same here," he rumbles in a low voice.

My breath falters when he gently lifts my chin with only a finger. He has green eyes. Gorgeous green eyes ringed with hazel. Mesmerizing.

"Willa?"

I blink my eyes a few times. "Sorry, what were you saying?"

"Dinner? I was suggesting if we get to know each other a little over dinner sometime this week, we can maybe avoid any future misconceptions."

As much as it excites me, it also sounds a little too much like a date. Although, it's just a meal not a lifetime commitment. We all have to eat.

"Why don't you sleep on it?" he says with humor in his voice, and I realize my inner dialogue may have played out on my face. "I'll give you a call tomorrow when you've had a chance to think it over."

He's already out the door and halfway down the steps when I come up with the only response I can muster.

"Okay."

DIMAS

I'm still wearing that grin when I get home ten minutes later.

Fuck, but she's cute when she's flustered, and I seem to have done a bit of that tonight. I get the sense her tough-guy persona is mostly something Willa wears on the outside to protect the warm-hearted woman I've only had glimpses of. It'll be interesting to see if she'll let me crack that shell.

I walk through my dark house—which coincidentally has much the same layout as Willa's, except mine looks out over the dry mesa of the Redlands instead of the Colorado River—heading straight for the fridge for another beer. I take it out on my back deck and pull out my phone.

"I'm off the clock," Radar grumbles.

"It's not even nine o'clock," I point out. "I've got a question."

"Shoot."

"Remember a while ago, you were approached at the gym for an unsanctioned fight?"

Radar may not look like a bruiser, but the man has some serious skills in the cage. Some guy came up to him after a sparring session and asked if he wanted to make an extra buck. Radar blew him off.

"I remember."

"Did he leave you a number or something?"

"No, I wouldn't take his card, but he still comes around from time to time."

"I need to get in."

"In? Like, on a fight? Jesus, Dimi, why—"

"Looks like a buddy of mine might be getting railroaded for that murder down the street from the office. Says he was approached a couple of months back at the shelter and declined. He knew the dead guy, though, and suspects he may have had a similar offer but accepted. Would fit the injuries."

This is something I didn't share with Willa, simply because I don't want her asking questions at work. She strikes me as someone who would.

"Look, I've heard some rumbles around the gym. Some idiots who imagine themselves to be MMA capable but couldn't knock over a goddamn garbage can to save their lives. They were talking about making money in this underground league. Pretty sure they were approached by the same guy. You don't wanna get mixed up in shit like that. Not with your limitations."

I fight hard to keep my anger in control before I answer. "I have no limitations," I correct him with the deadly calm he seems to recognize, because he stays quiet. "Challenges, maybe, but no limitations."

"I stand corrected. But that doesn't negate the fact you haven't seen the inside of a gym in how long?"

"I work out," I counter defensively.

"You lift weights," he says. "Which, as you well know, has dick-all to do with fighting."

He has a point. I want to get to the bottom of this but I'll need time without people cottoning in on what I'm doing. I can't get my ass whooped right off the bat. Besides, I may be a big motherfucker but if they have a scout going around local gyms looking for new blood, I need to be able to catch his eye.

"Next time you go take me with you. Introduce me around."

It's quiet on the other side and I take a sip of my beer, waiting him out.

"Fuck, man. Does Yanis even know about this?"

"It'll be on my own time, so there's no reason for him to know." My brother would have a fucking coronary if he knew what I was planning, so he's best left uninformed. With a bit of luck I can get this sorted without him needing to find out. "Nothing will blow back on you either way," I promise him.

"Famous last words," he mutters.

"The guy they're trying to pin this on, he's a good

man, a decent man who's had nothing but bad breaks."

"Killing me here, Dimi."

"I wouldn't ask if—"

"Holy shit, man. Fine. Five o'clock tomorrow morning I'll pick you up. Jesus, you're a pain in the ass."

"Five in the morning?"

"Change your mind already?"

Almost. Five in the morning is just cruel, but I'm not about to tell him that.

"Fuck no. I'll see you then."

CHAPTER 5

WILLA

I DON'T HAVE a chance to catch up with Brad until he knocks on my door right before the group session on Wednesday.

I saw him in the dining hall when I went to grab a coffee Monday morning, but other than a quick, "Hey, how are you doing?" and his responding "I'm good," we haven't really talked.

"Come have a seat." He closes the door behind him and sits down, looking around a little uneasily. I think he's only been in my office once before. "You okay?"

Almost distracted his eyes come to me.

"I'm good."

It seems to be a staple answer for him, but something must be up or he wouldn't be sitting here. Instead of prompting him, I decide to wait him out. I don't have to wait long.

"You're bound by confidentiality, right? Like a lawyer? Or a priest?"

Alarm bells go off but I keep my face straight.

"Similar, yes. Although if I feel someone is in danger of physically hurting themselves or others, I have a moral obligation to do what I can to prevent that," I answer honestly. "It's a bit of a gray area, really."

"What if it's illegal but it happened in the past?"

Now the hair on my neck stands on end, and I consider my response carefully.

"Unless it falls under the header of posing a current physical threat to themselves or others, it would still be privileged information."

He thinks on that before he appears to come to a decision.

"I killed a man with my fists."

It's very hard not to react to his blunt statement, and I struggle to keep my racing thoughts from showing on my face. I automatically nod to encourage him to go on but he's not looking at me, he's staring into space clearly somewhere else.

"We didn't see them coming. It was just a regular patrol like we'd done a hundred times before. I vaguely remember Dan yelling. They took us in broad daylight. My first clear memory after that is of the cell they kept me in. The only light came from a narrow slit in the door they used to check on me, or pass water and the occasional MRE through."

"How long were you held captive?" I ask in a soft voice when he seems to halt.

"I lost track of time. It was hard without outside light to guide me. They told me it had been five months, but it coulda been five years. At that point I wouldn't have been able to tell the difference. I didn't see Dan for a while. Didn't know if he was in the same situation. Or even dead. There's no frame of reference when you're stuck in a hole."

"I can't imagine," I gently interject, but it's like I'm not even in the room. I pray silently Ron sees my door closed and gets started with the group without knocking on it.

I don't want anything to interrupt what I hope is the story to explain Brad's initial statement.

"The first time I saw him, I was so relieved I fucking cried like a baby. We were thrown in the middle of a circle of insurgents, cheering and hollering. We thought for sure we were done for. That our heads would roll. Instead they told us to fight. Each other." He shakes his head and looks down at the hands he clenches on his lap. "We refused, but they were very convincing." I shudder at the coldly delivered statement that exposes so much more than it hid. "We fought and they placed bets until one of us couldn't get up anymore. Then we'd be returned to our respective cells until the next time they dragged us into the daylight. Only to do it all over again. It does something to your head. Who was your friend becomes your enemy. Then one day Dan went down, and I knew I'd killed him before he hit the dirt."

"I'm so incredibly sorry for what both of you went through," I opt to say, because telling him something inane like *"It was an accident"* would completely devalue the pain I'm sure he feels. "And thank you for trusting me enough to share it with me."

"I haven't lifted a finger to a single person since. Not ever. I can't," he says, looking me straight in the eye. "I had nothing to do with Art's death. They've approached me to fight, but would never do that again. Dimas knows that," he states with urgency.

"I never believed you did," I quickly reassure him, his friend's name leaving a bit of a sour taste in my mouth. The man, who showed up at my door out of the blue three nights ago, never followed through on his invitation for dinner. I hate that I feel disappointment. I shake my head to clear thoughts of him, and suddenly the rest of what Brad mentioned registers. "Someone approached you to fight? Do you mean like illegal fighting?"

Of course Ron picks that moment to knock loudly. "Your group is waiting."

"I'll be right there," I call out, without inviting him to come in when I see Brad's reaction to the interruption. Every emotion is at once wiped off his face, leaving behind the friendly but flat mask I realize he's been wearing since I met him.

"Brad, what do you mean—"

"You should get going," he interrupts me, getting up from his chair and moving to the door. "I just wanted you to know why I could never have done this."

He slips out before I can repeat my question about the fighting, and I don't have time to think about it because I have a group of residents waiting for me.

That doesn't mean I won't get back to it some time.

I'm surprised to see Dave Williams, our newest resident, taking a seat in the group as I walk in. He hasn't sat in on a meeting yet, and I'm not expecting much, but I'm glad he showed up.

"Sorry I'm a little late," I start as I take my seat. "I thought perhaps we can start today by introducing ourselves." I don't specify it's because we have a new resident present—I'm sure he wouldn't appreciate being put in the spotlight—but I'm sure everyone understands. "I'll start. My name is Willa Smith, I'm a veteran of the Army Medical Service Corps and I was stationed in Landstuhl, Germany, for eight years before coming back Stateside. After that I worked at the VA hospital in Grand Junction for five years until I started here a few months ago."

I look at Rupert sitting to my left, who introduces himself. Not everyone is as detailed with their intros as I was, but that's not surprising. We go around the circle until we get to Dave, and my ears perk up when he starts speaking.

"Dave Williams. Retired Navy." He looks around the group and then with his eyes on me adds, "Drunk and ex-con."

I almost feels like he's challenging me, but instead of biting, I simply smile and respond like I've done with each of the other guys. It isn't the first time I'm looked at with suspicion.

"Hi, Dave, so glad you're here."

I almost chuckle at the surprise on his face.

"You don't wanna know what I was in for?"

"Doesn't matter here, but you're welcome to share if you want to."

I get a quick shake of his head and this time a look of curiosity instead of suspicion. I'll call it progress, as I turn to the next resident in the circle.

It turns out to be a good session and although Dave doesn't say anything for the rest of it, he appears to listen carefully. Small steps.

Heartbreaking as some of these stories are, it's Brad's visit that is still on my mind when I return to my office. What he told me is horrific, but I know there's likely even more to his story he hasn't shared and it makes me sick to my stomach. I close my door for some privacy and unlock my desk drawer to pull out my laptop.

I've only just opened Brad's file, I keep with the others on my secure web storage, when my cell phone buzzes in my pocket.

"Oh, hey," I answer as casually as I can when I recognize the number on the screen.

"Busy tomorrow?"

DIMAS

Couple of days later and I'm still sore from the one early morning bout Radar put me through.

Yanis called me into his office the moment I staggered into the PASS. He thought I was drunk, or at least hungover, until I explained about my earlier visit to the gym, which he found hilarious. When he finished laughing at me, he told me to grab my gear and get to the airport with Bree for a flight to Reno, where a regular client—a celebrity with strong political views—was scheduled to speak at some convention the next day. The guy had received some threats that seemed directly related to the planned appearance in the prior twenty-four hours, so he wanted a little extra protection added to his regular detail.

Bree and I just got back to the office this morning, debriefed, and I just finished writing up my report before heading over to Sonic for a quick bite.

That's where I am now, parked at the drive-in, munching on some fries while I call Willa. Finally.

"Oh, hey."

Her casual tone is a little over the top and a clear indication she's not particularly happy with me, but I prefer to explain things in person.

"Busy tomorrow?" When it stays silent on the other side, I add, "Would love to pick you up for that dinner."

"Which dinner is that?" she asks with an edge, making me grin. I fucking love her grit, the fact she makes me work for it. Makes this game a hell of a lot more interesting.

"That would be the one I promised on the weekend, but never got around to calling about because I was out of town on a job. *That* dinner," I explain.

"As I recall, I didn't exactly agree to any dinner,

only to thinking about it."

This time I chuckle out loud. Yeah, she's making me work all right.

"I stand corrected. So let's try this again. Hey, Willa. Sorry I didn't call, but I was unexpectedly sent out of town on an assignment and just got back this morning. I hope that gave you enough time to think about my dinner invitation, which I was hoping to extend for tomorrow tonight, if you're available." I pause for effect before I add, "How's that?"

Her laugh is like her voice, full-bodied, slightly raspy, full of genuine humor, and sexy as fuck. My jeans are suddenly uncomfortable.

"Much better," she says with a smile in her voice. "But technically tomorrow tonight is laundry night."

"Again?" Sunday night when I stopped by she was doing laundry as well.

"Thursday night is my regular schedule. What you walked in on was me coping with stress."

"I see. I have to say, it's intriguing to me laundry would be put on a schedule. It's more of a need-based exercise for me. When the basket won't hold anymore dirty socks, it's time."

"Sacrilege," she fires back. "Although you get brownie points for putting your dirty socks in a basket."

"Cause for celebration, then. How about I add a bottle of wine to the dinner I can bring over, so you can still do your laundry?"

Once again, it's silent on the other side but this

time I wait her out, munching on a few fries in the meantime.

"You're pushy," she eventually concludes.

"I prefer thinking of myself as persistent."

"Fine, persistent then."

"I am. When I want something."

There's the slightest hitch in her breath and I wonder if I've shocked her enough with my bluntness for her to hang up on me.

"Why?" she asks me instead, and I don't even have to think about my answer.

"You don't take any shit. I like that about you. In fact, there are a lot of things about you that interest me."

Silence again, and then...

"Seven. You bring a bottle, I'm taking care of dinner."

I don't get a chance to protest before the line goes dead.

Yes. Willa Smith is interesting.

CHAPTER 6

DIMAS

I RUB MY hand on my jeans before I lift it to knock on her door.

Can't remember the last time I had sweaty palms before a date. Probably not since I picked Amanda Nichols up at her house for prom night twenty-odd years ago, and most of my anxiety had come from her implied promise I'd be getting lucky later that night.

I don't have those expectations tonight. Don't get me wrong; I don't generally have any objections to skipping preliminaries and getting to the good stuff. I'd be lying if I said I don't want my hands and mouth on those curves, but I'm not so sure that would be a smart place to start. Not with this woman.

"Goddammit."

The muffled curse sounds from the other side of the door, moments before I hear the lock turn.

Willa looks flustered. Beautiful, but out of sorts as she impatiently pushes a hank of hair behind her ear.

"Did I get the time wrong?" I ask, and am

immediately pinned with an annoyed glare.

"No, you didn't get the time wrong," she snaps, opening the door wide to let out a cloud of smoke and a smell that doesn't bode well for dinner. She waves me inside. "She said it was idiot-proof. Guess she gave me too much credit." She continues to mutter as she darts past me to the kitchen.

I'm curious as to whom the elusive *she* might be, but I know better than to ask another stupid question. Instead I follow her to check out the source of the heavy smoke, and almost trip over the remnants of a smoke detector on the floor.

Dropping the small bouquet of flowers and the bottle of wine I brought on the island, I move to the stove where she appears to be furiously stabbing at something. Dinner, I presume. I recognize an aluminum pan but the contents are an unidentifiable charred mess she is hacking with a dangerous-looking kitchen knife.

Instead of trying to intervene and risk pissing off an already angry-looking woman wielding a weapon, I start opening a few windows to clear the smoke. Then I pull out my phone and look up Pablo's number.

"What are you doing?" she asks, having thankfully put down the knife as she glares at me.

"Ordering pizza," I admit. "And before you say anything…" I quickly add when she takes a deep breath in, undoubtedly to tell me off, "…I was supposed to take care of dinner in the first place. Maybe next time we try for the home-cooked meal."

"Next time?" she notes, her eyebrows up in her hairline.

"You bet." I grin at her. "I get the feeling once won't be enough."

"I'm not a particularly good cook. I mean, I can do better than burn a ready-made lasagna—which I bought because Rosie recommended it and all I had to do was heat it up—but I'm far from a chef. I just got distracted and forgot about the oven."

"Not the first person that's happened to."

"I know, but…never mind." She shakes her head and I don't push it. She's clearly not having a good day.

"Why don't I get on that pizza while you pour yourself a glass of wine?" I indicate the bottle I brought in.

"You got me flowers," she notes, picking them up to give them a sniff.

"Florist is next to the liquor store."

"Thank you."

"My pleasure," I return. "Anything you don't like on your pizza?"

"I'll eat anything as long as it's on a pizza."

Then she sets about finding something to put the flowers in while I dial Pablo's.

An hour later the petrified lasagna is in the garbage can on the side of the house, the king-size pizza box has only a couple of slices left, and I'm pouring us the last of the wine.

"Best military movie ever made?" she asks, when

I hand over her glass.

After some general conversation over dinner, we seem to have progressed to the getting-to-know-each-other portion of the evening.

"*Apocalypse Now*," I answer immediately, having watched that movie about a hundred times. "You?"

"*Full Metal Jacket*. Hands down," she adds. "Your turn."

"Favorite vacation destination?"

"A remote cabin in the Rockies. You?"

"Really?" I'm surprised at her answer. "I had you pegged for some sunny, beachfront location like the Bahamas or something."

She exaggerates a shiver. "I could handle that for no more than thirty minutes before the heat, the sand, and the people would drive me to hide inside. Silence, nature, and fresh air is more my speed."

"Interesting. I'm not a beach bum myself, although I like being on the water. A mountain lake to be more specific. I don't care if it's a cabin, a tent, or just a sleeping bag under the stars, as long as it gets me away from people."

"Interesting, indeed," she mumbles, a small smile tugging at her lips as she takes a sip of her wine. "Okay, in that same vein, favorite vacation activity?"

"Hmm. There are several that make the top of my list, but let's stick with hiking and canoeing."

She rolls her eyes. "Oh, I bet," she mocks and I burst out laughing.

"Scout's honor."

"Somewhere W. D. Boyce is turning in his grave," she teases.

I shouldn't be surprised she knows the history of the Scouts. Willa is apparently full of surprises and all of them good, although I might do the cooking from here on out.

"So what's your favorite?"

"Reading. Love to read, I just rarely get a chance to sit and devour a book beginning to end. Vacation is good for that."

"Last book you read?"

The blush forming on her cheeks at my question makes me even more curious.

"It's been a while," she stalls, and I can see her eyes dart to a paperback upside down on the counter by the coffee maker.

Liar.

I recognize the name on the cover as that of the author who caused a stir in the literary world when she took erotica mainstream. I just don't recognize the title. As an avid reader myself, I checked out that first book to see what the hype was all about. Bit of a stretch, the story itself, but the sex was admittedly hot.

"For the record, she's not a new author to me," I admit, grinning when I see her discomfort. "But I prefer crime thrillers myself."

The blush only deepens as she empties her glass and gets up to clear it and the dishes into the dishwasher. It appears we're done with the question and answer segment, which is probably a good thing.

I quickly adjust myself when her back is turned, her round ass on display. I have a healthy appreciation for a woman with generous curves and I like a soft body in my bed, but Willa is stirring my blood with much more than her physical attributes.

That's why I get up from my stool and drain my own glass, setting it next to the sink. I don't want to come off like all I care about is how fast I can get her in the sack.

She looks at me surprised.

"You're leaving?"

"I started working out with one of the guys at work, and he likes to hit the gym at an ungodly hour."

She gives me a quick head to toe scan before smirking at me.

"You look fit enough to me."

"Could be better," I return, grabbing the spare tire that's been growing around my waist in both hands.

"Like I said," she repeats, her eyelids lowering. "You look fit enough to me."

Okay. That's my cue to get out of here before I let something happen I'm trying to avoid. I reach out and brush my thumb over her still-rosy cheekbone.

"I should go," I tell her gently. "But I'd like to see you again."

"I wouldn't mind that." She shrugs as she turns to the door, leading the way.

"I'll give you a call," I promise before joking. "But for curiosity's sake, what chores do you usually perform on your Saturday nights?"

That earns me a smile as she opens the door for me.

"Saturday I do groceries, but I keep my nights open."

"Good to know." I step out the door and turn to face her. "I'll give you a call tomorrow, and..." I add quickly since I promised her that once before and didn't follow through, "I will let you know if I'm sent out on assignment."

"Fair enough."

Even though the anticipation is going to be sweet, I can't stop myself from leaning in to steal a soft kiss, my tongue brushing over her lips for a quick taste.

"Night, Willa."

WILLA

Sooo...that wasn't in the plans.

At least that's what I convinced myself of when I said yes to dinner. I thought if things went well, we could enjoy each other for a night and then move on. No harm no foul. I thought that's all a guy like him would be after too. But then instead of making a move toward the bedroom, he made one toward the door.

The truth is I like him, and if that kiss was anything to go by there is a potential to like him a whole lot more, and that could be a problem. I promised myself years ago I wouldn't end up like my mother or sister, with a man for whom a wife and family would always come second to his loyalty and duty. A man who expects his woman to keep the home fires burning, not only while he's off to protect flag and country, but also at all times.

My father was always like that, and over the years my brother-in-law, Bill, has become the same way. I've never wanted to be in a relationship where it was expected of me to treat someone else like the center of my universe, while losing my own identity. I know myself well enough to realize I couldn't be happy like that in the long run, so I've always kept my expectations low and casual when it comes to the opposite sex.

Shit. I'm probably completely overthinking this, but tonight's easy banter with Dimas stirred more in me than most men managed during sex, and it freaks me out.

I snag my phone from the hall table and plop down on my comfy couch, pulling my legs up under me.

"And?" Rosie asks right away when she picks up, but follows it right away with, "Hey, wait a minute... it's not even ten?"

She had been all the way on board when I mentioned dinner with Dimas and hurried to assure me he was "such a great guy." She helpfully pointed out I should under no circumstances cook dinner for him. That's when she suggested the premade lasagna.

"He left fifteen minutes ago."

"Nooo." I can hear her yelling at Jake, who is no doubt somewhere near, "Dimi is an idiot!" Then she comes back on the line. "What happened?"

"Well, I burned the lasagna."

"Oh, Willa…"

"I know, but in my defense, I was doing laundry and got distracted. But it's all good because he brought wine and ordered pizza. It was nice."

"But?"

"No buts, he's calling me tomorrow. Wanted to know what was on my schedule for Saturday. So Rosie? You can call off your dog."

There's some mumbling on the other end before she's back with me. "Jake left the room. He says he doesn't wanna know. Give me the deets."

"We ate, we drank wine, we talked. It was nice and then he left but promised to call."

"And?"

I inadvertently snort at her un-Rosie-like persistence. "And it's freaking me out, if you must know."

"Why? Because he wants to see you again?"

A buzz from my phone alerts me to an incoming text. I quickly peek and see it's from Dimas.

Dimas: What are you telling Rosie?

"Rosie…how does Dimas know I'm on the phone with you?"

"Shit. Hang on." There's a rustling on the line and then I hear her call, *Jake, did you call Dimi?*

"Sorry," she says when she gets back on the line.

"Apparently my husband texted him and told him I called him an idiot."

"Christ," I chuckle, shaking my head. "It's high school all over again."

Dimas: Willa? Call me.

"I should go, now I have Dimas texting me. Look, I'll talk to you tomorrow, okay?"

"Yeah. Oh, but, Willa? I'm not sure why you're freaked out, but I wouldn't have told you he's a good guy if I didn't mean it."

"I know. Night, Rosie."

"Night."

I end the call and suddenly my nervous bladder necessitates a bathroom visit, and I stop off on my way back to the couch to grab a beer from the fridge. For reinforcement.

Instead of calling I shoot him a message.

Me: I'm off the phone.

I barely have a chance to take a sip of my beer when it rings.

"Hey."

"Why is Rosie calling me an idiot?" he asks right away, but I can hear the smile in his voice.

"I had nothing to do with that."

"But weren't you talking to her?"

"I may have been, but I never said anything about

you being an idiot."

"Wouldn't blame you," he says with a chuckle that ends on a groan. "I've been calling myself one since I left your place."

I'm not sure how to respond to that so stay quiet, but I'm smiling like a fool. I'm in so much trouble.

"Willa?"

"Yeah?"

"I had a good time tonight."

"I did too," I admit. "Even if I did burn dinner."

His deep chuckle sounds really good and I slide down, resting my head on a pillow.

"Pizza was good."

"That it was, and the wine. Thank you for that and the flowers."

"My pleasure," he rumbles and then falls silent.

I don't say anything either, happy to lie here staring at the ceiling with a smile on my face as I listen to him breathe.

"Willa?"

"Still here," I snort, which in turn makes him chuckle.

"Yeah. Not gonna lie to you, Saturday feels like a fucking long time away."

"Two days."

"I know. Still sucks, but I'm busy tomorrow."

"Me, too. Tomorrow is Friday, I've got chores," I joke and am rewarded with a full-out laugh. I imagine his white teeth showing through his beard while the lines around his eyes deepen.

"And you've got a schedule to maintain," he teases. "So as much as I don't want to hang up, I'm going to because I need to get some sleep. I'll find time to call you tomorrow so we can hammer out details."

"Sounds good. Night, Dimas."

"Sweet dreams, Willa."

CHAPTER 7

DIMAS

"FANCY."

I grin down into Willa's upturned face as we walk in the doors of Engine 36.

It isn't exactly fancy, but the restaurant is unique, located in an old brick firehouse downtown, and notoriously difficult to get into on short notice. The food is great and it has a rustic vibe I'm told is romantic, which is why it's a popular location for couples.

"Right this way, please," the hostess says, after I give her my name, and leads us to our table.

I help Willa into her chair and get an eyeful of her exposed back in the fitted emerald green dress she's wearing. We almost didn't make it out of her house when she opened the door looking like a wet dream. I've only seen her in casual clothing and wasn't sure what to expect, but it wasn't that.

"How did you manage this?" Willa asks. "It's been years since I've been here, and I hear these days you need to book weeks ahead."

"We've done some security upgrades for the owner," I explain, before giving in to the sudden unreasonable pang of jealousy when I hear she's been here before. "When were you here?"

"Must've been three or four years ago. My sister, Connie, came for a visit with my niece, Britt, and we ended up eating here. Haven't been back since."

I don't bother holding the smug smile that spreads on my face. Asinine, I know, but it pleases me to know she hasn't been here at some time with another guy.

"Is that so?"

She leans forward over the table and confesses, "I don't really date."

"This is a date," I point out.

"I know." She grins and turns her head when the waitress approaches the table for our drink orders.

Willa is a bit of an enigma to me. I like to think I'm fairly tuned in to the opposite sex, but she isn't as easy to read as a lot of the women I've been around. One moment I'm not sure if she's interested in pursuing anything, and the next I'd swear she was coming on to me. I admit I'm fascinated.

She's certainly one of the most uncontrived women I've met. Aside from the hint of gloss on her lips, and the surprise dress I really fucking like—both doing funny things to my libido—what you see is what you get with Willa.

Which makes that call from Yanis earlier when I was on my way to her house suck even more. Bree was supposed pick up a client, coming in on a chartered flight tonight, who needs a security escort from the airport to a property just east of Palisade, but she had a family emergency.

Ever since we took on production security for a movie filmed here last year, we get these quickie jobs from time to time, business people, politicians, or celebrities who either live here or are visiting. The money is good and the work easy enough. A couple of hours, that's all. Too bad I had plans for those hours.

"Unfortunately, it's a date that comes with a curfew," I share with her when the waitress leaves with our order.

"Oh?"

Her body language is loud and clear when she sits back right away, but as she moves, so do I. Leaning over the table I take one of her hands in mine.

"Work—one of our operatives was called away on an emergency, so I have to jump in. We have three hours."

That gives me enough time to drop Willa off at home, stop in at the office for my gear, and still be in time to meet the plane on the tarmac at eleven fifteen.

"Emergencies can happen," she says, visibly relaxing. "And three hours should be plenty for dinner."

"Yes, except I'd hoped dinner would only be the start of the evening," I share honestly.

"I thought—"

"That I was blowing you off? You couldn't be

further from the truth."

The waitress picks that moment to deliver our drinks and take our food orders. When she leaves, I purposely direct the conversation in a less loaded direction.

"So you have a sister. Any other siblings?"

"Just the two of us. Connie is two years older and married to Jim, a lifer like my dad was. Army. They have a twelve-year-old daughter, Brittany."

"You're an army brat?" She nods. "Is that why you joined the Medical Corps?" At that she laughs heartily.

"Good Lord, no. Let's just say Dad was *not* pleased his daughter had decided to enter a man's world. His words, not mine."

"Wow. That's a bit…" I let my voice trail off, not wanting to risk insulting her family on our date, but she finishes my sentence for me.

"Misogynistic? Yes, that would be an accurate description. What about you? Siblings?"

"My older brother, Yanis, and Jake's like a brother too. My parents took him in when we were kids. We all grew up together."

"Good childhood?" she asks. Somehow I get the impression hers was far from.

I tell her about growing up just outside the small town in Wyoming, where my parents still live. About the stray animals my mother was forever collecting, the vegetable patches we later discovered weren't just carrots and beans. She laughs when I tell her my parents still grow pot and supply the senior community they moved into a few years ago with my mother's version of digestive cookies.

Dinner is good, conversation is great, and when it's time to go, it feels natural to take her hand in mine as I lead her out of the restaurant.

"That was delicious," Willa comments when we get to my vehicle.

Knowing my time is limited and not wanting there to be any confusion about where I'd like this to go, I crowd her against the side of the truck, my hands braced on either side of her head. Her hazel eyes drop immediately to my mouth.

"Gonna kiss you, then I'm gonna drive you home, and kiss you again. You don't want that, now's the time to tell me."

When she raises her hands to my chest, sliding them up and around my neck, I have my answer.

There is no hesitation in the way her lips open under mine and her taste explodes in my mouth. I groan down her throat as my tongue strokes the bold touch of hers. Instinctively my body pins hers against the passenger door. I slip an arm around her and with my hand at the base of her spine; I press her hips against mine. I know she feels the ridge of my hard cock when her blunt nails dig into the muscles of my neck.

Fuck she feels good—tastes good—but we're in the middle of a parking lot in the center of town on a busy Saturday night.

"Wow," she whispers when I reluctantly lift my lips from hers.

"Yeah, wow."

I quickly hustle her in the passenger side and adjust myself as I round the hood before getting in behind the wheel. Pulling out of the parking lot, I reach for her hand and she slips her fingers between mine.

The drive to her place is quiet, so I hear her sigh when I pull in beside her parked RAV.

"I'm gonna walk you to your door, kiss you goodnight, and head to the office." I turn to her, sliding a hand around her neck. "But what I'd really like to do is follow you inside, strip you out of that ridiculously sexy dress the moment we enter the house, and fuck you hard against the wall."

Her breath hitches and her mouth opens, a flush darkening her cheeks. I brush my thumb over those lush lips.

"Yeah," I mumble before letting her go.

WILLA

Mercy.

If that first kiss last weekend stirred my blood, and the one in the parking lot earlier tonight set me on fire, this last one against my front door left me a quivering mess.

I could taste the hunger on his tongue, and if the way his large rough hands moved restlessly over the thin fabric of my dress is any indication, he knows how to use them.

My skin is still tingling ten minutes later when I walk out of the bathroom, ready for bed. Even just the slight brush of the sheets when I slip between them is enough to have me reach for the drawer in my nightstand.

By the time a couple of days have passed, with just an occasional text from Dimas, the glow of his kisses has worn off some. Once again I'm questioning the wisdom of starting something with him.

I'm not upset with him, I understand the kind of work he does isn't an easy nine-to-five. It's not him I'm questioning—it's me. Whatever is working its way to the surface between us has gone well beyond what I can justify as a hookup, and I find myself almost obsessively willing my phone to alert me to another text or maybe a call. I'm already losing myself.

He mentioned in his first text on Sunday what was supposed to be a few-hour job has turned into a longer, more involved assignment that would more likely take days. I'm sure this isn't the first, nor will it be the last time. I promised myself a long time ago; I would not be that woman who sits at home, waiting with bated breath for her man to come home.

Yet here I am, maybe not sitting at home, but most definitely waiting for a man to pick up life where we left it off. If this is a precursor of what a relationship with him might be like, I don't know if I'm woman enough.

"Okay, this is the second day I walk past your office to find you staring at the wall," Rosie says, leaning against my doorway. "What gives?"

"I'm fine." My words sound hollow, even to my own ears.

"Right." Rosie steps inside closing the door behind her. "Tell me how fine you are?" I sigh long and deep, causing her to snicker. "That bad, huh? Okay, let me guess. This wouldn't have anything to do with this emergency job that has the entire PASS team—including my husband—out of town indefinitely, would it?"

"Indefinitely?"

"I'm talking about the job. No telling how long their involvement is required, but they're not that far from home. Jake says they'll start rotating shifts so they can all have a break."

"Does Jake tell you about the assignments he's on?" I'm suddenly curious and she smiles at me with understanding.

"Depends on the type of assignment to be honest, but he talks to me about it after. Is that what is freaking you out? Their work?" She sits down across from me, subtly indicating she has time to listen.

"There's a reason I've never invested the time and energy to learn how to cook." Her eyebrows go up but she continues to listen. "We were celebrating my mother's birthday earlier this month. My mom and sister were in the kitchen, preparing her birthday dinner, while my father and brother-in-law first played eighteen holes at the local golf course, only to come home and sit down with their fucking drinks and a game on TV." Understanding dawns on Rosie's face but she stays quiet. "It's what we grew up with, it's what was expected, and it seems to be what my sister wants out of life, but it definitely is not what I'm looking for. So I have no interest in being Suzy Homemaker for anyone."

"And I completely understand that, but what isn't clear is what this has to do with the boys being on assignment?"

"I like him, Rosie," I try to explain. "I think I could like him a lot, but I don't want to wake up at some point down the line and find out I've turned into my mother, after all."

"That's the biggest load of crap I've heard in a long time," she snaps, and I sit up straight in my chair. "I don't know your mother or your sister, but I know you and there's no way you could ever be like that, not even if you tried. But more importantly, I know Dimas, and there is no way in hell he'd ever treat you like that."

"You don't—"

"Oh, but I do know. Once you meet his parents you'll get it." She gets up and moves to the door. "I get you think it's safer to avoid men like Dimas, but you're wrong. Trust me on this one, men like that will move heaven and earth to make sure you feel safe and cared for."

I don't know how long I sit there after she leaves, thinking about her words, when Ron knocks on the door. "Have you seen Dave?"

"Not today, no. Why?"

"No worries, I just want to clear up a few things with him."

"Yeah, I haven't seen him. Sorry."

"You heading home soon? It's after five." He glances at his watch.

"Probably," I answer, shocked at the time. "You have a good night."

I stop to pick up some sushi I have a sudden craving for on my way home. Changed into something comfortable and armed with a beer and my dinner, I sit down in front of the evening news.

My eyes are still watering from a piece of sashimi dipped in too much wasabi and soy sauce, when a knock sounds at the door. I'm still blinking when I find Dimas standing on my step.

"Are you crying?" he asks immediately, moving me backward into the hallway with a firm hand on my hip.

"Wasabi," I manage in a raspy voice.

"Can't handle the heat?" he teases with a grin.

"Oh, I can handle heat just fine," I snap.

I barely have a chance to identify the look in his eyes when the next instant his mouth slams down on mine.

Well, hello.

CHAPTER 8

WILLA

"TELL ME THIS fucking thing comes off."

I can't help the giggle bubbling up at his frustrated growl.

Somehow I ended up on my back on the couch, Dimas looming over me, struggling with the wrap shirt he's impatiently trying to divest me of.

"Let me," I snicker, pushing his hands—tugging at the faux wrap around my waist—to pull the whole thing off over my head.

A deep growl is his only response as he stares down at my naked chest. If I had any insecurities; the heat in his eyes as he peruses my heavy breasts and soft stomach would've instantly dispelled them. The man likes what he sees and isn't afraid to show it.

"Dimas…" I mutter when his mouth latches onto a nipple, his hand lifting my breast.

More growling as he sucks hard before releasing me, leaving the dark rose peak tight and erect. He trails the flat of his tongue to the other side, giving that nipple the same treatment before lifting off me, looking appreciatively at his handiwork.

"Fuck. Gorgeous," he rumbles, running his rough palm from my belly up over my chest to the base of my throat. "Tell me you want this." His eyes meet mine, searching for an answer.

"I want this," I whisper.

"I should probably explain—" he starts, but I immediately cut him off, curling a hand around the back of his neck, and pulling him down.

"You can explain later," I mumble with my lips against his.

As he kisses me hungrily, I slide my hands down and slip them inside the back of his jeans, my fingers digging into the firm butt cheeks. I can feel them clench as he rocks his hips into mine, and I wantonly open my legs.

"Easy, sweetheart. Waited long enough, so I'm not gonna rush through this."

I'm about to protest when he slides down my body, pulling off my lounge pants on the way to leave me completely exposed.

"You still have clothes on," I complain, and he immediately whips off his shirt.

Oh, yeah. A little more than just a dusting of hair covering his chest and running down his stomach. He's built. Not bulging and cut, but strong and solid. I instantly reach out, dragging my fingers from his pecs down his stomach, loving the feel of the bristly hair under my touch. He stops me when I reach his waistband, shaking his head with a smug grin. Then he hooks my legs behind the knees and spreads me open.

"Fuck, yeah," he groans before lowering his head.

He marks the inside of my thigh with his teeth and I hiss. Then he does the same on the other side.

"Yesss…" The word drags from my mouth when I feel the wet stroke of his tongue along my slit and my back arches off the couch.

The man knows how to put all his assets to good use. With teeth, tongue, lips, and even the slight abrasion of his beard on the sensitive insides of my thighs, he doesn't waste any time turning me into a shaking, quivering ball of need.

Then he slides a large, long digit inside me and I about levitate off the couch, whimpering pathetically. A second finger joins the first and he pumps a few times before rotating them inside me. I push my head back into the pillow; shamelessly grind my hips into his touch, and with his fingers curving deep inside me, he barely grazes my clit with his teeth, sending me flying in a million different directions.

When I catch my breath and finally lift my head, I find him looking down on me, the foil packet of a condom between his teeth. With brisk moves he unbuttons his fly, shoves jeans and briefs down his ass before palming the thick, very erect, and heavily veined cock jutting from the dense nest of hair.

A lazy couple of strokes and then he efficiently rolls on the condom before slicking the tip along my crease. With eyes burning into mine, he plants himself balls deep, filling me completely.

Fuck, yeah.

DIMAS

It's the fucking butt crack of dawn when my blasted alarm goes off on my phone.

Willa's naked body stirs against me, as I quickly reach for the damn thing on her nightstand.

Last night after milking another orgasm from her still quivering body, I let go of my own, leaving me almost cross-eyed. Somehow I managed to get us to her bed, where she rolled on her side the moment she touched the mattress and fell asleep. I lay awake for a while, simply watching her.

When my stomach started growling—I didn't stop to eat before I got here—I went in search of sustenance and found Willa's forgotten container of sushi on the coffee table which I promptly devoured. Sitting on her couch, I debated heading home. It would've been my usual MO, but for some reason sneaking out of the house didn't feel right with her. Instead I collected our clothes, strewn across the living room, and took them with me to the bedroom. There I stripped the jeans I never quite took off, removed my prosthesis, and slid between the sheets, where her body instinctively rolled against me.

It took me only seconds to drift off, her scent enveloping me.

I could do with another couple of hours after a few mostly sleepless nights, and I certainly don't want to leave the warmth of Willa's bed, but I promised Radar I would meet him this morning at the gym. After that I'm supposed to stop in at the office, pick up a few things for Yanis, and check in with our office manager, Lena, before picking up Bree and heading back to Palisade.

Pressing a kiss to Willa's bare shoulder, I ease myself out of bed and get dressed. I can take a shower at the gym after my workout. I scribble a note on the back of the sushi receipt and leave it under her phone on the counter before pulling her front door closed behind me.

We never did have a chance to talk.

"Jesus, man," Radar grumbles twenty minutes later. "You smell like sex."

Not at all bothered, I grin in his face. "I'm surprised you recognize it," I tease.

That earns me a swift left hook to the gut, knocking the breath out of me.

"I get laid, asshole," he grunts, right before I pay him back with a volley of punches on the body, ending with a solid hit to his chin.

Both of us are wearing protective gear—mandatory in the gym—but I still manage to rattle his cage.

"You're better pissed off," he groans, shaking his head.

We spend another twenty minutes going through the paces when Radar suddenly takes me in a headlock.

"He's here, and watching," he whispers close to my ear.

I twist out of his hold, at the same time hooking my leg behind his knees. He hits the mat hard when clapping draws my attention to the edge of the ring.

"Nice move." The guy looks to be in his late forties, fit enough and dressed for a workout. Looks like every other guy in here, so I wouldn't have looked at him twice.

"Thanks." I unclip the headgear, pretending disinterest.

"Looks like you may have spent some time in the cage."

I watch as Radar ducks between the ropes and heads for the showers before answering.

"Been a while ago," I lie. I've never fought in the cage, but that doesn't mean I never fought. Did plenty of that.

"Veteran?" he asks, indicating my leg when I pull off my gloves.

Grabbing my towel from the corner, I rub it over my sweaty hair before draping it around my neck.

"What's it to you?"

I'm being an asshole on purpose. I don't want to seem too eager and have him get suspicious. More credible if I let him bait me than the other way around.

"Nothing," he says, shrugging. "Just making conversation. I have a few buddies who were in the military. They do some recreational fighting; make a little money on the side. You look like you might be able to hold your own, but I can see you're not interested."

With that he walks away and I let him. If I read him right, he's not done with me yet.

I guessed right. When I walk out the door after my shower I spot him right away. He's standing beside a red, souped-up Challenger, decked out with a cheesy fucking racing stripe and a set of shiny-assed rims, trying hard not to look like he's been standing there waiting for the past little while.

He opens his door when I step off the curb and pretends to just spot me, giving me a chin lift. I play his game, move toward my vehicle and stop halfway there, turning back in his direction.

"Hey!" I call out, ambling over to him. "What's the catch?"

He shakes his head like he doesn't understand.

"Catch?"

"Yeah, you said recreational fighting and extra money. There's gotta be a catch. Is this like a fight club or something?"

"Or something. Lots of people enjoy watching a good bout, but not everyone likes the limitations of regulated fights or the often questionable judging," he explains, fishing in his back pocket for what I hope is a wallet. He hands me a card. "That's my number. Think about it. You decide you don't have what it takes, I understand. This kind of raw hand-to-hand combat is not for everyone."

His hook delivered—playing on my ego—he gets

in behind the wheel and starts up his ride. He revs the engine a few times, the loud rumble of the engine turning heads, before peeling out of the parking lot.

Typical small-dick move.

Still, I tuck the card away in my pocket, and smile as I walk to my vehicle.

Radar is already at the office when I get there.

"And?"

"Hook, line, and sinker." I hand him the card.

"Jason Krupcek. Sounds like a douche name," he observes, turning the card over in his hand. "Raw Vice talent scout. Jesus."

"Dig up what you can? On Raw Vice and that weasel. Something, anything. I want to know what, how, and where, but most importantly I wanna know who is behind it. Jason is a peon, not a big player. I need to know who he answers to."

"Sure thing."

"And Radar, keep this off the books, if you can—at least until I know the lay of the land—and find out if someone starts probing around my background."

"Of course."

Last thing I want is any of this to blow back on anyone else. I know Yanis is going to have a stroke when he discovers what I am willing to do to get to the bottom of this.

Hank has been instrumental in keeping Brad out of jail so far, but it's clear the cops have a hard-on for him. They've been sniffing around.

"You heading back to Palisade?"

"Yeah," I answer grudgingly, as I head out the door.

God, I almost lost my shit when Mercedes fucking Rockton came walking down the stairs of the private plane sitting on the tarmac, when I got to the airport earlier this week. I was about to turn on my heel and march right back to my truck, leaving her to fend for herself. Then her father came down the stairs behind her, waving me over.

Apparently his daughter had received threatening messages and phone calls in the prior week. Someone was apparently able to get into her apartment in Dallas, where certain 'gifts' were left for her. The last one had been found that morning in her bathroom; a message on her mirror that looked to have been written in blood.

No one but their regular security detail had entry to her apartment, so her father had freaked. He wanted her out of the way while he tried to find out who was doing this. The old man didn't even trust anyone else to accompany her to Grand Junction. He was so paranoid about anything happening to his daughter, he made up some story for Yanis, and then smuggled his daughter on board the private jet in a catering cart.

I was suspicious, especially after he mentioned she was the one who suggested coming here. A business associate of his, who is on a cruise in Europe for a few weeks, owns a sprawling property in Palisade.

I called Yanis on the spot, told him this wasn't a simple drop off and told him to meet me at the office.

Rockton got back on the plane, and I walked her to

my vehicle. She tried hard not to meet my eyes, which only confirmed my belief this was somehow by her orchestration, but since her dad thinks otherwise and he's footing the bill, who am I to argue?

She seemed disappointed when we stopped at the PASS office and Yanis got in the SUV with us.

It may appeal to some to be stuck in an opulent mansion, with more beds and bathrooms than fucking Buckingham Palace, but these past days have been far from fun for me. First of all, I don't care for fancy shit, and moreover, I don't care for Mercedes Rockton. The entire time I was there, she made suggestive remarks and dropped hints that had my brother looking at me funny.

Whether or not the claims of a stalker are true, she clearly came here with an ulterior motive, but I'm not touching that again.

Radar is staying behind, at my suggestion, running a few checks on her cell phone account and credit cards, just to see if anything looks out of place. I'm gonna drive back with Bree, who also had a night off, before taking over the detail for Jake and Yanis to get a break.

As much as it seems to annoy Mercedes that she can't have me out there alone, there is no way we can protect her properly without at least two people on her at all times. Already she's getting tired of being cooped up and unable to go anywhere.

Not that I give a shit. We're paid to keep her safe, not to cater to her needs. Her father can do that. She threw a fit right before I left yesterday, and I'm fully expecting my fifteen-minute indiscretion to be used as a weapon sooner or later.

I'm bracing myself for the fallout from that.

While I wait outside Bree's apartment, I quickly pull my phone out to turn the sound back on and notice a message from Willa.

Willa: Slept like a baby, thanks. :)

Me: Good. I'll try to give you a call tonight.

Willa: I vacuum on Wednesday nights. I might not hear your call.

Me: LOL. I'll try to catch you at bedtime. We can talk dirty.

Willa: Mmmmm. I'm deciding whether to be offended or excited.

Me: Excited. Definitely.

"Jesus," Bree says, as she climbs in the passenger seat. "What the hell's with the goofy smile?"

I try to straighten my face but it's impossible.

"Can't I be having a good day?" I ask as I start the SUV and pull away from the curb.

"Sure, but that smile is not it. That smile says you had some and you liked it, and I don't wanna spend an hour having to look at that mug, picturing you doing the nasty."

"You picture me doing the nasty? Wow, Bree, I had no idea," I tease, grinning wide. It earns me a solid punch in the shoulder, and Bree doesn't hit like a girl, she can make a grown man cry.

"Kiss my ass, Mazur," she snaps.

"Only because you ask nicely."

CHAPTER 9

WILLA

I'M ABOUT HALFWAY through my morning when the cops show up, interrupting what has been a really good buzz.

The first thing I noticed when I woke up was the slight soreness between my legs, taking me right back to Dimas's powerful thrusts last night. My disappointment was instant when I rolled to find myself in bed alone. I'd already worked up a decent head of steam when I found his scribbled note tucked under my phone.

Morning. Sorry I had to run. Hope you slept well. Call you later.

xo D.

It was the hug and kiss that had put a smile on my face. Most men would lose their mancard if they resorted to X's and O's, but for some reason Dimas can pull it off and still be a certified badass.

The happy buzz had lasted through a tough session with one of our residents this morning, who had broken shelter policy by bringing in drugs. We have a drug and alcohol-free policy in the shelter, but we don't really have any control once they walk out the front door. Turns out Art's death had hit Rick hard. The two shared a room and despite initially reacting like he didn't much care, he's feeling the loss.

I had to warn him; residents only get one second chance and this was his. By the time he walked out of my office, I'd been able to get him to unburden and he left with a promise he'd show up for group at noon.

But now, a heavy weight settles on my shoulders as I watch the same uniformed officer, who was here last time, walk in with a second man in civilian clothes.

"Can I help you, gentlemen?"

"Detective Craig and Officer Bergland, Ms. Smith," the shorter, stocky detective says. "We were hoping we'd be able to ask you a few questions."

"I'm afraid, as I explained to your colleague here, I'm limited as to what I can discuss with you. I'm not sure how helpful I can be, but please have a seat."

Bergland is an ass, but Craig seems a decent guy. We spend the next few minutes setting the parameters to what I can and cannot answer.

"Do you feel you know everyone living here well?" he asks.

"The residents? As well as they'll let me, I guess. Some are more reserved and cautious than others."

"Was Arthur Hicks? More reserved than others, I

mean?"

I pull up a mental image of what he was like.

"He struck me as a normal guy. Was friendly with some and didn't care much for others—no different than anyone. Mostly went his own way, but I wouldn't consider him more reserved."

"Any violent tendencies? Arguments or fights? Was he quick to use his fists?"

"Arguments happen, but we haven't had a fight here yet, to my knowledge."

Craig looks at Bergland, before turning back to me.

"Really? From what I understand there was a fight in the kitchen not long ago that involved Mr. Hicks?"

"That wasn't a fight," I insist, throwing Bergland a glare when he chuffs. "Unless fists are involved—and they weren't because I was there—it's considered an argument."

"No punches exchanged?" Craig asks.

"No. Don't get me wrong, it was heated but over quickly, just like most arguments are. There are at least a couple a week."

That's when Bergland speaks up.

"Except people don't turn up dead after."

"What is your impression of Brad Carey?" Craig fires off, before I have a chance to voice my opinion of Bergland's comment. "I'm not asking for a professional opinion, just your personal observation. Does he have violent tendencies? Get into fights?"

I can't believe they're persisting with this.

"Never," I state firmly before adding sarcastically, "from my personal observation. In fact, I've only seen Brad Carey as quiet but friendly, he works hard in our kitchen on a volunteer basis, and participates in weekly group sessions as required of all our residents."

"I see," the detective comments, but I can tell he's not convinced. "Just one more question, Ms. Smith, and we'll let you get back to work. Are you familiar with a club by the name of Raw Vice?"

"Never heard of it. What is it?" I ask, a little confused as I note both men observing me closely.

"The name of an underground fight club we have reason to believe Arthur Hicks was part of."

I can't hold back the small gasp as a flashback to a conversation I had with Brad not that long ago hits me. Craig narrows his eyes on me and I quickly blank my expression, but the damage is already done.

"Nope. Never heard of it," I reiterate, reading the disbelief on the detective's face.

The two men leave my office, not long after, with a warning they may have more questions for me. The moment they're gone, I close my office door, open my laptop and type Raw Vice in my browser.

When my alarm goes off on my phone, warning me I have five minutes until today's group session, I slam my laptop shut. An hour of sifting through vegetarian sites, WWE articles, and some disturbing shit about cannibalism, my search hasn't netted me a single viable lead to an underground fighting ring. I realize it was wishful thinking it would be that easy to dig something up on mainstream media, but I had to start somewhere.

I'm pleased to see both Brad and Dave in the community room, although neither contributes during the session. I corner Brad after.

"Do you have a minute?"

He looks over his shoulder where I can see Dave watching us.

"Sure." It's clear he'd rather not talk to me, but he follows me to my office nonetheless.

"The cops were in this morning," I inform him, but it doesn't appear to come as a surprise, he just nods.

"Heard that."

"Did they come to see you?"

"I won't talk without my lawyer present, they know that. They seem to have talked to everyone else, though." I hear a resignation in his voice I don't like.

"Look," I start, leaning forward on my desk. "I think you should know, they really seem to be pushing a theory that somehow has you involved in Art's death. The detective guy—"

"Craig?"

"Yeah, him. Something he said worried me. Remember you mentioned something about fighting? A fight club?" Immediately his eyes narrow. "Don't worry," I quickly say. "I didn't say anything, but he wanted to know if I'd heard of Raw Vice. He said it was an underground fight club. Is that the same—"

"*Shit*," he curses, startling me. "Forget you ever

heard that name."

"But I thought maybe—"

"Willa, please. For your own safety." Without another word he abruptly leaves my office.

I lean back in my chair and pull out my phone to dial Dimas, but there's no answer, so I leave him a message instead.

Me: If you have a minute, can you call me?

DIMAS

"She's some piece of work," Bree mumbles, annoyed as she walks into the cavernous kitchen.

The whole place is ridiculously pompous and oversized. Its only saving grace is the view from every window in the house. Located in the Cottonwood Creek valley, with nothing but mountains surrounding it. Eight miles south of the highway and no other buildings out this far; the place is remote enough we can see anyone coming. Especially since Radar spent the first few days here installing cameras along the only road to the property.

When we arrived this afternoon, Jake and my brother were in a hurry to get out of here. Our client's daughter had not stopped whining, and both men had been ready to slap duct tape on her to shut her up. As it turns out, her whining consisted mostly of asking when I was going to be back. That earned me a sharp look from Yanis, but luckily he was more concerned about getting out of here than giving me the third degree.

Protection detail is boring as fuck if you're doing it right. Trying to stay sharp when nothing's happening, just so you can act quickly should the shit hit the fan, is a challenge. That's why we switch it up; one of us is with the detail, the other mans the monitors, and then we trade places.

When I switched with Bree after dinner, it did not make Mercedes Rockton happy. She's one of those women who sees every other female as competition, so where Jake and Yanis got the whiner, Bree got the flaming bitch.

"That woman has her sights set on you," Bree says, pouring coffee from the thermos on the counter and holding it up to me. I shake my head. I've had enough coffee to keep me awake for a week.

"I know."

"Word of warning," she cautions, sipping her reinforcement. "If she's been hinting to Jake or Yanis the way she's been hinting to me, your little encounter with her is gonna be common knowledge soon."

"What?"

She shrugs. "Maybe it's only obvious to me because I'm a woman, but before it becomes clear to everyone you slept with her, maybe you should give your brother a heads-up, or I can see this going sideways in a hurry."

"Jesus. I swear it was only the one—" She cuts me off when she holds up her hand.

"Really not looking for details, Dimi. Just thought you should be warned."

I'm such a fucking idiot.

"I'll handle it."

"Good. Get in front of it. This kind of thing can wreck the dynamics of a good team." She pulls something from her pocket and tosses it on the counter in front of me. My phone. "Found it tucked in the couch pillows when she went up to bed."

Shit. I'd let Mercedes use it before dinner when she wanted to call her father. For security purposes we'd confiscated her phone and laptop when we got here. I forgot to get it back.

I quickly scan through messages, but the only one I missed was from Radar with a file attached.

"Thanks," I tell her, as she settles with her laptop on the couch in the family room, and flips on the TV. "I can take first watch," I offer.

We alternate using a bedroom beside the master to get a couple of hours of sleep, while the other stays alert downstairs, and we switch halfway through the night.

"I'll be good for a few hours," Bree says, holding up her mug, so I head upstairs.

The door to the master is closed and I tiptoe past to the second bedroom. I take off my boots, and lie back on the bed, fully dressed, my phone in my hand.

It rings five times before my call gets kicked to voicemail. I'll try again in a few minutes; maybe she's having a shower. But when I try five minutes later and then again ten minutes after that and she still doesn't answer, I leave her a message.

"Hey, sweetheart. It's me. Guess you're already sleeping. Sorry I missed you. Gonna catch a couple of hours, but give me a call when you get up, I'll be awake by then. I—"

"Who are you talking to, honey?"

I shoot up in my bed at the sight of a half-naked Mercedes coming into my room. I quickly end the call and swing my legs over the side.

"What the hell game are you playing at, Mercedes?" I bark, and not too softly either.

I stalk toward her but instead of her backing up, she takes a step forward and puts her hand on my chest.

"Don't be like that. I came here for you."

For the life of me I can't stop myself slapping her hand from my chest as I take back a step.

"You what?"

"Oh, come on. You know you want me," she says, moving too close a-*fucking*-gain. "You can't tell me you weren't flirting with me all week." She pushes whatever that flimsy thing is she's wearing off her shoulders.

The bitch is off her fucking rocker.

"You're delusional, woman! I want nothing to do with you."

She looks shocked, tries for a wobbly bottom lip, but then decides on anger instead.

"You weren't saying that when you were fucking me," she hisses.

"Christ. Here's a newsflash, when a guy doesn't bother taking off his pants, he's not in it for the long game."

Her mouth drops open and she makes a strangled sound.

"You'll change your tune when I've had a word with your boss," she snaps, tugging the thing back over her tits, which almost spill out of that mini-bra she's wearing.

Then she swings around and almost bumps into Bree, who looks quite comfortable leaning against the doorframe. With a huff Mercedes passes by her, and a second later I hear the door to the master bedroom slam.

"How much of that did you hear?"

"Trust me. More than I cared to," she says calmly. "Good time to make a few phone calls."

"Shit." I run both hands through my hair. This is not going to be fun. Then something occurs to me. "I fucking knew it. She mentioned something about coming here for me."

Bree straightens up. "What do you mean you knew it?"

"Had a suspicion the moment I saw her coming off that damn plane. This stalker story never sat well with me."

"She staged it?"

"Wouldn't put it past her. Maybe she had help, maybe she didn't, but I'd bet my left nut she set this up."

Bree shakes her head. "Do me a favor, don't mention your nuts, I already heard enough to traumatize me tonight." She turns toward the stairs and says over her shoulder, "Might as well come downstairs. I'll make another pot of coffee. Have a feeling we won't sleep much tonight."

It's not until after Yanis reams me a new one, and has me fess up to Bruce Rockton on a fucking conference call, that I realize I never called Willa back to clarify what she may have heard on that message.

I'm so fucked.

CHAPTER 10

WILLA

I DON'T CHECK my phone again until I'm getting ready for work after a restless night.

The first thing that pops up is the text exchange with Dimas from last night that finally had me turn off my phone.

Me: If you have a minute, can you call me?

Dimas: Busy.

Me: It's important.

Dimas: Don't have time for you now.

The abrupt dismissal had been a punch to the gut. It still is this morning. This is the exact reason why I was hesitant to start something in the first place. Christ, I've spent one night with the man and already the honeymoon is over. Relegated to the back burner.

Well, if he thinks I'll put up with that shit, he's in for a rude awakening.

Then I notice a series of missed calls and a few voicemails left overnight—all from him—and a stubborn sliver of hope springs alive as I check my inbox.

"Hey, sweetheart." My cold resolve not to let myself be swayed immediately melts at the sound of his voice. So different from the cold messages last night. *"It's me. Guess you're already sleeping. Sorry I missed you. Gonna catch a couple of hours but give me a call when you get up, I'll be awake by then. I—"*

He cuts off and I hear someone talking in the background before the voice comes on to tell me to press one to play again, seven to delete, or nine to save this message. I press one and turn the volume way up high.

Then I hear the second voice in the background, clearly a woman's.

"Who are you talking to, honey?"

That sonofabitch.

Seething, I promptly delete my entire inbox and tell myself this is good. I knew I was taking a risk going in. Better to know now what kind of guy he really is, than find out after I lose my heart to him. Although judging from the ache in my chest, it may be too late already.

I quickly block his number and tuck the phone in my pocket, fighting to keep my eyes dry. I will not shed a goddamn tear over that man.

"Are you okay?" Rosie asks, when we arrive at the same time and walk into the lobby together. "You look pissed."

"Woke up with a headache. Don't mind me," I tell her. "I'll take some ibuprofen and I'll be right as rain."

"If you need to leave, just let me know, okay?" she offers, as she heads for her office.

Another thing to be angry at Dimas for. I like Rosie a lot. I'm a bit of a loner and don't easily let people in, but I like having her for a friend. Now that's going to be awkward as hell since her husband is best friends with him.

I head for the dining room, where some of the residents are having breakfast, and stop to chat with a few of them before I make my way over to the coffee station.

"Morning," I call out to Brad, who is serving up scrambled eggs at the food counter.

"Hey, Willa. Want some breakfast?"

"Will you join me?" I ask him.

He hesitates for a beat as he looks around the room, but finally shrugs.

"Sure. It's dying down."

We settle at a table near the window, and despite feeling like death warmed over; I dig into the pile of scrambled eggs Brad served me.

"How are you doing?" I finally ask after a period of silence as we eat.

"I'm good, Willa. Don't worry about me."

"I can't help it. It's in my job description," I tease,

trying to make light of things. "I just want you to know, I'm here to help with whatever I can."

"There's no—" He stops abruptly, looking over my shoulder. I turn to look and see a couple of police cruisers stop in front of the building. His hand grabs my wrist and I swing back to face him. "Call my lawyer. There's an envelope in my locker I need you to give him." With his other hand he presses a key in my hand. "You want to help me? Go now. Please."

The hair on my neck stands on end when I hear the urgency in his voice.

"Please," he repeats before letting my wrist go.

I don't hesitate and get up, slipping quickly out of the dining room, just as a group of police officers come in through the front door. I don't want to risk having to wait so I bypass the elevator, but the moment I hit the stairwell I start running up the stairs.

I'm breathing hard when I slam through the door on the third floor. Hurrying to the group of lockers on the far side, I look at the key in my hand. Number three-oh-five. I find the matching locker, slip the key in the lock, and open the door. Luckily he doesn't keep too much in there, and I easily find the large manila envelope with the name, Hank Fredericks, and a phone number written on the side.

With the envelope tucked in the waistband of my jeans covered with my shirt, I pull open the door to the stairs when I hear the elevator ding behind me.

I don't stop running until I'm in my office, closing the door behind me. I copy the handwritten number into my phone and slip the envelope and the locker key in my drawer, just in time, when there's a sharp knock on my door.

"Come in!"

A flustered Rosie opens the door.

"They're arresting Brad. They have a warrant to search his room and locker. I already called Jake but he was halfway to Palisade. What should I do?"

Jesus. A few seconds later and whatever's in that envelope would've been found.

"Cooperate," I tell Rosie. "Can't stop them if they have a warrant. Is Ron in?"

She acknowledges with a nod. "He's out in the lobby keeping an eye on a small mutiny threatening to break out. Some of the other guys aren't exactly fans of the cops."

"Ron can handle it for now. Why don't you head upstairs and make sure they only go through Brad's stuff. I'll give his lawyer a call, and then I'll give Ron a hand with the residents."

She nods and ducks back out of my office. I hit send on my phone.

"Good morning, Fredericks and Associates, how may I direct your call?"

"Hank Fredericks, please."

"I'm sorry, I'm afraid Mr. Fredericks is busy. Can I take a message?"

"It's urgent I speak with him. It's about one of his clients, Brad Carey."

"One moment, please. Let me check for you."

Only seconds later I have him on the line and quickly explain who I am and what is going on.

"Also, I have something he asked me to give you," I add.

"What is it?"

"It's an envelope. I have it locked in my desk here at the shelter."

"Keep it there. I'm heading out to the police station to wait for him. I'll swing by the shelter after."

He doesn't wait for my acknowledgement and ends the call.

I turn the lock on my drawer, slip the key in my pocket and head out to the lobby, where Ron is doing his best to keep a few of our residents from getting themselves arrested. They're blocking the door to prevent the cops from taking Brad outside. The poor guy is already in handcuffs.

It takes some convincing, but eventually the two of us get our guys away from the door so the officers can take Brad outside. I follow behind them, but all I can do is give Brad an assuring nod when they place him in the back of a patrol car. Feels pretty helpless to watch them drive off.

The lobby is empty when I walk through on the way back to my office.

"Be careful."

I'm about to step inside and swing my head around at the sound of the whispered voice. Dave is leaning casually against the wall behind me.

"I'm sorry?"

"I saw you. Upstairs," he clarifies, and my heart jumps in my throat. "Dangerous game. Don't wanna see you get hurt."

Before I even have a chance to react, he turns on his heel and disappears back to the lobby. I dart into my office, slam the door shut, and take a deep shaky breath in.

What the hell was that all about?

Was that a threat?

DIMAS

"The number you have dialed cannot be reached."

For fuck's sake.

I slam my phone down on the kitchen counter, drawing the attention of Bree, who is bent over her laptop at the dining table.

Life couldn't get any fucking better already, and to top it off, now it appears Willa has blocked my number. What a shit show.

Fucking Mercedes is still holed up in the bedroom upstairs after her father demanded to speak with her. He'd already finished with me and that hadn't been pretty. She'd sworn high and low she had nothing to do with the threatening messages and notes, but it didn't look like her father was buying it this time. She threw a temper tantrum and ended up stalking to her room.

Yanis had been the voice of reason and suggested before we call this whole thing a hoax, we make absolutely sure. Rockton was going to talk to his head of security in Dallas, and Yanis and Jake were on their way here to have a sit-down with the princess.

"It'll blow over," Bree says, a sympathetic smile on her face. "It always does with Yanis."

I grunt. It may blow over with my brother, but I'm not so sure about Willa. Although I have to say if she's that quick to dismiss me—even after I left her another three messages to explain the situation—I'm not so sure she's the woman I thought her to be.

On the video feed I can see my brother's Yukon approaching.

"You're a fucking pain in my ass," he tosses at me, when he walks in the door moments later. I'd expected much worse than that, to be honest. "Better hope you're right and she staged this whole fucking thing, because that'll be the only thing that will get us paid. Think of that next time you can't keep your fucking dick in your pants."

Okay, that sort of stings—especially since he makes it sound like I make a habit of it—but before I can voice an objection, footsteps come pounding down the stairs and Mercedes throws herself crying into my brother's arms.

"Oh my God, I'm so glad you're here. Everyone's been so horrible to me."

Shit. The look on my brother's face almost makes me laugh out loud, but I hold back. Bree has no such compunctions and snicker-snorts behind me, earning her a dark glare from Yanis, who is trying to pluck

Mercedes off him.

Jake walks in, takes a look at my struggling brother and busts out laughing.

Yanis eventually manages to coax the woman back upstairs, and Jake sits down beside me.

"Before I go up there, take me through it from the beginning."

Mustering up patience I don't have a spare supply of, I describe events leading up to last night. At that point, I'm grateful for Bree to jump in occasionally, confirming she was witness to most of that exchange. Being stuck in a he said, she said scenario is never a comfortable situation.

When Jake heads upstairs, I take my phone outside and call Radar.

"Have you found anything on Krupcek or Raw Vice?"

"Been working on it hard since I heard your buddy got arrested."

It takes me a minute to realize what he's saying.

"Arrested?"

"This morning. Charged with first-degree murder. I just heard from Hank."

"Jesus F. Christ. I didn't think they had enough to pin on him."

"Apparently the cops were dumpster diving on garbage day. Pulled a T-shirt with your buddy's name written in the collar, and covered in the victim's blood out of a trash bag a couple of days ago."

"Why the fuck would his name be in the collar?"

"All the residents put their names in their clothes to make it easier to sort the laundry."

"Unreal. The guy is smart as a whip. Even if he did this—which he didn't—he'd never be fool enough to stuff a bloody shirt with his goddamn name on it in the garbage, right outside where he lives. Son of a fucking bitch. He's being railroaded."

"I'm on it, but, Dimi, you're going to have to get the others in on this. I won't bore you how I got there, but I found a chat room, where crazy fuckers looking to get their heads bashed in can sign up to challenge a selection of fighters, for a price. They use zip codes and intersections to identify locations. They're all over the fucking states."

"How many around here?"

"Depends on what date you're looking at. Most of these dates look to be Wednesdays and Saturdays. I count twelve in Colorado for this month alone. I have to look a bit closer, but it appears to be a league of some sort. Let me dig into it a bit more."

"When is the next fight in this area?"

"You sure you wanna do this, man?" Radar asks cautiously.

"Can't leave Brad in there too long, Radar. We don't have much time. Next fight?"

"Next Wednesday. East of town, out in Loma."

"Book me in."

"Got two grand? That's your buy-in."

"Book me in," I repeat.

Now I really want to talk to Willa and see if there

is anything at all I can salvage from this fucked-up day.

"Bree, can I borrow your phone?" I ask, walking into the house.

She raises her eyebrows but doesn't question me. I take the phone back outside with me and dial Willa's number.

"Hello?"

"Hey, sweetheart, it's me. I had to borrow—"

And click.

Fucking brilliant.

CHAPTER 11

WILLA

*B*ASTARD.

I slam my phone facedown on my desk. Then I drop my head in my hands.

It's been a crap day so far and unless I find something to keep me busy, I might lose it.

What I'd like to do is have a look at what is in that envelope—the key to my desk drawer has been burning a hole in my pocket—but so far my sense of propriety has kept me from peeking. I'm about to throw propriety out the fucking window.

First I close my door with a soft click before sitting back down at my desk. I fit the key in the lock and slide the drawer open to slip out the envelope. It would've ended there if it had been sealed, but it isn't. The flap is tucked in. Inside are a couple of sheets of paper with what looks like a schedule.

Dates, numbers, and under each of those, anywhere from four to eight names. Or rather, nicknames, since I'm pretty sure no parents would be so cruel as to call their kids Hulk Walker, Bone Crusher Perez, or Lights Out Davis.

I grab my phone and snap pictures of each page when I notice a name handwritten on the back of the second page. Jason Krupcek. I take a shot of that too.

I jump a foot in the air when I hear someone at the door.

"Willa? Are you available?" Rosie calls from the hallway.

I scramble to get the papers back in the envelope, tuck under the flap, and shove it back into the drawer.

"Come in," I call out, flipping my phone upside down as she pushes open the door.

"Sorry," she mouths, as she walks in followed by a tall gray-haired man in a suit. "I don't think you've met Hank Fredericks yet."

I get up and round my desk.

"We spoke on the phone. Willa Smith."

"Nice to meet you," he says, shaking my offered hand.

His gray hair threw me for a second, because when he smiles it takes a decade off his age. Too bad I'm not into suits and ties, or I might at least flirt a little.

"I'll just leave you to it." Rosie backs out of the office, closing the door.

"How's Brad? Please, have a seat," I throw out as an afterthought, indicating a chair while I slip back behind my desk.

"Hanging in there. He says you know he was held captive for months, so being locked up is not easy for him."

"He's talked to me," I confirm, without going into details.

"Right, he said he trusts you, which is why he gave you that envelope."

"Oh, yes, of course."

I pretend to unlock my drawer and pull it out, handing it over. He pulls the sheets out, giving them a brief look before tucking them back. I do my best not to fidget in my seat and draw attention to the fact I must have guilt written all over my face.

I almost let out a sigh of relief when he gets up.

"Well, I'd better get going. Better start the wheels turning if I want to get Brad out of that jail cell."

I stand up as well.

"If there's anything I can do…"

"Other than keeping this…" He pats the envelope. "…to yourself, I'll let you know if there's anything else."

"Of course."

I move to open the door for him and with a smile and a nod; he walks past me and down the hall.

Rosie lifts her head when I stick my head into her office.

"Everything okay?"

She waves me in and I take a seat across from her.

"Yeah. I just wish there was something more I could do to help Brad."

"Is that why he was here? Hank?"

"As a courtesy. Brad asked me to call him the

moment he saw the cops pull up outside. Guess he figured they were here for him."

Rosie is far from stupid, and I'm sure my weak explanation for the lawyer's visit isn't cutting it, but she doesn't probe further. I feel like a heel lying to her.

"How's the headache?"

"A little better."

"Did you talk to Dimas today?" she asks, her head tilted slightly as she closely observes me.

"Briefly."

It's not exactly a lie, although I didn't do any talking and I barely gave him a chance to say much either, I just hung up on him.

"Did he tell you about this mess with their client?" When I shake my head, she leans forward on her desk and continues in a lower voice. "Apparently this woman faked a stalker, just so her rich daddy would hire PASS for her security."

"Why?" I can't for the life of me imagine why someone would do that—attention?

"Who knows why people do the things they do," she says after a bit of a hesitation. "I'm sure Dimas can tell you."

I look down at my hands.

"About that…the last thing I want is for things to get awkward between you and me, but I don't think I'm gonna see him again."

"Oh no, what happened?"

"I just don't think we're compatible." That sounds

like a lame excuse, even from my own mouth.

"Bull. I think you're just running scared," she challenges me. "He's one of the best guys out there. You could do a whole lot worse."

There it is, the awkwardness.

"I'm sure, but…"

"Is it because of his leg?"

My mouth drops open in shock.

"Of course not. That's a ridiculous thing to say," I snap.

"No more ridiculous than saying you're not compatible. That's the dumbest excuse ever. If you're not into him, just say that."

"More a case of him not being into me, Rosie."

To my surprise she bursts out laughing.

"Oh my, that's priceless. Are you kidding me? He's so into you it's almost pathetic."

"He has a funny way of showing it."

I get up, cross the hallway into my office to snatch my phone and return. I find my messages, pull up the exchange with Dimas from yesterday and show it to her.

"You can scroll down."

"That's not like him," she finally says. "I'm sure there's an explanation."

"Apparently that's how he is with me, and as far as his explanation, that left a lot to be desired. A lot." I take a deep breath in and soften my tone. "The truth is, I'm already hurting, Rosie. I've done well on my own most of my life. Why would I risk getting hurt by letting myself fall even deeper? It sucks that he's your friend, but I really think this is for the best."

"We'll see."

It's obvious she's not convinced, but at least she seems to be backing off. Until I turn to walk out of her office and she pipes up behind me.

"My money is on Dimas."

That headache is no longer fake, and I manage to hang in there for another hour before I throw in the towel. Rosie quickly waves me out the door, telling me to get some rest.

I plan to do just that as soon as I've picked up a bulk-sized bottle of aspirin and a couple of things I'm running low on at the grocery store.

Of course those couple of things somehow multiply into a cartful by the time I head for the checkout lines. Only one of the twelve registers is open. Figures. The headache I'd managed to dull with a couple of aspirin flares up in full force, when I see someone I'd rather avoid standing in line already.

"Willa. How wonderful to see you."

Maris Dietrich.

I haven't missed the program coordinator since leaving the VA hospital, so I can't say the same. The woman had been a thorn in my side ever since the object of her obsession, Dr. Brantley Parker—who is responsible for the veterans' outpatient programs—decided I would be next on his vast menu of conquests.

Maris, in her narrow-minded wisdom, decided it had to be my fault he didn't look at her twice, and proceeded to make my life miserable enough I jumped at the job opportunity at the shelter.

Still, I plaster a smile on my face.

"Hi, Maris. You look good." I reluctantly push my cart in line behind her.

"Why, thank you. How sweet of you," she gushes and I wonder what happened to that sharp tongue of hers. "I'm engaged now," she says, waving a giant rock in my face. "Happier than I've ever been, which is probably showing."

"Must be." I make what I hope are the appropriate sounds of admiration as I'm made to study the ring. "Who's the lucky man?"

"Why, Brantley Parker, of course," she says, eyeing me intently.

It's on my tongue to congratulate her on finally landing the man, but manage to contain myself.

"Well, congratulations. I'm thrilled for you both." I'm very proud of my mature response, even though I mentally add, "You deserve each other."

When the cashier calls for the next person in line, Maris mumbles a distracted, "Thank you," before turning her back.

My mind is still on the interesting encounter when I push the cart toward my RAV. My eyes scan the parking lot for a glimpse of the woman, but instead they catch on a figure a couple of rows over.

I could've sworn I just saw Dave Williams duck between two parked cars.

DIMAS

"Rosie tells me you've been sniffing around Willa."

I shouldn't be surprised he's calling me out on that. As disgustingly happy as Jake and Rosie are, it stands to reason they don't keep secrets.

We're finally on our way back to Grand Junction after a day I'd like to erase from memory. Yanis and Bree are driving the Yukon in front of us, with Mercedes in the back seat.

Yanis got her to confess to setting this whole stalker thing up with the aid of one of her equally clueless girlfriends. Hard to believe that a thirty-one-year-old woman—let alone two—would be that stupid. And why? Because of a dumb crush?

From what I understand, she'd tried to throw me under the bus by claiming it had been more than what it was and I'd supposedly made her promises. I consider myself lucky neither Yanis nor Jake bought into that.

Then of course there's this fucked-up situation with Willa that I don't fully understand.

"If you mean have I been seeing her, then yes," I answer curtly. "Although that may well be a thing of the past, so you don't need to go all big brother on me."

His chuckle annoys me.

"Fuck it up already?"

"She blocked my phone number and I don't even fucking know what I did."

"Willa doesn't strike me as a flighty person, so I'm sure she felt she had a good reason."

I shoot him a glare.

"Is that you being supportive? Because if it is, you suck at it," I grumble.

"No, that's me being observant and if you weren't in such a pissy mood, you would've noted I didn't say she *had* a good reason, I said she must've *felt* she had one."

"All I know is I tried calling her last night as we'd agreed, and she didn't answer. I was leaving her a message when Mercedes walked into the bedroom, running her mouth. Fuck, as soon as that situation was under control I left another couple of messages to explain. This morning she'd blocked my number and I ended up calling from Bree's phone, but she hung up on me. You tell me what I did wrong."

"Shit, brother. That goes beyond my pay scale, but according to Rosie…" he pulls out his phone and looks at the screen, "and I quote; you suck and should grovel until Willa forgives you for being an asswipe, or Rosie won't ever talk to you again." Then he pins me with a glare. "Clearly you did something. You should go talk to her."

"Not helping me," I grind out, attempting to keep my focus on the road. If I could've talked to her, whatever this is could've been sorted out already, but she won't fucking listen.

Ahead of me the Yukon turns off toward the airport. I keep going straight to the next exit.

"Hey, baby," I hear Jake on his phone beside me. "We're on our way home. Yeah, I'll tell you when I get there. Dimi's dropping me off at the office so I can pick up my truck. Yes, he's here. I already—. Okay, hang on one sec." He turns to me. "Rosie wants to talk to you."

"Oh, for fuck's sake," I grumble.

"Yeah, that's him. Okay, hang on, gonna put you on speakerphone."

"You're an idiot," Rosie's voice is loud and clear.

I press my lips together before I say something Jake is not going to be happy about. The asshole is chuckling beside me.

"He's clueless," he informs his wife. "Put him out of his misery, baby,"

"Dimas?"

"What, Rosie?" I sigh, frustrated out of my mind.

"You want a clue? Check your last text message to Willa."

My last text? That was yesterday morning when I was picking up Bree to head up to Palisade. That's when I told her I'd call her later.

"The one about talking dirty?"

Jake's chuckles turn into a laugh and I throw a sharp glance his way as I turn into the PASS parking lot.

"What?" Rosie squeals. "Your memory must be failing you. I suggest you check again. Jake, honey, I'll see you when you get home."

The moment he gets out of the vehicle, I pull out my phone and check.

Me: Excited. Definitely.

That's the last text I sent her.

I toss my phone in the cup-holder and drive off, still no wiser. I don't even think I touched it until I let…

Fucking hell.

I get to Willa's place in record time. Relieved to see her RAV in the driveway, I pull in behind it. The door opens as I walk up. She must've seen me pull in.

"What do you want, Dimas?" she asks, sounding and looking tired.

"I want you to look at this." I hold my phone up in front of her. "Read it," I prompt her when she doesn't take her eyes off me.

"Why am I looking at this?"

"Because that's the last message I sent you."

"Bullshit."

"Here." I shove the phone at her and watch as she tries to scroll down.

"I don't understand," she finally says.

"That makes two of us. Can I come in so we can sort this out?"

For a moment it looks like she's going to say no,

but then she steps out of the way and I quickly move past her inside.

"Where's your phone?"

"I'll get it."

I follow her into the kitchen where her phone is charging on the counter. She unplugs it, punches in a code, and hands it over. I immediately go to her texts and my blood boils when I read what I'm supposed to have sent.

"That goddamn bitch," I spit out, and almost fling Willa's phone at the wall, just catching myself at the last minute.

"Okay. I am so confused. Are you saying you didn't send those?"

"Fuck no, I didn't send those."

I'm barely holding on to my temper when she turns around and opens the fridge, taking out a couple of beers and setting them on the counter.

"I'm going to grab a sweater and we'll go outside. You can punch a tree if you need to, but then I'd really appreciate an explanation."

When she disappears down the hallway, I grab the beers and head out on her back deck. If I regretted fucking Mercedes before, I do even more now. The last thing I want to do is explain what already was a really bad decision at the time. One with consequences worse than I could've anticipated.

I set the beers on a small table between two Adirondack chairs and move to lean on the railing, hanging my head as I take a few deep breaths in. I turn when I hear the sliding door open.

"First of all, I'm so fucking sorry. I couldn't figure out why you weren't taking my calls, but I get it now." I take the bottle she hands me and take a swig when she sits down in one of the chairs, pulling her knees up to her chest. I stay where I am so I can look at her. "The day before I met you I made a monumental mistake."

I don't hold back and tell her everything. She sips her beer and keeps a mostly straight face; until I get to the part where we came to the conclusion Mercedes Rockton had faked a stalker just to get close to me.

"What a fucking psycho."

"Pretty much," I agree, relieved at her reaction.

I toss back my beer, set the bottle on the railing, and move toward her, leaning down. But when I try to kiss her she stops me.

"Hold on. Not so fast."

Fuck.

I was afraid that was too easy.

CHAPTER 12

DIMAS

"MOTHERFUCKER!"

I quickly reach down and pull Radar to his feet. Blood is streaming from his nose.

"Fuck, brother. I'm sorry."

I grab a towel off the ropes and toss it at him before he bleeds all over the floor.

"I think you broke it." His voice is muffled as he presses the towel to his face with one hand, and unclips the strap of his headgear.

"We'll get you checked out. Jesus, Radar, you're like a goddamn faucet."

I've been in a foul mood since Willa put the brakes on a few days ago. I'd been ready to pick up where we'd left off, but apparently that doesn't work for her. She needed some time, so I gave her some, but it's been four days and it's starting to mess with my head.

I was taking my frustration out in the ring, when Radar mumbled something about me needing to get laid, and I hauled out.

"Save those hits for your bout, fucker," he says, climbing between the ropes. "You're gonna need it."

Radar put my name in as a challenger for this coming Wednesday night in Loma. I could've called Jason Krupcek, that scout, to set something up, but it works better if I can decide who I fight and when I fight.

I've chosen not to share this with my brother yet and have sworn Radar to secrecy. After the fiasco in Palisade, I'm afraid he wouldn't be too open to my plans and I can't afford to be slowed down. Hank tells me Brad is hanging on by a thread and I need to get him out of there.

So I'm going ahead, with only Radar to back me up, and hope I can get some answers for Brad. I'll deal with my brother after.

Lena is the first person we encounter when we walk into the office a couple of hours later, after a visit to the emergency room, and her mouth falls open.

"Holy shit, what happened to you?"

Radar's nose turned out not to be broken but is pretty swollen, and he's starting to look like a raccoon from the bruising around his eyes.

"Gym mishap," he mutters, darting by her desk and disappearing into his office, slamming the door shut behind him.

I head for the small kitchen in search of coffee. Bree is just coming out.

"Yanis was looking for you earlier. He's on his way to Panama to deal with some issues at the copper mine."

There are a few North American mining companies with interests in Central and South America we have contracts with. Mostly for personal security of the executives when visiting the mines, but the contract for the copper mine includes site security since it started commercial production last year. We had to hire local staff for the project.

"What issues?"

"Theft. One of our guards was caught with his hand in the cookie jar. Yanis is flying out to try and salvage the contract."

Copper is a valuable commodity. Hell, copper is stripped from houses and commercial job sites because it's worth a pretty penny even as scrap.

Theft is one of the main things we're supposed to be there to protect against. Having one of our own employees do the stealing does not look good. I'm glad putting out fires like that isn't my job.

"What did he need me for?"

"He wants you to take his meeting at The Red Apple today. One thirty. He left the file on your desk to go over."

We're supposed to install security and cameras throughout the new nightclub scheduled to open in six weeks. For the past couple of months, the inside of the freestanding commercial building has been gutted and is being turned into a high-end, two-story club not too far from where I live.

Yanis had done the front-end work on this contract,

but I guess we're getting close to installation.

"No problem."

While I spend most of the morning going over the plans and Yanis' notes, Radar was the subject of some intense ribbing by Jake and Bree. Every so often he'd throw a dirty look in my direction until Jake picks up on it.

"You wouldn't have anything to do with the state of Radar's face, now would you?"

"Me? Don't know what you're talking about."

"Hmm. You're a shit liar." I decide ignoring him is the best course of action until he adds, "Is this about Willa?"

Shit. I managed to distract myself all morning, but hearing her name brings back all the frustration. I pile all the paperwork back in the file, tuck it under my arm and get up.

"I'm gonna head out."

"Your appointment isn't until one thirty," he points out.

"I've got a stop to make first."

Ignoring the smug smile on Jake's face, I walk over to Lena's desk to let her know I'm off before heading out.

On the way downtown I wonder if, with Yanis out of the way, I should include Jake in my plans. Wouldn't be a bad idea to have both him and Radar at my back Wednesday night. Just in case.

I find a parking spot a few doors down from the Dream Cafe and head inside to put in my order for two of their Malibu chicken sandwiches. The place already has a healthy lunch crowd going, so when the girl behind the counter tells me it'll be ten minutes, I head next door to Grand Valley Books to kill some time.

Fifteen minutes later, I walk into the South Avenue Shelter, heading straight for Willa's office.

"She's not in there."

I swing my head around to find Rosie behind the desk in her office, with the door open. She's grinning at me.

"Where is she?"

"She's got a group session. Just started ten minutes ago, she'll be at least an hour, if not more." She points a finger at the bags in my hand. "What's that?"

"Lunch." When I see her eyes light up I quickly add, "Willa's."

"You can put it on her desk. I'll keep an eye on it."

"I don't trust you, Rosie," I tease her. "I've heard stories from Jake. Pregnancy has turned you into a food thief."

"I am not." To my horror she looks like she's about to cry.

"I'm just kidding, Rosie, I've got two sandwiches. Here, let me put hers on her desk and you and I can share mine."

I walk into the empty office and set the bag on Willa's desk. Then I grab a Post-it note and a pen and jot down a quick line, sticking it to the bag before I return to Rosie's side of the hallway.

"This is good," she says with a mouthful of Malibu chicken a few minutes later.

"Mmm. It is."

"But didn't you wanna wait for Willa?"

"I can't. I have an appointment in half an hour," I explain, before taking another big bite of my sandwich.

"She'll be disappointed she missed you."

I almost choke. "I don't know about that."

"I do."

WILLA

That was a good session.

Small, with only four of the residents attending, but it turned out to be the right mix.

It started when one of the guys asked if I knew how Brad was doing. Unfortunately I didn't have a good answer for that, but it launched a discussion on the fear of being confined to a small space. Two out of the four guys admitted to panicking when they're closed in a small room or elevator. That led to a good discussion about triggers and responses, and how different they could be from person-to-person.

With conversation flowing so freely, I could've gone on forever, but the last ten minutes my stomach started complaining loudly.

I clean up the discarded cups, toss them in the garbage, and close the door behind me. Passing Rosie's office, I see she has the door open.

"Hey, I'm heading out to grab something for lunch, want me to bring you something?"

"Already had lunch," she says with a grin. "And you don't have to go out. Lunch is on your desk."

I swing around and see the bag sitting on my desk.

"Sweet. Thanks, Rosie."

As I head into my office I swear I hear her mutter, "Don't thank me."

I notice a Post-it note stuck to the bag, pluck it off and sit down in my chair, reading it.

Sorry I missed you. See you tonight.
xo D.

Tonight?

No wonder Rosie had that smug look on her face. When I was on my way to the group room, she'd called me into her office, asking me when I was going to stop making Dimas pay for the sins of others.

Making him pay wasn't the reason why I asked for some time, but I did want to make a point. To myself. It would've been easy to give in a few days ago, when he showed up at my door with explanations. To just let him kiss me and take me to bed, forget how upset I'd been the twenty-four hours prior.

That hadn't been his fault, it had been my own, because I jumped to conclusions when just calling to ask for clarification after that last text message, or taking his calls, or listening to his messages, could've saved me a sleepless night and a miserable day.

Asking for time was so I could get my own head straight, because one thing I've learned in this profession, if you expect the worst of people, eventually they'll live up to those expectations.

I open the bag, and fish out the sandwich, when I notice there's something else at the bottom. I pull out what looks like a gift-wrapped book, an envelope taped to it. Inside the envelope is a card that has me burst out laughing so hard, Rosie comes running.

"What?"

I hold up the plan white card so she can read what it says:

YOU SUCK LESS THAN MOST PEOPLE.

Dimas added a written message.

I'll bring dinner. Do. Not. Cook.
xo D.

"Looks like he's got your number," she says, grinning. "Told you he's a good guy."

"Yes, you did."

"What's that?" She points at the package.

"Not sure."

I tear off the wrapper to uncover a very pretty ring-bound planner. I flip it open and notice he's written something on the inside of the cover.

Pencil me in. Please.
xo D.

—

I get home a little after five thirty to find him already waiting on my front step.

Grabbing my things, I get out, hit the locks, and walk straight up to him. I lift up on my toes and press my lips to his mouth.

"Thank you. That was very thoughtful of you and I loved it, but it wasn't necessary."

His arm snakes around the small of my back and he tugs me closer.

"Maybe not, but if it gets me invited inside, it was well worth it."

I smile up at him. "I would've invited you in regardless."

He leans down and brushes my lips with his.

"Good to know." Then he lets me go and holds up a bag from one of my favorite Chinese restaurants. "Dinner's getting cold."

Over dinner we chat easily about odds and ends, until Dimas suddenly puts his chopsticks down.

"I never asked you what you wanted to talk to me about. The text you sent?" he clarifies.

Part of me wants to tell him about what Brad told me and what I've discovered since, but then I'd also have to confess I took a peek at something that wasn't meant for my eyes. I feel guilty and not just a little ashamed, but would likely do it again. Brad has been locked up for five days, and I can't imagine—given what I know about him—that he's doing well. I also don't trust those cops.

It took a bit for me to sort out the numbers on that schedule are actually zip codes and street names, but now I have a general location and a date where I think the next fight will be. I haven't really thought about what I can do, and I'm not stupid so I'll keep my distance, but I can at least have a look at who shows up.

"I was worried about Brad. The police had been in to ask me questions again," I give him a limited version of the truth. "Mainly about him, which concerned me."

He reaches over and lightly strokes the pad of his thumb along my jaw.

"I'm sorry I didn't answer."

"Water under the bridge," I assure him with a smile. "Do you know how he's doing, though? What's happening?"

"I've been in touch with Hank. He says he's hanging in. I don't want you to worry about it though, Hank's got it covered."

Well, I'm glad Dimas seems to firmly have his trust in Hank, but I don't really know the man so I'll reserve judgment.

"Are you done?"

I get up from my stool to clear the dishes, but Dimas turns and pulls me between his legs, his arms banding around me.

"We'll get those later," he mumbles, even as his mouth descends on mine.

His kiss is thorough and overwhelming. In about one-point-two seconds my mind is drained of all coherent thought. With his hands tracing my curves and his tongue exploring my mouth, my whole body is sensitized.

"Love your taste," he mumbles, when he drags his lips along the column of my throat.

"That's the Szechwan pork," I point out.

He buries his face in my neck and chuckles. The vibrations are like a high-voltage charge straight to my core. I can't control the resulting full body shiver and Dimas lifts his head to study me.

"Are you cold?"

I shake my head. "The opposite," I confess and watch as his eyes darken.

"Fuck, sweetheart, you're killing my plan," he groans.

"What plan?"

"To woo you, win you over."

I let out an inadvertent snort at his word choice.

"Woo? I don't think I've ever had anyone woo me before." I press my lips together but don't succeed in keeping the smile off my face.

"Are you laughing at me?"

I lift my hand and show my thumb and index finger

close together. He grabs the hand, gets on his feet, and pulls me behind him to the bedroom, where he unceremoniously shoves me backward onto the bed. I plant my elbows in the mattress to lift myself up so I can see him pull his shirt over his head. Next he unbuckles his belt, undoes his fly, and shoves jeans and underwear down his ass. I'm momentarily distracted by his erect cock, almost flat against his stomach, before I notice he's struggling to get his jeans over his prosthesis.

I scramble off the bed.

"Sit down."

He looks like he's going to protest, but when I give him a little nudge; he turns and sits. Without a word I sink on my knees between his and quickly remove the boot and sock from his right foot. I feel his eyes on me when I turn my attention to his prosthesis, which I quickly figure out and remove before sliding his jeans off. Then I carefully roll down his prosthetic sock, revealing his stump before I look up at him.

His eyes scan my face, maybe looking for any aversion, but he won't find any. Every part of him is beautiful. Bracing myself with my hands on his knees, I hold his gaze as I lean forward and run my tongue from his balls to the tip of his engorged cock.

There's something about having a gorgeous, strong, and virile man shiver at your touch. I'm still fully dressed, while he is completely exposed. It takes a confident man to let himself be controlled, which is even more of a turn-on.

His head drops back and he loudly groans when my tongue traces the crown before I slide him into my mouth. His hand comes up and he twists his fingers in my hair, helping me set the pace. When I use a hand to play with his balls, he lets out a muffled curse and pulls me back.

He's breathing hard when I look up at him. His nostrils flared and a dark flush on his cheekbones.

"Need you naked, Willa," he says in a low voice, and I'm so turned on, I don't hesitate.

Getting to my feet, I kick off my shoes while pulling my shirt over my head, and in seconds I'm as naked as he is.

"Condom," he grinds out, as he pulls himself further onto the mattress until his back is against the headboard. "Right front pocket of my jeans." I get what I need, climb on the mattress after him, and hand over the foil wrapper. "Come here," he says when he has himself sheathed, and I swing a leg over his hips, straddling him. With both hands on my hips, he agonizingly slowly guides me down on him. "So fucking beautiful. So wet for me. So perfect."

"Yes, God, yes," I mutter breathlessly, as I adjust to the feeling of him so deeply seated inside me.

His thumb slides down to where we're connected and brushes lightly over my clit. Every pass is like an electric charge.

"Fuck me, Willa. Take me there."

Slow at first, but once I find my rhythm I ride him with full abandon, encouraged by his rumbled words of appreciation. When his hips buck up underneath me, I know he's as close as I am and I grind myself down on him shamelessly in my quest for release.

I may have screamed as the sudden pull of his lips around my nipple tips the scale, and my whole body seems to convulse around him.

"Fffuck, yeah," he growls, his face pressed between my breasts. "I could stay like this forever, with you filling all my senses."

CHAPTER 13

DIMAS

I DON'T PARTICULARLY want to get up, but I have to get my ass to the gym for one last workout.

Not sure it will make a difference in the beating I stand to receive tomorrow night, but at least I'll have done what I can to prepare.

Reluctantly I move away from Willa's warm, soft curves pressed against me. She moans a sleepy complaint, but then turns over and is back asleep. I hop to the bathroom, hoping she has something that doesn't smell like flowers or cake I can wash myself with. I'm pleasantly surprised when I find the plain bar of Dial soap in her shower.

Two towels hang on the rack, one of which looks unused, so I grab that to dry myself off with. Back in the bedroom, I recover my stump sock and free my prosthesis from the tangle of my jeans and, as quietly as I can, get dressed in the dark.

I'm just tugging my shirt over my head when Willa rolls over, blinking her sleepy eyes.

"You leaving?" she whispers.

"Yeah. I have some things to take care of this morning."

"Oh." The single syllable is expelled on a breath and followed with a cute pout I feel compelled to kiss off her lips.

"I could be back here tonight, though." That earns me a pleased smile. "And maybe we can sleep in a little tomorrow morning." The smile stretches wider.

"I'd like that," she mumbles.

"Good, because I'll be busy tomorrow night and won't be able to see you then."

I'm tempted to let her know where I'll be but I'm afraid she may put up a protest, so I keep it to myself.

"I've got stuff to do as well," she mutters, her eyes already closing again.

I bend down and kiss her softly.

"I'll be in touch later, okay?"

"Mmm."

"Sweet dreams, Willa."

Her response is no more than a little grunt before she snuggles under the covers. For a moment I just sit there, watching as her breathing deepens with sleep. Then I sneak out of the bedroom and out of the house.

By the time I get to the office, I'm almost dragging my knuckles on the floor. Radar had me work the bags this morning. His face looks pretty bad and we decided it would probably be best not to risk stepping in the ring. He put me through my paces, though, and my arms and shoulders feel like I've been quartered.

Bree comes over the moment I sit at my desk.

"How was the meeting yesterday?"

I shove the file her way.

"Only a few changes from our original plan. Shouldn't have any impact on our timeline, though. They'll be ready to get us in there next Monday."

"Okay, I'll get Lena to add it to the schedule. You and Radar on this?"

"Yeah. I just need to check materials to see if we need to order extra."

"Just let me know."

"Did you talk to Yanis?" I ask her.

"He called this morning. Says it looks like he'll likely be there until at least Sunday, maybe longer."

"That bad?"

She shrugs. "The guy they caught appears to have been only the tip of the iceberg. Yanis promised the client he would stay until this is resolved."

"Pretty bold promise."

"Guess that was the only way he could convince them not to pull the contract."

"Gotta do what you gotta do." I look around the office. "Where's Jake?"

"Ultrasound this morning. He should be in before lunch."

"Can fucking barely believe he's a married man, let alone gonna be a father," I mutter, shaking my head.

"Who knows," Bree says with a shrug, "by next year that could be you. Provided Willa puts up with you that long."

"How'd you...? Goddammit, you guys are like a bunch of gossiping old ladies," I grumble when she grins widely. "Jake talked."

"No more than you did when he started hanging around with Rosie."

I pin her with a stare.

"You know what that means, right?" I tease her with a straight face. "You're next."

"Never," she states, but a blush is creeping up her cheeks. "That'll never happen," she reiterates, but does it walking back to her desk.

"Never say never," I call after her.

Jake walks in half an hour later, a ditzy smile on his face and a dazed look in his eyes.

"You okay?"

His eyes slowly focus on me as he sits down at his desk.

"It's a girl," he says as his smile widens. "They couldn't say for sure last time, but she gave us a clear view today. A girl," he repeats.

I can't help but match his grin.

"That's great news, brother."

Bree walks over and gives Jake a hug before pointing out, "You know you won't have a moment's rest in about fifteen years or so, right?"

Suddenly shock washes over his face.

"I need more guns."

Radar comes out of his office to see what the hilarity is all about. Not that Jake thought it was one bit funny.

With everyone in one place and the mood uplifted, I decide I may as well fill Jake and Bree in. Hank emailed me a copy of the same fight schedule Radar had found online. He got it from Brad. With him in the know as well, there really isn't much point trying to do this quietly. The fact Hank asked me to look into it validates my involvement. Somewhat.

"I might need your help," I start.

Jake knows Brad's story, but Bree doesn't, so for her benefit I give some background, his current situation, the so-called evidence law enforcement has on him, and my plans for tomorrow night.

"Does Yanis know about this?" is Bree's expected reaction.

"No, and I'd prefer it to stay that way. At least while he's stuck in Panama. Nothing he can do from there anyway," I point out.

"What is it exactly you hope to accomplish tomorrow?" Jake wants to know, eyeing me sharply.

"Blend in. Get people comfortable enough to talk to me if they think I'm one of them. Someone has to know something, but I doubt they'd be eager to share. There's a lot of money involved in these unsanctioned fights."

"It looks like a well-organized outfit," Radar adds. "And the chat room where I found information on the fights boasts over sixty-thousand members nationwide."

"Jesus," Bree mutters.

"Yeah. It's a thriving business. From what Radar

uncovered, they have a roster of fighters who can be challenged by any enthusiast," I expand. "Buy-in is two grand. It's a simple elimination structure, and with eight scheduled fights to start off, there's a potential for fifteen bouts to decide an overall winner. Aside from the total sixteen grand buy-in proceeds, it's gonna generate a whack of betting income with each bout."

"You're not a trained fighter," Jake observes dryly. Radar makes a choking sound, catching his attention. "Wait, that was Dimas?" he asks, indicating the sorry state of Radar's face.

"He may not be trained, but he's got a hell of a punch."

"What about your leg?" Bree wants to know.

"What about it? As long as I can keep to my feet, I'll be fine."

"Anything on the T-shirt they found? If it wasn't him, someone went through a lot of trouble to make it look like it was," she observes and it's Radar who answers.

"Easy to nab one of his shirts. They do common laundry at the shelter."

"Implying it would've been someone with access to shelter laundry taking it."

"Probably. I'm checking into all the other residents, but short of someone coming out and claiming responsibility, it's gonna be hard to pin on one person," Radar admits.

It's quiet for a few moments when Jake speaks up.

"I'm in."

He looks at Bree, who rolls her eyes dramatically as she sighs audibly.

"Fine. Count me in too."

WILLA

"A girl? Oh my God!"

I get up and round my desk to give Rosie a hug.

She's beaming: a high blush on her cheeks and her eyes shiny with happy tears.

"I can finally pick out the right paint color," she says, making me laugh.

From what I understand, this will be the third time the nursery will be repainted. She'd tried for gender neutral colors—soft green, butter yellow, and finally a periwinkle gray—but apparently still not to her satisfaction.

"Does Jake know?" I tease her and her face goes soft.

"He says he doesn't care if he has to paint the damn room a different color every week, since I'm giving him a little princess," she answers quietly.

Okay, I'm not one for easy tears but that makes my eyes sting. I wouldn't have thought Jake could be so sweet. Rosie is a lucky woman, and from the expression on her face, it's clear she knows it too.

"What color are you thinking?"

"A cream base with lilac diamonds."

Not being particularly fashion or color coordinated,

I'm having a hard time picturing it, but I tell her, "I love it," anyway.

"Me too," she says dreamily. "I'd love to turn her room into something out of Arabian Nights, with lots of rich fabrics and textures. Maybe a canopy bed when she gets older. I already saw this perfect light fixture at Wayfair." She smiles to herself. "I used to wish for a room like that growing up, but there just wasn't enough space in our trailer house."

"How lovely you get to create it for your own little girl."

Kids have never been on my radar in any serious way. Don't get me wrong, I love my niece, I love kids in general. It's just that I've never seen myself as a mother. Of course I never considered myself relationship material either, and look at me now. This thing with Dimas is sure starting to look like one.

"We should celebrate," I blurt out, in an attempt to distract myself from the direction my thoughts were taking. "We can't do cocktails, but have you had lunch?"

"Not yet." She smiles. "What did you have in mind?"

"I think we should hit up Be Sweet for some of their champagne cupcakes."

Her mouth falls open and her eyes light up.

"I would *love* that…but I have to be back here at one thirty."

I check the clock on my desk and then grin at her.

"How many cupcakes can you put away in an

hour?"

"Let's go find out."

An hour later, we stumble back into the shelter, sugar-drunk and giggling like a couple of schoolgirls. Be Sweet cupcakes are the bomb, but I may be a tad nauseated after downing four with the latte I ordered.

Coming down the hall, I find Rupert waiting outside my office. Rupert is our oldest resident at seventy-two, a sweetheart, and more than a little confused most of the time. He occasionally pops in for a chat.

"Have you been waiting long?"

"It's all good," he mumbles when I open the door for him and let him lead the way inside.

Usually Rupert will talk about his wife, who passed away twelve years ago. He'd looked after her for the years she battled cancer and was by her side when she died. Without children to support him, he disappeared into the bottle and ended up losing everything he and his wife had spent a lifetime building. The night after the first time I heard Rupert's story, I cried myself to sleep.

Sadly his is not an uncommon story. He served in Vietnam, came home at twenty-seven, married his Cora, and led a relatively normal life until she got ill. She was the love of his life.

"How are you, Rupert?" I ask when he sits down in one of the club chairs across from my desk.

"Doin' all right. Hear anything about Brad? He ain't gonna last in there."

"I actually heard from a friend yesterday, he's hanging in."

"He the guy droppin' off food here for you yesterday?"

"Dimas, yes. Brad and he are—"

"Friends, I know. He your boyfriend?"

There's no confusion whatsoever in Rupert's eyes this time.

"I'm seeing him, yes."

"Could do worse 'n that boy," he concludes. "He'll look after ya."

I grin at him. "You know I've been looking after myself most of my life, right?"

"Never hurts to have an extra pair 'a eyes on ya. Especially these days."

I lean forward with my elbows on my desk.

"These days?" I probe, and he shakes his head.

"Gotta watch your back, girlie. Everybody ain't what they look to be. They got Brad, didn't they?"

The hair on my arms stands on end.

"Who are you talking about, Rupert?"

"They think I don't know nothin'...I don't see what they're up to. I ain't stupid, though. I see plenty."

His voice gets louder and his eyes are darting around the room, never quite focusing on me anymore.

"What do you see, Rupert?" I ask, keeping my voice as calm and level as I can.

Behind him I see the door open and Ron sticks his head in.

"They're everywhere," he yells agitatedly, as he

gets to his feet. "Waiting, watching. They got Artie, but they're not gonna get me!"

He starts moving to the door but stops in his tracks when he sees Ron and Rosie in the doorway. Then he turns his head around to me and hisses, "Watch your back."

As Ron leads him down the hall, I notice Dave stepping out of their way. His eyes are on me.

CHAPTER 14

WILLA

I HAVE NOTHING to wear.

I mostly dress myself blindly in the morning since seventy-five percent of my wardrobe consists of jeans and tees. Tonight I'm at a loss.

The day started off well enough, waking up to a very warm, very firm body pressed against me. It turns out Dimas likes to take his time when he doesn't have to get up at some ungodly hour. By the time he was done with me my body was Jell-O, and I almost ended up late for work.

At the shelter is where nerves started plaguing me, when I slip into the dining room for a coffee and spot Rupert sitting by the window, watching me.

Last night Ron had gently guided him out of my office while Rosie slipped in to make sure I was okay. I won't lie; the incident had shaken me. I know the old man has episodes where his mind leaves him, but his passionate ramblings last night felt more rooted in reality than fantasy.

The clear eyes that were staring at me from across the room this morning seemed to confirm it.

He showed up for this afternoon's group session but didn't say much. Normally, he's the most vocal resident and as a result of his silence, it had been a struggle to keep the group going for the allotted hour. Could be just my anxiety, but it felt like all the guys were kind of subdued today.

Then Rosie dropped in after, asking if I wanted to go shopping for the baby tonight since Jake was working late. She wasn't quite able to hide her disappointment when I told her I couldn't because I had *things* to do. So by the time I got home, I was anxious *and* felt guilty.

Now I'm standing in front of my closet, trying to figure out what one should wear when planning to spy on an illegal fighting ring. I have yet another moment filled with second thoughts, but then I snatch a pair of dark jeans and a navy Henley shirt off their respective hangers.

I quickly change, shove my feet in a pair of dark blue Skechers and pull my hair into a ponytail, when my phone rings.

"Hi, Mom," I answer, when I see my parents' number on the screen.

"How are you, honey?"

The endearment puts me on alert. Mom uses it on rare occasions when something is expected of me or to precede bad news of some kind.

"I'm fine, Mom. Is everything okay there?"

"Your father and I are fine, dear," she assures me, but then she clears her throat and I know there's more coming. "We have Brittany with us this week."

I'm a little confused. My sister is a stay-at-home mom, so why would Britt be with my parents?

"You do? Is something wrong with Connie?" When she doesn't answer right away I prompt her, "Mom?"

"Well, Connie and Jim need some time alone."

"Are they on vacation?"

"No…"

"Mom, what's going on?"

I'm getting annoyed having to pull teeth to get whatever the story is out of her, so my tone is a little sharp.

"No need to get snippy with me, Wilhelmina."

When the full name comes out, it's usually followed by a lecture and I don't really have time to sit through one.

"Mom, I'm meeting someone and I'm going to be late. Can you maybe get to the point?"

"Oh? You're seeing someone?"

I roll my eyes to the ceiling. Of course she would focus on that.

"I said I'm meeting someone, Mom. Can we get to the point, please?"

"Your sister and her husband have hit a little bump in the road. That's all. They just wanted a little time to sort things out."

I would love to know what that little bump is, but I won't get it from Mom. Connie and Jim are the perfect couple in my parents' world, and she'd protect that image at any cost.

"So they dropped Brittany off with you."

"Yes, and she's fine here until the weekend, but after that…"

"What happens after that?"

"Well, you know your father always plays golf in Southern Pines the first two weeks of July, dear."

My father has had a golf schedule since he retired from the armed forces. Summer is North Carolina, where he golfs with one of his army buddies—always the same two weeks—and he doesn't go anywhere without Mom to cater to him like some personal assistant.

I'm starting to get the picture.

"You want to drop her off here?"

"Well, her last day of camp is Friday and your father wants to leave on Sunday."

Of course. Nothing can come between my father and his all-important golf game. Familiar anger bubbles up, not just at my father for being a narcissistic asshole, but also at my mother for continuing to facilitate him, and blowing off her only grandchild to do it. Worst of all, my poor niece is being shuffled around like an inconvenience from household to household.

As much as I'd like to stand firm, I know the only person who'd get hurt in all of this would be her, and she doesn't deserve that.

"Of course she's always welcome here, but I have to work, Mom. I can't take time off, I just started a few months ago."

"She's twelve, she can stay by herself during the day."

This from the mother who hovered like the proverbial helicopter parent over my sister and me until we moved out of the house. I bite back a sharp comment and instead take a deep breath in before I respond.

"I'll have a look to see what summer programs are out there. She needs something to do during the day."

I hope it's not too late. I'm sure most summer camps have been long booked up.

"Has Connie said anything about how long?"

"Not really."

I'm pissed. At my parents whose lives are so regimented they can't even stop to deal with a crisis, and at my sister and her dick of a husband, who ship off their daughter like she's a piece of furniture in the way.

"What time were you thinking of dropping her off?"

"We'll be there at noon and, Willa? Thank you."

The last is delivered in a soft voice that pulls at my heart. I know she means it, and I'm aware my father was behind the call in the first place, but I wish Mom had a little backbone.

"Mom? I've gotta run, but tell Britt I can't wait for her to get her cute butt over here."

My mind is going a mile a minute, trying to think of things to do for a twelve-year-old in Grand Junction on my drive out to Loma. At least it keeps me distracted from the anxiety around what I'm doing.

I had the presence of mind to grab a few bottles of water, some granola bars, and a portable charger for my phone, in case I run out of juice. The plan is to stay at a distance, get a peek at who enters.

Nerves win again when I turn right on 14 Road. Loma isn't particularly densely populated and I'm heading into farmland now. I should probably have looked at Google satellite before I came out here. Somehow I had it in my mind I'd have a parking lot to hang out in, or some buildings to hide behind, but that may not be the case.

It's already dark out and other than from the odd farmhouse, the road has no lighting. My eyes are squinting under the bill of my ball cap as I lean over my steering wheel to see where I'm going. Then I spot something flashing in the sky.

Clever, they're using laser to pinpoint the location.

The closer I get, the more cars I see on the road. There's a steady stream turning onto a dirt road running between two cornfields to a large equipment barn set back from the road. Cars are parked on one side in the field where the corn is partially cleared.

This is not exactly what I envisioned. I'd stand out like a sore thumb, just surveilling from my RAV. I briefly contemplate giving up altogether and turning right back around, but the dirt road is barely more than one set of tracks currently used by vehicles coming this way.

The other option is to go in. Go with the flow of people. Blend in.

Shit.

DIMAS

"You sure about this?"

I glance over at Bree in the passenger seat. Radar and Jake are in the vehicle behind us. Bree is going to mask as my girlfriend—which may give her a different behind-the-scenes perspective—while the guys are going to mingle with the crowd. The objective is to gather as much intel as we can between us.

"Positive," I confirm, even though the prospect of getting obliterated by someone nicknamed Bone Crusher—the fighter challenged by Radar on my behalf—isn't something I'm looking forward to.

She'd suggested earlier we could all simply go as observers, and I didn't need to get the snot kicked out of me, but we both know the best way to avoid suspicion is to jump in with both feet. Let them think I'm like the other idiots paying prime dollar to be used as punching bags. I'm pretty sure that's what this is going to amount to.

"Your funeral," she mumbles beside me. I hope it doesn't get that far.

We're out in the boonies here, nothing but farm fields and the odd building on either side. Law enforcement in Loma is provided by the Mesa County Sheriff's Office and Colorado State Patrol, but it's unlikely they'd be patrolling through farmland unless out on a specific call. Besides, you can't even see the cars parked from the road.

There's no room close to the dirt road leading in, but I find a spot at the far edge and pull right up to the cornfield. If for some reason we have to bail out of here, at least we're not stuck behind other cars and can just plow through the field.

I drape my arm around Bree as we walk toward the large barn and she leans into me, settling in our roles. There is no one guarding the large doors we walk through. There's a decent crowd gathered around the raised cage, where two guys are already fighting. Yelling and cheering go up with every impact of fists or feet. Bloodthirsty bunch.

I don't waste time looking for Jake and Radar, I know they're in here somewhere, scoping out the betting. Bree points at a sign that says *Challengers*, and we follow it to the back of the barn where we're stopped by a large guy. His shirt says STAFF and he's wearing a large semi-automatic on his hip.

"Fighters only," he grunts.

I hand him the ticket Radar printed off for me and try to move through, but he holds me back with a hand on my chest.

"Fighters only," he repeats.

I look at the makeshift locker room behind him and notice several females milling about.

"She's comin' with me," I challenge him. "She'll get eaten alive if I leave her alone out here. Look at her."

Bree's innocent looks and short stature work to our advantage, because he takes one glance at her and steps out of our way. He has no idea the set of lethal skills he's just invited in. Bree may come in a small package but she's not one to mess with.

I strip down to my shorts and take a seat, pulling Bree on my lap. She pulls rolls of narrow fabric from her purse and starts wrapping my hands, doubling up across my knuckles. After that we kill time pretending to make out while keeping an eye on the fighters coming and going, mentally noting things like general descriptions and identifiers like tattoos and scars. Some of the guys coming back look like their faces were run through a grinder.

I hear the crowd yell when the Bone Crusher is introduced, when the sleezeball from the gym walks in. Jason Krupcek. It doesn't take him long to spot me, and he ambles over.

"See you found your way here without my help."

He's not very good at hiding his annoyance.

"Thought I'd test the waters first," I share casually.

"Who'd you challenge to get in?"

"Bone Crusher."

He grimaces and sucks air in through his teeth.

"Shoulda called me. You could've gone on the roster and probably have an easier match. Woulda saved you the two grand buy-in as well."

"I'm a cautious kind of guy," I return, keeping my eyes steady on his. "I prefer to know what I'm getting into before I commit. I'll let you know after tonight."

"Fair enough." He shrugs. "Provided there's anything left after the Bone Crusher is done with you."

He barely gives Bree a second glance and walks off to chat up some other guys.

"Not too late to change your mind," she says, nuzzling my neck, but I can hear the humor in her voice.

"Yeah, it is," I point out when two minutes later the Bone Crusher's first victim is carried out on a stretcher, his arm slipping off the side and dragging along the dirty floor.

I grab Bree by the hips and lift her off me, so I can get up. I know the name I used is going to be called next.

"Stay here," I instruct Bree, loud enough to be heard, before tagging her behind the neck and planting a hard kiss on her mouth.

Kissing Bree is like kissing a sister, this is a role we've played before and it's all part of the job. I pull her arms from around my neck when the announcer calls me out, and walk down the narrow walkway they built to the cage.

If the crowd wasn't already intimidating with its roar for blood, the behemoth stalking around the cage with sweat rolling off his bulging muscles and blood soaked into his hand wraps would do the trick. Jesus, the guy is massive. I'm not small myself, but I'm a doughboy in comparison.

The older guy manning the gate to the cage checks my hand wraps to make sure I haven't hidden anything sharp or hard in them. Fuck, I could hide brass knuckles under there and I doubt it would make a difference in this fight.

I guess I passed because the gate is opened and I'm almost shoved in the cage. It's basically a round platform with heavy netting affixed to a metal frame. I try to ignore the sea of faces, heckling and yelling, and focus on my opponent instead. But before I have a chance to scope out any weak points he might have, the announcer yells, "Fight!" and I see a fist coming at my face.

One of the benefits of having a prosthesis is people tend to underestimate your agility, but aside from leaving me with a slight limp, I'm as agile as I was before I lost my leg. I made sure of that. It still presents a weak spot, simply because a well-aimed kick could seriously mess with my ability to defend myself.

So far agility wins, since I'm able to duck the first few punches he aims at me. The next ones I'm not so lucky and catch one on my jaw and one to my shoulder. I duck and dodge, trying to keep the much slower man off balance as much as I can and even manage to land a few hits to his body. It's almost like he's toying with me to get the crowd riled up.

I don't realize how true that is until he suddenly steps into my body, and plants his foot on the toe of my prosthesis. He uses the momentum of his body to knock me to the ground, ripping the suction socket off my stump. Fuck, that hurts.

I try to push up from the mat when his ripped arm rounds my neck, pulling me partially up.

"Dimas!" I hear the voice over the roar of the crowd and my eyes catch on a familiar face.

Before my brain has a chance to process Willa in the middle of the bloodthirsty mob, a solid hit lands on the side of my head and it's lights out.

CHAPTER 15

WILLA

THERE WASN'T MUCH security walking into the large barn.

I'd waited for a sizable group of people to tag on to and easily followed them inside. No one looked twice at me.

I stayed on the periphery of the crowd, weaving in and out, scanning faces to see if I recognized anyone. The energy in the place was intimidating, and the spectators were almost frenzied in their excitement when the first bout was announced. I had to look away a few times from the brutal fighting, wondering how people could enjoy two men beating each other to a pulp.

At some point, I pushed and shoved my way a little closer to the cage to change my vantage point. I'd been mostly looking at the backs of people's heads and figured if I had my back to the ring, I'd be able to see faces.

That's where I've been for the past ten minutes.

Scanning faces and getting pushed around. Good thing I've got some height and a little mass on me, or I could've been trampled a time or two.

Then I hear a heavy thud of one of the fighters going down hard. I turn my head and see a few men entering the cage to check on the guy. A stretcher is brought in and the unconscious fighter is carried off.

That's when I get a glimpse of one of the guys walking alongside it. A familiar face that looks so out of place, at first I have trouble identifying him, and when I do, I'm positive I must be wrong.

The announcer calls out the next fighter—*Gladiator*—another idiot with a name I'm sure his mama didn't give him, unless she was high on something. I ignore what is happening on the stage and try to make my way through the crowd to the back of the barn where I saw the stretcher disappear.

I don't get much farther than the doorway, where I'm held up by a massive guard, putting an unapologetic hand in the middle of my chest.

"Fighters only," he growls, giving me a little shove.

"Hey! Don't touch me," I snap, trying to sidestep the looming figure.

"Or what?"

He takes a threatening step closer when a hand appears on his shoulder.

"What's going on here?"

My breath falters when I recognize the voice, and when his face appears over the guard's shoulder I take an inadvertent step back.

His eyes narrow when he catches sight of me. "Willa?"

I promptly turn on my heel and dive into the crowd. *Jesus*. I have to get out of here.

Anxiety overwhelms me when the crush of bodies pushes me closer to the side of the cage. I try to brace myself on the edge of the platform to prevent getting flattened, when I catch sight of the man being held in a chokehold on the mat.

"Dimas!" I yell in surprise, when a pair of eyes that look as surprised as I am zoom in on me.

Disbelief freezes me for a second, before full-fledged panic hits as I realize what I'm looking at. I swing around, and with my head down shove forcefully through the bodies, with only one thought in mind; get out.

I'm breathless when I get to the RAV and with shaking hands try to fish my keys from my pocket, looking behind me to see if someone followed me out. I open my door, dive behind the wheel, and immediately lock up before starting the car.

I peel out of my parking spot, thanking God I had the presence of mind to back into it. When I pass by the barn I see the big guard coming out the doors, looking right at me.

It's not until I hit the highway leading back to Grand Junction and no one is behind me, that I dare let myself think.

Seeing Dimas in the cage surprised me, and for a brief second I wondered if I could've misjudged him so badly, but I quickly dismissed that. He was probably there for the same reason I was, to find anything that might help Brad. I'm actually infuriated with him for taking a stupid risk like that, stepping in a cage with that giant.

But it's the other man I recognized that scares me.

First of all, what are the odds that the last few months I've been able to forget he exists and suddenly within a week he pops ups twice on my radar. Once at the grocery checkout, talking to Maris of all people, and now here?

Dr. Brantley Parker. The man who tried—and failed—for five years to get in my pants, and didn't do well with rejection. The same guy I saw tending to the injured man *at a fucking illegal fighting ring.*

I can't even begin to process that information.

My heart rate settles into a more normal rhythm when I pull into my driveway, but still I find myself wishing I had a dog.

Inside I flip on lights and lock the door behind me, before going around the house, making sure all windows and doors are secure. Then I grab a beer from the fridge and pull my legs up underneath me on the couch while I contemplate what to do next.

I'd hoped to have an opportunity to ask if anyone knew Artie, but once there, I didn't have the guts to approach any of the excitable spectators. Finding out Brantley Parker is connected to illegal fighting more than makes up for it, but what do I do with the information? Tell the cops? They're likely to brush it off, seeing as they're so eager to pin things on Brad. They probably won't even want to acknowledge the existence of a fight ring, let alone consider a prominent physician might be involved.

My other option is to tell Dimas, who is clearly doing some investigating of his own. He'd seen me there now, so the fact I snooped is bound to come out anyway, if he hasn't figured it out yet. I know I have to tell someone. I'll call Dimas tomorrow.

I turn on the TV for some mindless distraction before I head to bed. While I watch an old episode of *Bones*, my mind starts drifting to my earlier conversation with Mom. That's another call I plan to make tomorrow morning, Connie. I should know what's happening so if Britt wants to talk, at least I'm not in the dark. I also want a letter from my sister giving me authority to enroll her daughter into a summer program somewhere. I don't like the idea of Britt alone for hours on end. Too much trouble a twelve-year-old can get into.

It's almost midnight when my eyes start to get heavy and I turn off the TV. I take my empty bottle to the kitchen and set it beside the sink before I start turning off the lights. I'm about to flick off the outside light in the front entrance when I about jump out of my skin at the rusty sound of my doorbell.

The sight of two uniformed policemen outside my door at midnight won't do much for my anticipated night's rest.

"Ms. Smith?"

The unpleasant Officer Bergland is accompanied by a much younger, and uncomfortable-looking, officer.

"That's still me," I answer, snippily. "What can I do for you in the middle of the night, officers?"

"Where were you tonight?"

"Excuse me?"

"It was a simple question, Ms. Smith," Bergland reiterates. "Where were you tonight?"

"What is this about?" An uneasy feeling crawls up my spine.

"Just answer the question."

"I'm not answering anything unless I know what it is that has you show up on my doorstep in the middle of the night."

"We found the body of Rupert Lezlo in the rail yard, less than a thousand feet from the shelter's parking lot," the younger officer clarifies, earning him a dirty look from the other man.

I slap a hand to my chest, unable to speak.

"Stabbed to death and clutching your business card, Ms. Smith." Bergland's expression is almost pleased when he gives me that devastating news. I know for sure I'm in a boatload of trouble when he follows it up with, "We're gonna need you to come with us for questioning."

DIMAS

"Fucking Willa?"

Jake barks, and I wince.

"Not so loud, for fuck's sake," I plead.

I'd been out for the count until someone shoved an ammonia capsule under my nose. Instead of letting someone there have a look at me, Bree got me dressed, grabbed my artificial leg, and helped me right out of the barn where Jake and Radar were already waiting. Collectively they got me into my truck and Bree took the wheel.

I kept insisting I was fine, but everyone ignored me and Bree drove me straight to the Community Hospital emergency room on our way into Grand Junction.

Apparently I will live—something I could've told them a couple of hours ago—and we're just waiting for the doc to give the all-clear so I can go home to nurse my battered face and ego.

"I'm gonna have a talk with her," Jake grumbles.

"You're not," I tell him firmly. "I'll handle Willa. Anyone know where my phone is?"

Bree hands it over, but before I have a chance to dial, the nurse sticks her head around the corner.

"You're good to go as long as you have someone to check on you. Any changes, dizziness, nausea, blurred vision, slurred speech, you come back here right away."

I give her a two-fingered salute and swing my legs over the side of the bed, and Bree hands me my prosthesis. My stump is pretty tender after that bout, but not nearly as tender as my pride. Found out firsthand why they call the guy Bone Crusher, and I hate to admit I was not even close to a match with him.

Bree refuses to give me my keys so I grudgingly get back in the passenger side.

"Call her," she urges me.

I dial Willa's number but don't get an answer. Then I try again with the same result.

"Can you swing by her place? I just want to make sure she got home okay."

I give Bree directions. I'm both worried about and pissed at Willa. The first for being there at all, without letting me know, and the second for apparently not sticking around long enough to check on me.

Her RAV is parked safely in the driveway and her outside light is on. She's probably asleep and turned her phone off or she's ignoring my calls. If not for Bree sitting beside me, and my body aching from the beating I'd received, I'd be banging on her door.

"Looks like she's home," Bree volunteers.

"Yeah, I'll deal with her tomorrow."

Less than ten minutes later, we pull up outside my house. To my surprise Bree gets out as well and locks the truck.

"What are you doing?"

"Staying here tonight."

"You can take my truck, we'll sort the rest out tomorrow."

She ignores me and keeps walking to the front door.

"You heard the nurse. You need someone to check on you. I'm staying."

Without slowing down, she fits my house key in the door, and leads the way inside. I'm too tired to argue, so while she makes herself comfortable on the couch, I walk into the kitchen, toss my phone on the counter, and grab myself some ibuprofen and a glass of water. Then, with a casual, "Good night," I head to my bedroom, manage to get stripped down to my boxers, and flop face-first on the bed. The shower will have to wait until tomorrow.

"Dimi...Dimi, wake the fuck up."

I blink and open my eyes to Bree standing beside my bed, my phone in her hand.

"Wha—"

"It's Willa, she's at the police station."

I grab the phone with one hand, while wiping the sleep from my eyes with the other.

"Willa?"

"They're not giving me much time. Can you call Hank for me? I need help. They say they're charging me with murder."

"Don't say a word, Willa. Not a single word." I swing my legs over the side.

"I'm not an idiot. I asked for a lawyer right away. It just took them four hours to—"

Suddenly the line goes dead.

"*Fuck.*" I throw the phone at Bree while I hop to the bathroom. "Get Hank on the phone, tell him to get his ass to the police station right now. Willa's being charged with murder."

It takes me two minutes to shower and by the time I get back to the bedroom with a towel around my waist, Bree has already put some clean clothes on the bed for me. I dress and walk out of the bedroom, to find her in the kitchen. A glass of water and more ibuprofen is sitting on the counter, and she's putting another travel mug under the Keurig.

"Hank?"

"On his way there," she says, while adding milk and sugar to what I assume is gonna be her coffee. I drink it black.

"You know you're gonna make someone an awesome wife some day, right?" I tell her, tossing back the pills and the water.

"Don't hold your breath," she warns me with a smile, but I can tell her heart is not in it. She twists the lid on the second mug and hands it to me before snatching my truck keys off the counter. "And I'm still driving."

We're made to sit in the small waiting area by the front desk, for close to an hour before Hank comes out, his face grim.

"What's going on? Where's Willa?"

"She's been arrested for suspicion of murder and is gonna be spending a few hours in the holding tank until the DA can file official charges when he gets in."

"What the hell?" That's from Bree, who steps up beside me. "Who is she supposed to have murdered?"

"One of the residents at her shelter."

"That's bullshit!"

My outburst draws the attention of the officer manning the desk and I raise my hands in apology. It won't do anyone any good if I get charged with disturbing the peace or some such nonsense.

"They found evidence."

CHAPTER 16

WILLA

For TWO HOURS they have me sit in a small room with nothing more than three uncomfortable chairs, a small table, and my thoughts.

I can't believe Rupert is dead. That poor man did nothing to deserve that.

Stabbed? Who would do such a thing?

My emotions are all over the place: sadness, frustration, anger, and even fear. How could they think I had anything to do with this? I have no idea what they think they have on me.

I need a lawyer.

The moment the door opens, I'm on my feet. Bergland walks in with Detective Craig.

"Sit down, Ms. Smith," the officer says.

"I'd like to make a phone call."

"Sit down," he barks.

Shocked at his ferocity, I sit my butt down.

"We're simply here to ask you some questions, Ms. Smith," Craig says in a disarming voice. I guess he's supposed to be the designated *good* cop versus Bergland's *bad* version.

"Where were you tonight?"

"I'd like to call my lawyer."

"Only people who have something to hide need a lawyer," Bergland snaps.

"You haven't even Mirandized me."

"No need for that, we're simply on a fact-finding mission at this point," Craig assures me. "I understand you knew Rupert Lezlo?"

I can't help the tears filling my eyes, despite efforts to keep them at bay. I nod, not trusting myself to speak.

"We would like to notify the family, do you know if he has any?"

"Not that I know of."

"Ms. Smith, we understand you had an altercation with Mr. Lezlo in your office the other day. Can you tell us about that?"

An altercation?

The need to defend myself is too great, and I blurt out, "That's not what happened."

"Maybe you can help us understand what happened?" Craig prods, and I almost fall for it.

"No. That's privileged information."

"Don't bother," Bergland interjects, looking at Craig. "We already know she's guilty. We've got plenty of evidence."

My mouth opens to ask what they think they have in evidence, when I see the calculating gleam in

Bergland's eyes.

"I'd like to call my lawyer," I repeat instead.

"Told you it was a waste of time," the officer directs at Craig, clearly upset.

Craig turns to me.

"Ms. Smith, I wanted to give you an opportunity to tell your side of the story. Perhaps Rupert attacked you and you had no other recourse than to defend yourself? Perhaps you blacked out? If there's anything that could help you, I strongly suggest you share it with us."

It's a game. They're trying to scare me into saying something that might incriminate me further by keeping me off-balance.

"I'd like to have my lawyer present."

"Quite a coincidence that this is the second resident of your shelter who ends up dead holding your business card."

"Could I please have my phone so I can call my lawyer? I believe you're violating my rights by ignoring my repeated requests to have my lawyer present."

"Let's go," the detective says to his partner, getting up.

I'm relieved to see them go, but it takes a long time before Officer Bergland is back with my phone. Instead of handing it to me, he slips it in his pocket and motions for me to get up and turn around.

"Place your hands behind your back."

"What about my call?" I try, but he grabs both

arms and twists them behind my back, grabbing onto my hands. I feel the cold steel of the handcuffs snap around first one and then the other wrist.

"You're under arrest on suspicion of the murder of Rupert Lezlo."

I'm so stunned; I barely register when he reads me my rights.

"You have the right to remain silent. Anything you say can and will be used against you in a court of law. You have the right to speak to an attorney, and to have an attorney present during any questioning." Then he pulls my phone from his pocket and holds it in front of my face to unlock. "Phone number?"

"Sorry?"

"What's the phone number?"

I rattle off the first number that comes to mind. He dials, hits speakerphone and continues to hold it up in front of me. I try to ignore his glare as I listen to it ring.

"Dimas?" I ask when a woman answers.

"This is Bree. Willa?"

"Is Dimas there? I need to talk to him; I'm at the police station."

"Hang on, let me get him."

When I hear his voice I almost lose it, but manage to explain the situation in as few words as possible before Bergland ends the call mid-sentence.

I don't resist when he grabs my wrists and propels me in front of him toward a holding cell in the back of the station. I'm still numb with disbelief when I'm left sitting on a bench, staring through bars at the door Bergland just disappeared behind.

My mind is trying to make sense of everything that happened in the past hours: the barn, the fighting, Brantley Parker's face, Dimas, Rupert dead, and my arrest. It's too much, my thoughts are jumping all over the place until I finally give up, curling on my side on the hard concrete bench and closing my eyes.

I'm not sure how long it's been when the door opens and Hank walks up to the other side of the bars.

"Willa?"

"Please help me," I manage, making my way over to him. "I don't know what's happening."

"We'll figure it out," he says, and I believe him.

DIMAS

Hank hustles us out to the parking lot, out of earshot.

"What evidence?" Bree asks.

"A letter opener from her desk was used to kill the victim. It was left in his chest. They also found blood in her office, the dining room, and the kitchen of the shelter."

"It wasn't her," I insist.

"I believe you. Heck, I believe her, but—"

I shake my head. "You don't get it. I know for a fact it couldn't have been her, because I saw her tonight." Hank looks at me curiously and I explain. "We were looking into that fight ring you and I talked about. Last night there was one in Loma and Willa showed up."

"So that's where you got the face. Yeah, she told me she was there, but she never mentioned seeing you. Wonder why that is?" he adds with a grin.

Goddamn, Willa must think I need protecting. If I wasn't still so pissed at her for going there by herself in the first place, it might warm my heart.

"Stubborn woman thinks she needs to cover for me," I conclude.

"Holy shit," Bree exclaims, throwing up her hands in exasperation. "Don't put this just on her. Both of you two seriously need to try communicating."

"We did. I told her I was busy and she said she had stuff to do."

"That's not communicating, that's blowing each other off."

"As enlightening as this conversation is," Hank interjects, with a heavy dose of sarcasm. "I have an impromptu breakfast meeting with our Mesa County District Attorney."

"How'd you get that set up so fast?" I ask.

"I didn't. Our DA is a creature of habit and he owes me a favor."

"Wait," I call after him when he starts walking to his car. "What about Willa?"

"She'll walk. Cops were so eager to get at her; they completely bypassed proper police procedure. I'll call you."

I watch him get in his car and drive off before I turn to Bree.

"How's your head?" she wants to know.

"It's fine." I automatically bring my hand to my face, where I can feel the swelling under my fingers.

"Good enough to drop me at home? We can't do anything here, it's almost six, and I want to shower and get to the office to meet up with Radar and Jake. We never had a chance to debrief last night."

"I'll drive you home but I'm coming straight back here. I don't want to go too far."

We start walking to my truck when Bree bumps her shoulder into my arm. She holds out the keys and I snatch them from her hand, unlocking the doors.

"You've got it bad," she teases.

"Whatever," I brush her off and get in behind the wheel.

"It's cute," she persists when I drive off the parking lot. "I mean, it's a new look for you. Never thought I'd—"

"Unless you want me to start harassing you the next time I catch you staring at my brother funny, I'd stop if I were you."

"I don't look at Yanis funny," she snaps.

I give her a side-eye.

"He may be blind, honey, but the rest of us aren't."

She presses her lips together, folds her arms over her chest and stares out the side window.

Shit.

I'd promised myself, a long time ago, I wasn't going to insert myself in whatever is or is not happening between my brother and Bree, and I shouldn't have said anything now. Sure, she'd been riling me up, but that was no excuse.

I reach over and put a hand on her leg.

"That wasn't cool. I was outta line and I'm sorry."

"Not like you were lying," she mutters.

I hate the flat tone of her voice. I've avoided it so far, but maybe it's time I smack my brother upside the head, shake him awake.

I want to apologize again when I pull up outside her building, but she doesn't give me the chance.

"Give me a call when you hear from Hank?" she asks, as she gets out of the truck.

"I will. Look—"

I try but she cuts me off, "Talk to you later," and slams the door shut.

I fucked up.

It's almost eight when the door swings open and Hank walks in, an older portly man following behind him.

I jump to my feet to intercept them.

"Give us twenty minutes, Mazur," he says, as the other man keeps walking past him. "I'll bring her to you."

It's actually forty-five, very long fucking minutes, but relief floods me when Hank walks toward me, a rough-looking Willa by his side.

I reach her in two strides and pull her into my arms, feeling her body sag against me. My eyes meet

Hank's over her head.

"Let's walk outside," he suggests.

I press a kiss to her head before dropping one arm, keeping the other firmly around her waist as we follow Hank to the parking lot. She leans heavily against my side, and I have a feeling she's at the end of her rope. She hasn't said a word yet.

"My truck."

Hank glances back, takes one look at Willa and changes direction to where my vehicle is parked. I unlock the doors and help Willa in the passenger seat, leaving the door open.

"What happened?"

"DA decided the officers jumped the gun on Willa's arrest. They're currently being instructed on proper police procedure, and on why this case is going to be handled by someone else. He's also looking into the validity of the charges against Brad Carey."

"Good. Brad's been in too long already. And for your information, I've never liked Bergland, he's an asshole," I share.

"There's something else you need to know. Willa mentioned she recognized someone last night."

I turn to Willa, whose eyes are on me.

"Brantley Parker," she says, the weight of the world in her voice. "He's the physician in charge of the veterans' outpatient program at the VA hospital where I used to work."

"Did he see you?" I ask immediately and she nods. "That's not good, sweetheart."

"I know," she whispers, staring down at her hands.

"We'll fix it, though."

"Won't bring Rupert back," she says without looking up.

Fuck. She cared about the victim.

"Okay." I turn to Hank. "I'm getting her home and then I'll call the team. We'll make sure she's covered at all times."

"Glad to hear it. I'm gonna head back in to see what's happening for Brad, but I'll be in touch." Then he turns to Willa. "I'll call you when I hear something, and don't hesitate to get in touch with me for anything. Get some rest."

I close her door and round the hood, getting in behind the wheel. When I see she hasn't buckled in yet, I reach over and do it for her.

"Thank you."

"No problem."

"I'm tired."

"I bet. I'll get you home in no time."

"How badly does that hurt?"

I glance over at her and see she's taking in the state of my face.

"Not gonna lie, it's sore. I got KO'd by the Bone Crusher."

"Oh no, should you be operating a vehicle?"

"I'm fine now. My team insisted I get checked out, so we stopped at the ER on the way home. That's why Bree was at my place. She was making sure I didn't croak during the night," I quickly add, in case she got the wrong idea.

"Guess we should talk about last night," she says, but I can tell it's the last thing she wants to do.

"We should, but first you need some rest."

"Okay."

The rest of the drive to her place is quiet and when I pull into the driveway behind her RAV and look over, she's asleep in her seat. When I get out and round the truck to her door, she's blinking her eyes against sleep. I open the door and help her out.

If I were in better shape, I'd pick her up, but I feel every fucking muscle in my body. We stumble to the front door together.

"Where are your keys, sweetheart?"

"My pocket," she mumbles, trying to reach them.

"I've got it."

I manage to fish her keychain from her jeans and get the door open. We don't stop walking until we get to her bedroom and she falls on the bed. I struggle to get her shoes and jeans off and pull the covers up over her. She doesn't even lift her head.

But when I start moving to the door she calls my name.

"Yeah?"

"Are you leaving?"

"No, sweetheart. I'm just gonna lock up. I'll be right back."

I quietly close the door and walk into her kitchen, pulling out my phone.

"Is she out?" Bree wants to know.

"Yes, we just got home. She's done for and needs a few hours of sleep."

"Are you coming in?"

"No, that's why I'm calling. I think it's time to fill Yanis in."

"You sure?"

"Yeah, we need to come up with a plan to keep Willa safe."

CHAPTER 17

WILLA

"WHY ARE WE here?"

I stare at the sign on the decrepit building he parked in front of *Center Shot Gun Range*.

It had been the first question Dimas asked yesterday, after I'd woken up disoriented in the middle of the day: if I owned a gun, which I confirmed.

My first concern at the time had been the fact I wasn't at work, but he assured me Jake had filled Rosie in and I wasn't expected. I can't say I was happy that decision was made without me, but seeing as I'd already slept the bulk of my day away, there wasn't much I could do about it.

Then he'd taken me to the PASS office, where I was asked a million questions about Brantley Parker and was told—not asked, but told—I needed security. I'd balked, but only until Bree calmly pointed out that Brantley wasn't their only concern; someone had murdered Rupert and gone through a lot of trouble to pin it on me. That reminder scared me into agreeing to the security they offered.

What it means is that Dimas is my shadow, which I didn't mind at all last night when he was doing magical things with his fingers and mouth. Having him attached to the hip while I went in for the group today was not so much fun, nor was being hustled out of the shelter after. I wasn't allowed in my office, which was sealed by the police for further investigation. Rosie was able to tell me they said they'd be done over the weekend and I should have access by Monday.

Group was a somber affair. Rupert had been well-loved, both here at the shelter and outside on the streets, apparently. Everyone seemed to have a story to share and mine weren't the only tears shed.

I was looking forward to crawling into bed at home to escape from the emotional and mental drain of the past few days. So I'm a bit out of sorts to have been dragged to some gun range on the outskirts of the city.

Dimas twists in his seat to face me and reaches for the glove box where, to my annoyance, he apparently stored my gun when it's supposed to be on the closet shelf in my bedroom.

"A gun for protection is useless unless you keep it within reach," he educates, only annoying me more. "I want to make sure you know how to use it."

I roll my eyes, but get out of the truck anyway. Despite my irritation with Dimas, I won't say no to an opportunity to fire off a few rounds. It's been a while.

Judging from the backslaps exchanged with the old guy behind the counter, Dimas is well-known around here.

"Rocket, meet Willa."

The old man gives me no more than a cursory nod and—clearly categorized as arm candy—dismisses me as he leads the way out the back door.

The weather is nice so I'm glad to see the outdoor range. Rocket points out a lane for us to use.

"Need ammo?" he asks Dimas.

"Box of 9 mm."

The 9 mm Smith & Wesson M&P Compact had been a gift from my father on my twenty-first birthday. My sister got the same thing. Despite being firmly stuck in the fifties' role division, he felt it important Connie and I were able to protect ourselves. At least until we had a man to do the protecting for us.

He had me go through a gun safety training that included a few hours at a gun range. After that he took me to a range a few times, but when I started shooting better than he did, he stopped taking me. I haven't been since. That was eighteen years ago. I clean the gun maybe once a year—usually before Christmas so when my father asks if I have, I can tell him yes—but it hasn't been fired in all that time.

Dimas dismantles my gun as if he does little else every day and mumbles his approval before putting it together again. Rocket comes walking back with a box of ammo and sets it and a stack of paper targets down on the stand.

"Call me if you need anything else," he mutters, before ambling off inside.

"He's a ray of sunshine," I observe wryly, grabbing the ear protectors from their hook.

"Don't let it bother you. He's an asshole to everyone." Dimas winks at me as he loads my weapon.

"Seems nice enough to you."

"Only because I bring him a bottle of his favorite whiskey every so often." He shrugs, handing me my gun. "Show me what you've got."

The first magazine I empty misses the paper target more than it hits, but by the time I'm halfway through the second, my shots are starting to group nicely. Dimas nods in what I assume is approval as he goes to replace the target with a fresh one.

"Again."

Instead of focusing on the biggest part of the target—the torso—I put half of the next clip in its head, and the other half in his crotch area. When the second clip is empty I slip the earmuffs around my neck.

"Now you have me worried and turned on at the same time," he mumbles, as he plucks the weapon from my hand and pulls me flush against him.

I chuckle against his lips, giving his tongue easy access. For a moment, I lose track of where I am, until I hear the rustle of paper and turn my head to see Rocket approaching with the target in his hand.

"Thought I was fucking seeing things," he grumbles before pinning me with bloodshot eyes. "What was your name again?"

"Willa," I supply, propping a hand on my hip.

"Nice shooting," he comments, and I glance at Dimas who is looking at me with an unidentifiable smirk on his face.

"I'm a little rusty, it's been a while."

He harrumphs to that and turns to Dimas. "You keeping this one?"

"Thinking about it," he mutters in response, his eyes fixed on me.

"Figures," the old man grumbles, before making his way back inside without so much as another glance in my direction.

"What was that all about?" I ask when the door slams shut behind him.

"Rocket has a thing for women who can handle a gun. Last woman who impressed him was Bree, but Yanis almost bit off his head when he tried hitting on her."

It wasn't that part of the conversation I was questioning but I decide to let it go.

"Hate to insult your friend, but I'm not so sure he's Bree's type. Or anyone's under seventy for that matter."

Dimas barks out a laugh.

"I've seen some of his lady friends. You'd be surprised."

"Well, there's no accounting for poor taste," I conclude with a shrug, before turning to hang the ear protection back on the hook.

"Not gonna argue with you there."

I roll up the target Rocket left behind for a souvenir

while Dimas collects my gun.

"I'm thinking I may frame this and hang it over my bed."

"Let's go, Annie Oakley," he says, chuckling as he wraps his hand around the back of my neck.

"Are you sure you don't want me to shoot some more?" I tease.

"I'm good. Let's grab something to eat and go home."

I tilt my head back and smile up in his green eyes, letting him know I like the sound of that.

As soon as we get back in the truck, I check my phone I left in the center console. One message from my sister.

Connie: Thanks for taking Britt. I'll check in next week.

Oh shit.

Dimas

Willa has been in a state since we left the gun range.

Apparently with all that happened the past few days, she'd forgotten her parents were to drop off her niece tomorrow to stay with her for an undetermined period of time. At least that's what I've deduced from her rambling. There was some more about golf trips, summer camps, and marital problems I couldn't make heads or tails of, but I listened, hummed, and nodded my support anyway.

"They can't know," she insists before taking

her first proper breath, giving me a chance to say something.

"Can't know what?"

"That I was arrested. That I'm a suspect in a murder case. They can't know any of it. My mother would have a nervous breakdown and my father…" She doesn't finish the sentence, but I get the sense whatever the news would do to her father would not be good.

"So don't tell them. It's a bogus charge anyway. We'll get it cleared up," I reassure her. "You won't need to say a thing if you don't want to."

I glance to the side and see her distraught dark eyes on me.

"But Britt's gonna be here. She's smart, she'll figure out something is up." She clasps her hands in her lap so hard her knuckles turn white. "She's going to wonder why someone is always keeping an eye out. Why you're there. Oh God, and what am I gonna do with her when I work? I can't leave her alone, and now I can't send her off to camp."

"Why can't you?"

That seems to have been the wrong question because she shoots an indignant glare at me.

"I can't send her to camp when she may not be safe. Someone was murdered!"

I'm learning interesting things about Willa. She seems able to take things on the chin better than most when it only affects her, but she seems almost frantic in her need to shield the ones she loves.

Time to break it down to bite-sized pieces.

"Here's what we'll do; we're going to stop at the grocery store and stock up on food. Your fridge is empty and kids eat. A lot. We'll get your spare bedroom in order and then we call Bree. She's kickass at problem-solving, knows just about everything going on in this town, and can help us come up with a plan for your niece. We'll get this sorted, sweetheart."

"You can't be there."

"Sorry?"

"After tonight. You can't be there when they come."

The turnoff into the Safeway parking lot is up ahead, and I wait to respond until I've parked the truck in a vacant spot. Then I turn in my seat.

"Yes, I can," I tell her firmly, putting my hand on her wringing ones. "You won't even have to lie. Tell them I'm your manfriend."

It takes her a minute, but then she snorts out a laugh.

"My *manfriend*?"

"Sure. Unless you want to call me your lover, I'm good with that too," I tease, glad to have succeeded in breaking through her panic. Even if it is for a moment.

"You don't understand. My mom's going to turn this into a big deal and make it embarrassing. Oh my God, the moment my dad finds out you're a veteran, you'll be invited to his next golf game. Seriously, meeting my parents is the kind of pressure you'll regret."

"Why?" When she shakes her head like she doesn't get it, I repeat, "Why would I regret it?"

"Because they'll make it uncomfortable."

I shrug, unclipping my seat belt before I lean over the console and press a kiss to her stubborn mouth.

"They can bring it on, sweetheart. If I can handle being drawn and quartered by my brother yesterday—talk about uncomfortable—I can handle your parents."

My brother had not taken well to the news I'd gotten myself—and my teammates—involved in what was an active police investigation. He'd been less than complimentary about my admitted involvement with Willa; reminding me of the not so great track record I have with women and thus should not have messed with a friend of Rosie's.

Now granted, I may have a tendency to dine and dash so to speak, but in my defense, there has never really been anyone who affects me the way Willa does. I don't pretend to have any idea where this is leading, but what I do know is I want to stick around and find out. That in itself should've told him this isn't the same, but he wasn't exactly receptive.

My brother is a hard-ass, or at least he pretends to be. Our parents to this day live the kind of idealistic and romanticized life that only sheer luck and my brother's levelheadedness and leadership has sustained. If not for his deep-rooted sense of responsibility—something entirely lacking in my parents—life could've looked a lot different for them, and for us.

I'm neither a dreamer, nor a pragmatist—I hover somewhere in between—but those are the only two defining qualities Yanis recognizes, so if I'm not one, I must be the other.

Willa seems pensive in contrast to her earlier ramblings, as we zip around Safeway choosing stuff that doesn't require a huge skill set in the kitchen. Neither of us have one.

It's clear she does better with stress when doing something, so once we have the groceries tucked away back at home, she heads to the spare bedroom to get it ready for her niece. I give Bree a call and fill her in.

"Give me an hour," she suggests before asking, "You have plans for dinner?"

"Not particularly." We did buy stuff, but that would require turning on the stove or firing up the almost brand-new grill on Willa's back deck, and given the current stress levels I'm not sure that would be a good idea.

"I'll pick up some takeout on the way."

"Sounds good."

⌒‿⌒

"Oh my God, this is delicious."

Willa's fingers and face are covered in barbecue sauce as she gnaws on the ribs Bree showed up with.

I love that she doesn't give a shit. Aside from the stress her current situation puts her in, she has to be one of the most easygoing, unpretentious women I know. Bree is another, although she's more reserved. You always get the sense there is more to what she is showing on the outside.

Willa simply is.

Sure she's beautiful, kills it at the gun range, is fearless in bed, and has a banging body, but that authenticity is arguably the most uniquely appealing thing about her. It seems like every new thing I discover about Willa only settles her deeper under my skin. Even her earlier panic, the hurt I sensed when talking about her parents, and the vulnerability that showed were not at all a turnoff for me.

"Texas Smokes, that new place on Colorado Avenue," Bree says around her own mouthful of ribs.

She brought a huge paper bag with ribs, brisket, potato wedges, and the best damn coleslaw I've had since I left home.

"It's good," I agree.

"Mmm." Bree grabs a napkin and wipes her hands and mouth. "Okay, let's figure this out. So your niece is twelve? What is she interested in? Any sports? Dance? Tomboy or princess?"

"Tomboy, definitely. Loves doing outdoorsy things with her dad to my sister's annoyance."

"She doesn't mind getting her hands dirty?"

"Nope."

"Does she like animals?"

"She's been begging for a dog since she was three years old, but my sister is allergic. Absolutely loves animals."

Bree grins wide.

"Perfect. I have a friend who runs the Humane Society here in Grand Junction. He's always looking for part-time volunteers. She'll be helping with feeding, taking some of the dogs out for a run, and giving cuddles to whatever animal needs some lovin'."

I watch as Willa's mouth falls open before spreading into a wide grin.

"Get out. For real? Holy shit, she's gonna flip."

CHAPTER 18

WILLA

"I THINK IT'S clean."

I turn to find Dimas leaning against the doorway of the guest bathroom.

I'm on my knees, scrubbing the tub. Never mind I already did this last night before Dimas finally pulled me up and dragged me to bed. There he pulled every trick out of the book to get me to relax, which worked until my eyes opened this morning. I've been back at it ever since.

Cleaning is my way to deal with stress. The mindless tasks normally helping my body to relieve the stress and get some control of myself, but in my current situation control is so far out of reach, I'm afraid I'll implode if I stop moving.

If only I could bake, that might be a more satisfying way to work off all this nervous tension. At least I could eat the results. Scrubbing an already clean bathtub for the second time yields nothing.

"Come have something to eat," he urges me, finally

plucking the sponge from my hand and pulling me to my feet.

"I'll throw up," I inform him, not sure my stomach can handle anything more than the three coffees I downed in record time this morning.

"You're wired. Maybe we should go back to bed where I know how to mellow you out."

If I wasn't coiled tighter than a spring, my body would've responded to the touch of his hands on my hips and the promise behind the grin on his face.

"We can't! They could be here any minute." I twist out of his hold and grab the sponge from the tub, tucking it and the bottle of cleaning solution in the cupboard under the sink. "I have to change."

"Hold up," Dimas says, as I push past him to head to my bedroom.

I don't, so he follows me and sits down on the bed while I strip off my wet T-shirt and my ratty old sweatpants, diving into my drawers for a bra and a clean shirt.

"Explain to me what has you so on edge."

I open my mouth to snap at him but think better of it. Why am I so on edge? I mean, aside from the shit storm I seem to have landed in, why is the fact my parents are going to show any minute freaking me out?

My whole adult life I've marched to my own drum, done my own thing without apology or regret. I've steeled myself against their disapproval of my choices and let it slide down my back. So why is the thought of my parents meeting Dimas suddenly such a big deal?

"I don't know," I confess, musing out loud while I pull a brush through my hair. "I've never cared what they thought. Not as an adult anyway. Maybe I care for your sake, although I almost rather they dislike you than the opposite."

His face scrunches up in confusion. At least the swelling has gone down, and the faint bruising on his jaw is mostly hidden by his beard. Evidence of a fight on his face would have prompted questions from my father I'd prefer to avoid.

"You want them *not* to like me?"

"No, that's not what I mean. What I'm saying is I don't need their approval, but I'm worried I'll get it."

"And that would be bad, because?"

I sink down on the bed beside him, leaning my shoulder into his.

"When Connie and Jim first started dating, I actually liked the guy. He could be funny, was head over heels for my sister, and I remember thinking at the time I should be so lucky to find a guy like him." I snort. "It was like that movie *The Stepford Wives*— you know the one with Nicole Kidman? My father slowly pulled him into his vortex—his good old boys' club—and Connie, well, she eventually became a robot like my mom."

"You're worried you'll become like them?" he asks, and I shake my head.

"No, that'll never happen," I state firmly.

Dimas shifts so we're face-to-face, and his hands come to rest on either side of my neck as he bends close.

"I don't know if you've noticed this about me, sweetheart, but I'm a bit of a rebel myself. All you have to do is ask my brother. I have a history of not doing what's expected of me. The chances of me ever becoming part of an old boys' club are slim to none." I try to hide my face, embarrassed he seems to have put his finger on my exposed nerve, but he won't let me. "Can't tell you what the future holds, Willa, but what I can guarantee you is, no matter what, I will never expect you to be anything other than exactly who you are."

Okay. Even though his ability to read between my lines freaks me out a little, that may well have been the perfect thing to say.

I grab his wrists and lift my mouth to his for a soft kiss.

"Thank you."

"You can do better than that," he teases, with a twinkle in those green eyes.

"Yes, I can."

I grin, throw my weight against him, knocking him to his back, and land on his chest. My mouth finds his as I feel the texture of his beard with my fingertips. As I deepen the kiss, I throw a leg over his hips and straddle him. Deep sweeps of my tongue sync with a soft roll of my hips over the hardening ridge of his cock. I moan in his mouth when his hands grab on to my hips and grind me down on him.

So easily he makes me forget everything until my focus is like a laser point on anywhere he touches me: my mouth, my hips, my core, ...my heart.

"Dimas..." I mumble against his lips when his hands slide up to cup my breasts. His thumbs roll my erect nipples, sending a ripple down my spine and between my legs.

The sound of the doorbell is like a cattle prod to the skin.

DIMAS

At this moment, I don't care who's outside the door; I want to end them.

Willa jumps off the bed, a sudden flurry of movement as she pulls at her shirt and smooths the hair I never got a chance to mess up.

I reach a hand down to push my happy dick into submission and scissor up from the bed. She's already out of the bedroom by the time I get to my feet, and the sound of voices fills the house by the time I feel presentable enough to follow her.

The first person my eyes land on, walking into her living room, is the young girl with shockingly purple hair latched to Willa's midsection. That must be Britt, the niece. Her father is next, his rigid military stance unmistakable—shoulders squared, legs slightly apart, hands clasped behind his back—as he glares at me, ignoring my polite smile. Appropriately halfway hidden behind him is a small, rotund woman, smiling almost eagerly as she catches sight of me.

I glance over at Willa to take my cue but she looks like a deer caught in the headlights, so I move forward to introduce myself. Her father first.

"Dimas Mazur," I say, extending my hand. "Pleased to meet you."

It takes the man a second before upbringing wins over suspicion, and he shakes my hand, clearly trying to establish alpha dog with an unnecessarily firm grasp. I maintain an impassive face, unwilling to wince or wiggle my fingers to restore blood flow before I turn to Willa's mother.

"Ms. Smith, so nice to meet you."

Fuck if the woman doesn't blush when I gently press the hand she puts in mine.

"Likewise," she says breathily, and I note how similar her voice is to Willa's. Except Willa's isn't timid by any stretch of the imagination.

"And who might you be?" her father demands when I turn to the cute girl, who has let go of her aunt and is staring at me with big eyes. Ignoring him, I smile at Willa's niece.

"You must be Britt." I reach out to shake her hand, holding it a little longer. "Your aunt has told me about you."

Her eyes grow big.

"She has?"

"Oh yeah. You're twelve, you like nature, love animals, and eat Mini-Wheats for breakfast."

The girl's face splits open in a big smile.

"Excuse me," her father says behind me, and I turn around, moving to stand beside Willa and putting my arm around her stiff shoulders. "I'm not sure who—"

"Dad," Willa interrupts, finally having found her voice. "Dimas is my…" I grin, wondering what she's going to call me. "…boyfriend. Dimas, these are my parents, Chuck and Josie Smith."

"I didn't know you had a boyfriend," Britt pipes up, eyeing both Willa and me with blatant curiosity.

"Neither did I," Chuck mutters, pinning his daughter with a glare.

"Oh, how wonderful!" her mother gushes, her hands clasped against her chest.

"Why don't I put on a pot of coffee?" I offer, giving Willa's shoulder a squeeze. She looks up at me with a sparkle of humor in her eyes. She knows exactly what I'm doing and approves.

"Surely you've managed to learn how to make coffee by now?" her father sneers at her, and I'm about to say something when Willa grins at me before turning to her father.

"I have," she states calmly, "but Dimas does it so much better."

"Oh, but surely…" her mom starts, her eyes darting between her husband and her daughter, before settling on me.

I wink at her and turn to Britt.

"Wanna give me a hand, Short Stack?" I ask, already moving into the kitchen.

There's silence at first, but then I hear footsteps and a voice behind me.

"I'll have you know I'm the tallest girl in my class."

"Oh yeah? Good, you can reach the cups in that cupboard then. You drink coffee?" I glance over at her while scooping coffee into a filter.

"No," she scoffs, making a face. "It's gross."

I chuckle. "An acquired taste. You'll grow into it. Four cups then, and check the fridge, I think your aunt got some orange juice and chocolate milk. Take your pick, glasses are in…"

"I've got it," she says.

A quick glance inside shows Willa and her parents have taken seats in the living room, but most of their attention is on the kitchen.

I grab the tray on top of Willa's fridge and give it a quick wipe with the dishrag before setting the cups Britt hands me on it. I pull the small container of creamer out of the fridge, grab the sugar bowl from the counter, and add those and a bunch of spoons to the tray.

I note the girl has opted for chocolate milk.

"You know what would go well with that? Cookies. Check in the pantry, we have some."

Five minutes later, we walk into a very quiet living room, Britt leading the way with a plate of cookies she put together, and me with the tray.

"You seem to know your way around my daughter's house."

It's not so much a question as a statement, but I still feel compelled to answer.

"I should. I spend enough time here."

"Let me do that." Josie jumps up when I start pouring coffee.

"Thanks, Josie, I've got it, but you can add your own cream and sugar. Britt, offer your grandma a cookie, will you?"

"What is it you do?"

That's a question I was expecting, I finish pouring coffees and sit down next to Willa on the couch before I answer.

"I work for PASS: Protection and Security Services."

"Never heard of it."

"That doesn't surprise me," I tell him with a friendly smile. "We're not the kind of business to advertise to the general public. Most of our work is generated through word of mouth and referrals."

"And what kind of work is that?"

"I'm a security specialist. We cover corporate security, cyber security, installations, personal protection, that kind of thing."

"Interesting. What exactly qualifies one as a security specialist?"

There's an insult wrapped in that question somewhere, but I can't be bothered to be offended. Not worth feeding into the negative energy.

"In my case, former Special Forces."

As Willa predicted, that grabs his attention. His

eyes narrow on me.

"That so? You're still young, why former?"

I look over at Willa, who seems to be observing the interaction with more than a little interest. I raise an eyebrow in question and she clues in when I tug on my pant leg. Her slight shrug is answer enough.

I reveal my prosthesis and note Josie's sharp intake of breath.

"Cool!" Britt exclaims, immediately followed by, "I mean not cool that you have no leg, but cool I've never seen a fake one up close."

"Brittany, hush," Josie stage-whispers.

I grin at the girl. She is just like Willa. No pretenses. I like it. Willa herself chuckles softly.

"I'll show you later," I tell Britt, who looks almost giddy at the prospect.

Hey, I remember my own insatiable curiosity at twelve, and I would've been morbidly fascinated with a prosthesis myself at that age.

"IED," Willa answers her father's unasked question.

"Where?" he directs at me.

"Iraq."

He seems to mull on that before he leans forward, his elbows on his knees.

"Say—do you play golf?"

Willa and I simultaneously burst out laughing.

CHAPTER 19

WILLA

"OH MY GOD, look how cute she is!"

I smile watching Britt sit on the concrete floor at the shelter, being licked to death by the most unsightly dog I've ever seen. Something of a mix between a pug and a schnauzer, with bristly hair sticking out all over her face and back, while the rest of her fur was short and flat. She was so ugly it was adorable. The big brown, bulging eyes, and slight underbite, combined with the rapid wagging of her ratty tail made her impossible to resist.

"What the fuck is that?" Dimas whispers behind me, making me snort.

"A dog."

"That's not a dog, it's a fucking gremlin," he grumbles, and I elbow him in the gut.

"Hush. Britt's in love."

My niece was up early this morning, bouncing to get the day going. We'd told her yesterday about the possibility of volunteering at the animal shelter, and she'd been over the moon.

When my parents left on Saturday—after my father finally accepted that Dimas would not be a new golf buddy—Britt settled in easily. We took her out for dinner and a movie that night, and she rolled into bed the moment we got home. Not even once did she question why Dimas was around.

He's good with her, funny, attentive, and I have to admit my ovaries may have tingled a little watching their easygoing interaction. It's fun having Britt around. It distracts from the mess I seem to find myself in.

Yesterday after breakfast Dimas had taken off for a few hours, making me promise to stay home with Britt until he got back. She and I had a great time, just hanging out and catching up. She mentioned her parents briefly but I didn't push it. Lots of time to open that dialogue.

Dimas came back late afternoon with steak and baking potatoes, using my barbecue to cook a surprisingly delicious meal. I was allowed to chop vegetables for a salad and Britt surprised me by helping. As it turned out, my twelve-year-old niece is sadly more adept at handling food than I am.

Last night I discovered Dimas had also brought back a large duffel, holding his laptop, a good amount of clothes, and his toiletries. He was settling in too, something that happened silently and without fanfare. Never having lived with anyone but family, or a roommate while I was in Germany, I would've expected it to feel invasive to have him everywhere in my space, but it's not.

I'm aware circumstances are the reason for him temporarily moving in, but that doesn't mean I'm not enjoying it. Maybe even hoping...

"She seems to be getting along well with the animals."

I turn to find Bree's friend, Steve, watching Britt handle the dog. She already has the schnug sitting and giving paws.

"I knew she'd love this," I tell him. "Are you sure she'll be okay here?"

"She'll be fine," he reassures me with a smile. "Natasha is our other volunteer. She just turned fourteen and this is her second summer with us. I'll put the two of them together until Britt is settled in."

We don't stay long after that. Britt barely notices us leaving.

Rosie had called earlier to let me know my office was cleared, and I'm eager to check in with my residents. Dimas is supposed to drop me off before he heads into the office for a few hours. PASS apparently has had eyes on the shelter since Rupert was found, and although I'm not sure what that means exactly, it does give a sense of security. Besides, Rosie and Ron are there as well, it's not like I'll be alone.

"What are you doing?" I ask, when he gets out of the truck at the shelter.

"Walking you inside," he says, casually draping his arm around my shoulders.

"It's twenty feet to the door, I think I can manage," I scoff.

He stops us and steps in front of me, his hands sliding down to my upper arms.

"I can't open the door for you when I'm sitting in the truck," he points out the obvious. "I can't kiss you properly leaning over the center console." I'd have to agree with that. "And I don't want you walking into the next potential crisis without me there to back you up." He leans in closer. "That's why I'm walking you inside."

Oh, boy. I'm having a melty moment.

I've always thought of myself as tough and self-reliant, but apparently I have a softer side. One Dimas seems able to tap into with ease. Not sure if that is worrisome, or cause for celebration. I'll reserve judgment on that. For now.

A couple of the guys are playing cards in the dining room off the lobby and I wave as we pass. Rosie's door is shut but I can hear a boisterous, deep laugh filtering from inside. Opening the door to my office, I notice traces of black dust in a few places and see my carpet's been removed. A small shiver runs down my spine at the thought Rupert may have been stabbed right here. Dimas seems to guess my thoughts.

"He wasn't killed here. All they found was a small blood smear on the carpet. They likely took the whole thing to the lab for processing. Someone must've cleaned up the fingerprint dust."

"Probably Rosie."

"Yeah." He pulls me in his arms. "Are you sure you're going to be okay here? Say the word and you can just tag along with me."

Tempting, but I have a job that needs looking after, and besides, it's not like me to cower in someone's shadow. Even if the someone comes in as enticing a package as Dimas.

I lift my face and put my hands on his shoulders, pulling myself up to kiss him soundly on the lips.

"I'm fine," I barely have a chance to mumble before his mouth covers mine. His arms band tightly around me, keeping me partially suspended as his tongue plunges deep. He grunts down my throat as he slowly lowers me, the prominent ridge of his hard cock brushing my lower belly.

He makes me feel safe and surrounded. His strong arms at my back making me feel treasured, and his hungry mouth conveying his desire. I softly groan when he lifts his head, those clear green eyes fixed on mine.

"Be careful."

"I will."

"I'll be back at four so we can pick up Britt."

"Okay."

Once again he kisses me, short but thoroughly, before letting me go. I reach behind me to grab the edge of my desk as he turns to leave, stopping suddenly.

"Whoo-wee! That kiss about blistered my eyeballs."

Two men are standing with a smiling Rosie in the hallway, right outside my door. One a fiftyish, nicely dressed, gray-haired man, the other a broadly grinning black man in a loud Hawaiian shirt and board shorts. I'm guessing he's the one who spoke.

"Grant. Richard," Dimas rumbles in greeting, clearly knowing the men.

"I was hoping to introduce you," Rosie says, looking at me. "This is my best friend, Grant." She indicates the black man. "And this is his husband, Richard. They just came back from a three-month honeymoon in the Bahamas. Guys, this is the Willa I've been telling you about."

I step around Dimas, who is lingering in the doorway, and first shake Richard's hand before turning to Grant. He completely ignores my extended hand and instead wraps me in a bear hug.

"Dayumn, Sunhine, but you've got great taste," he booms.

I look up to find that wasn't directed at me but over my shoulder.

Sunshine?

"Thanks, I think." I chuckle, looking at Dimas behind me. His head is tilted back, eyes on the ceiling, which only makes me laugh harder. "Weren't you going to work…Sunshine?"

"I fuckin' am now," he grumbles. "Richard, good to see you survived your honeymoon. Grant, it's been real. See you later, Rosie." Then he turns to me, hooking a hand behind my neck before planting a quick kiss on my mouth. "Four."

"You're perfect," Grant declares before Dimas is even out the door. "Isn't she perfect, Ricky?"

"She is." The other man smiles indulgently at him.

"Like a beautiful Amazon warrior. I just wanna bet you really blew that boy's hair back. Did she, Rosebud?" He turns to Rosie, who is grinning wide. Seems Grant has a nickname for everyone.

"From the moment he laid eyes on her," she confirms, leaving me with my mouth hanging open.

Really?

"We should get going, honey," Richard announces. "We haven't even checked if the house is still standing." To me he clarifies, "Grant had to see Rosie as soon as we got in."

"Of course I did," Grant says, bending down to kiss Rosie's baby bump. "Had to see for myself how much Little Bitsy's grown."

That's sweet. Must be so nice to have friends like that. I can't help smile at the contrast between petite, redheaded Rosie and Grant.

I watch as he kisses her cheek before he takes a step toward me and does the same.

"See you, Rosebud."

With a wave the two set off down the hall when Grant turns his head and shouts over his shoulder.

"Later, Xena!"

Dimas

"Good to see you back, Bro," I tell Yanis when I walk into him outside his office. "When did you get in?"

"Last night. Don't get comfortable," he says, when I'm about to sit down at my desk. "We're meeting Hank at the courthouse. Bring your checkbook."

I follow him into the garage and hop in the passenger seat of his Yukon.

"What's happening?"

"A meeting with the judge. Hank says the DA is willing to consent to a request for his release without prejudice. We may have to step up to guarantee Brad won't skip the country, by word or by bail. Either way, Hank doesn't think the judge will go for it on his word alone."

"Whatever needs to be done," I vow, and I can feel him look at me.

"It may be necessary for you to speak to Brad's mental condition, Dimi," he cautions me. "You're the only one who knows what it means for him to be locked up."

"Whatever needs to be done," I repeat through clenched teeth.

The rest of the drive is silent.

Hank is waiting outside the courthouse when we pull up.

"Let's go. The judge has allowed us fifteen minutes to make our case. We'll need every last one of them."

I've been in the newer courthouse a few times, but have never visited a judge's chambers. Not too shabby. Judge Marshall's office is lined in oak paneling and bookshelves spanning both walls. Impressive. As is the judge behind the massive desk. I didn't know Judge Marshall was a woman. A very fine-looking woman at that. Already seated across from her is the same older man I briefly saw at the police station with Hank last week.

Hank takes care of introductions and I find out the name of the DA is Edward Russell. No one bothers shaking hands, it's not that kind of gathering, and Judge Marshall directs us to sit down.

"Tell me why I'm giving up a good chunk of my lunch recess to listen to something that would be more appropriately dealt with in an in-court session?"

Not exactly a promising start.

"Your Honor," Hank starts. "We've put in a motion for the court to release Mr. Carey without prejudice, based on new developments in this case."

"Mr. Fredericks, I have the motion in front of me. I can see right here the DA is not contesting, but what I'd like to know is why this can't wait for a proper court appointment. Get to the point. You're wasting my time."

I like an assertive woman. Heck, I love that about Willa, but this woman has me crossing my legs and covering my jewels. Talk about a ball-buster.

"Very well," Hank concedes. "Your Honor, Brad Carey is a former POW. He was captured by insurgents on his last tour in Iraq, and held prisoner for five months before a special operations team was able to extract him. His conditions had been deplorable, but

Mr. Mazur here can better tell you that. He was one of the men who rescued Mr. Carey."

The judge's eyes come to me appraisingly before she simply says, "Please."

I decide to keep it brief and to the point.

"Your Honor, aside from the daily torture Brad had to endure, he'd been kept in an underground cell too small for an adult to stretch in any direction. When I pulled him out, he was barely able to stand, let alone straight. We were on our way to the rendezvous point where the bird—I'm sorry, helicopter," I explain but she holds up her hand.

"I know what you mean by *bird*, Mr. Mazur. Please continue."

"Right. So I was half-carrying Brad when the IED went off. I lost part of my left leg and Brad almost all of his right one. We ended up in the same hospital." I uncross my legs and lean forward, looking her straight in the eye. "You Honor, Brad couldn't even handle it if someone closed the curtains around his hospital bed. Like a lot of us, he suffers from PTSD, but one of his triggers is being confined to small spaces. It's one of the reasons he ended up on the streets. At the shelter where he stays, his bed is under a window and his door is always wide open."

I stop talking. I want to tell her what he confessed to me, half delirious, right before we hit the IED, but I've already shared too much that isn't mine to share.

She doesn't say anything but starts flipping through the file in front of her. I sit back and shrug at Hank.

I've done what I can.

"Your Honor, if I may?" the DA pipes up.

"Just a minute, Mr. Russell," she interrupts, holding up her hand as she turns to me. "Mr. Mazur, first of all, I'm sorry for the loss of your leg and I thank you for your service." Then she turns back to Russell. "Now you may speak."

"Your Honor, on closer investigation, my office has come to the conclusion the circumstantial evidence we have in this case against Mr. Carey at this point in time is not sufficient to obtain a conviction. My office has no objection to the motion as submitted by Mr. Frederick, release without prejudice."

"Perhaps if your office had more closely examined the evidence provided, you could have saved the court precious time." She pins him with a glare and I'm glad I'm not in his shoes.

"Yes, Your Honor."

Forty minutes later, Yanis and I are waiting in the parking lot when Hank leads a rough-looking Brad out of the county jail.

I clap him on the shoulder.

"Good to see you, buddy."

"Yeah, thanks," he mumbles, his eyes darting around.

"Let's get you out of here," I suggest.

"And go where?"

"Buddy, I'll take you anywhere you wanna go."

He hesitates for a moment and then he says, "Shelter."

"You've got it. Hop in front." I let him get in beside Yanis before turning to Hank, extending a hand. "Thank you, brother."

"My pleasure. Take care of him. I'll be in touch."

I get in the back seat of the Yukon and pull out my phone.

Me: Bringing Brad to the shelter. He may need you.

Her response is instantaneous.

Willa: OMG. I'll be here. Thank you!

CHAPTER 20

WILLA

"*A*ND I BOTTLE-FED two kittens someone brought in. They barely had their eyes open. Oh, and Twister followed me around all day. She's so cute. You should get a dog, Auntie Will."

Britt hasn't stopped rambling since we picked her up at the shelter.

"Maybe some day, honey."

Her enthusiasm is like a balm on the raw emotions left by my impromptu session with Brad.

I let her voice drift to the background, my mind going to earlier this afternoon.

When Dimas walked Brad into my office at the shelter, he looked like some of the patients I'd encounter at Landstuhl, brought in freshly injured from the front lines and still shell-shocked.

Dimas left with a quick press of his lips to my forehead, closing the door behind him. I sat down across from the chair Brad had taken and stayed silent, waiting for him to lead the way. It had taken a few drawn out minutes, but eventually he started talking. I wasn't sure where he was in his mind at first, but then he mentioned he felt like drowning in the ever-present dust every time he took a breath. I clued in he was in that underground bunker in Iraq.

I let him talk his way into the present, only every so often nudging him along. By the time I could sense he was in the here and now, his eyes clear, mine were red and gritty and my emotions were rubbed raw.

I'd said no more than maybe a dozen words during the session, but I'd touched him, tentative and brief at first, attempting to keep him connected, but eventually I was leaning forward holding on firmly to his hand.

My reward had been a bone-crushing hug and a whispered, "Thank you."

The moment Brad left my office Dimas slipped in and, taking one look at my face, wrapped me tightly in his arms. He told me he'd run out to get his truck from the office—his brother apparently had been driving—and had been waiting outside the rest of the time.

"I'm fine," I'd mumbled into his shirt before leaning back. "We should get going."

When Dimas pulls his truck in beside my RAV in the driveway, Britt is the first one out, running up to the door.

"That was a good call by Bree, setting her up at the shelter," Dimas says, as he waits for me to get out.

"Absolutely," I agree. "Although I have a feeling she's going to hound me until I get a dog—no pun intended."

FREYA BARKER

He chuckles beside me as we join Britt on the front steps.

I like the sound of his chuckle. Deep and resonating, it makes me want to burrow into him, absorb it into my skin. In the two nights since my niece arrived, we've done little else than snuggle up in bed. Usually spooning, my back to his front, and although the feeling of his larger body surrounding me is bliss, I already miss him inside me.

"How about we try for spaghetti and meatballs tonight?" Dimas suggests, walking into the kitchen.

I snort and raise an eyebrow.

"Hope you're not looking at me to attempt that."

"How hard can it be? We have all the basic ingredients," he offers, when Britt pipes up.

"I can show you," she says with all the confidence of a preteen.

I try not to look too doubtful. After all, it wouldn't be too much of a stretch of the imagination a twelve-year-old could outcook me.

"Grandma showed me."

Well, what do you know? Just because I avoided the kitchen like the plague doesn't mean Britt didn't actually pay attention to my mother's tutelage.

"Perfect." Dimas grins at her. "I've made it before and it was halfway edible, so between the two of us we should be able to make it actually taste good."

"Hey. What about me?"

Britt turns to me and pats my arm.

"You can roll the balls," she decrees.

I shoot Dimas a scathing look when he busts out laughing.

It's a little after nine when Britt can't keep her eyes open and heads to bed already half-asleep.

We just finished watching an episode of *Bones*, a show I was afraid might be too graphic at times, but Britt assured me she watches it all the time and has seen "way worse."

Dinner had been good; my niece appears to have paid close attention because the spaghetti was almost as I remember it growing up. As delegated, I rolled meatballs and stirred. That was about as much responsibility they dared hand over. I did, however, pay close attention to what they were doing. You never know, I might learn a thing or two.

"Beer?" Dimas asks, getting up from the couch.

"Please."

I watch his ass as he bends over to grab a couple of bottles from the bottom of the fridge. It's a good ass. No. It's a *great* ass. He doesn't wear his jeans as tight as some, I assume in part because of his artificial limb, but it certainly doesn't take away from his nicely sculpted behind.

"Are you checking me out?" he asks, grinning when he catches me with my head bent back for a better look.

"Don't flatter yourself," I fire back, but I do it

grinning as he stalks toward me.

My head bends back even farther when he leans in for an upside down kiss, before rounding the couch to sit next to me.

"Tell me what happened?" I ask, when he hands me a bottle.

I sit sideways with my knee pulled up on the seat, sipping my beer as he tells me about the meeting in the judge's chambers. His hand is resting loosely on my knee as he talks. His touch is comforting and already familiar.

"I popped into the office earlier when I was picking up my truck. Bree had been busy chatting with her connection at the GJPD and found out some interesting information."

That has me sit a little straighter.

"Like what?"

"For one thing, it turns out that your tip about Dr. Brantley Parker was never followed up on. The DA apparently called in to follow up on it this morning, and the new detective says there was no mention of Parker in the case file."

"Wow."

"Yeah, apparently he got so loud in the chief's office, half the force could hear him. Being accused of corruption in his ranks did not make the chief happy. After the DA left, he called everyone on the mat who'd even looked at that file. Apparently it's loosened some dirt on your favorite couple; Bergland and Craig."

"Good. I hate them."

He reaches out and strokes the back of his fingers down my cheek. Such a sweet gesture that seems entirely out of place for the rugged man before me, and yet it's all Dimas.

"It's great," he confirms. "The whole incident prompted the DA to agree to Brad's release. Not that he's out of the woods yet; the evidence, although circumstantial, keeps him on the list of suspects, but the sole focus is no longer only on him."

The fingers of the hand on my knee slowly stretch up the inside of my leg and a warm tingle starts deep in my belly.

"What about the case against me?" I ask, a little hoarse and all too aware of his touch.

"Her contact didn't have anything specific on that, but I'm sure after this morning that evidence will get the proper scrutiny as well. It was all a little too convenient..."

His hand is slowly traveling to the apex of my thighs and I have a hard time concentrating on his words.

"Sweetheart?"

"Mmmm," I mumble, my eyes closing and my head falling back against the couch when his fingers brush along the seam of my jeans, creating a deliciously subtle sensation.

"I was asking if you were tired."

My face cracks a grin at the promise of my bed.

"Exhausted."

DIMAS

I watch her pupils dilate as I strip out of my clothes by the side of the bed. She doesn't even have to move to have an effect on me.

I sit down with my back to her to take off my leg. I've been respectful of the fact there's an underage girl in the house. I've kept a firm control on my need for Willa since Britt's been here, but after a day like today, I need to feel her around me.

First there'd been the story of Brad's rescue. It's one he and I share, but never talk about. Sharing it with others—some of whom I don't even know— was not easy. I kept it as matter-of-fact as I could and left lots unsaid. Still, even if I didn't say the words, I relived the memories of what was left to read between the lines.

Yanis said little as we drove Brad to the shelter, but once we dropped him off and we were on our way to pick up my truck, he talked. Asking me why I'd never talked to him about that incident. All he knew was I ran into an IED in Iraq.

Jake is the only one who knows a lot of it because he'd been part of the same unit at the time. He doesn't talk about what he's seen either; it's not that easy to explain what things are like out there. It's one thing to share stuff with guys who've experienced it, but not easy to talk about with civilians. Not even my own brother.

Trying to explain why I'd kept the story from him

had not been easy. He seemed upset. Yanis hadn't been particularly supportive when I first enlisted with Jake, many moons ago. Part of it was he didn't like the idea of something happening to me, but I suspect there was also resentment. I was bailing after he spent most of his teenage years parenting me since Mom and Dad had their heads in the clouds. Quite literally most of the time.

I was a bit rebellious. Didn't want to be held back or weighed down by responsibilities like he seemed to be, so I took off. It took him a few years after I left, but he eventually left Encampment, Wyoming—where he'd served a few years as a police officer on the small force—as well. Resigned to leaving my parents to what they were, a couple of hippie potheads, he moved to Grand Junction, where after a short stint with the GJPD, he eventually started up PASS. After my honorable discharge for medical reasons, I joined him.

We get along fine, but he'll always be the big brother, which is why I'm sure he's upset.

Finally there'd been Brad, who seemed a mess, worrying me, and Willa who looked so incredibly sad after talking to him.

"Dimas?" I hear her pensive voice behind me and realize I've been sitting here lost in thought. "Are you okay?"

I turn to face her and with my eyes locked on hers, reach out to undo the fly of her jeans, pulling them along with her underwear down her legs. Then I crawl up and silently divest her of her shirt and bra until she lies naked on the bed, the question lingering in her eyes.

I lower myself on top of her so we're skin to skin, her soft breasts yielding against my chest as I give her my weight. I know I'm large and possibly too heavy for her, but Willa is strong, built to last. Her curves able to support my body. Me.

Our faces are inches apart when I finally answer her.

"Now I am," I whisper, brushing my lips over hers. "Do you realize how right you are for me?"

A blush creeps up her cheeks and her mouth pulls into a soft smile, even as she shakes her head.

I lift my head a little so I can see her better.

"Yeah. Tough as nails under all those beautiful soft curves. You fit me perfectly."

Her hand drifts up and she lets her fingers trail along my jaw, brushing my beard.

"I think so too," she whispers, lifting her face for a kiss.

As I lazily explore her mouth with my tongue, I move a hand down her body. I hook her behind the knee and pull up her leg as I roll us on our sides, our mouths still fused. Then I run the palm of my hand up the back of her thigh, smooth it over her lush ass cheek and dip my fingers in her crease, finding her warm, slick, and ready for me.

I quickly reach behind me to grab a condom from the bedside drawer where I stuck them and have myself covered in seconds.

"Dimas…"

"Yes, sweetheart," I respond, as I roll her to her back and settle myself between her legs.

"We have to be quiet."

"We will."

I brace myself on my elbow and take my cock in the other hand, teasing her clit with the crown until she sighs my name again.

"Right here, baby," I murmur against her lips, as I slowly enter her. "I'm right where I want to be."

CHAPTER 21

DIMAS

"THEY'VE GOT HIM," Bree announces when I walk into the office.

"Got who?"

I turn my chair to face her and sit down at my desk.

"Krupcek. I just got a call from my contact who watched them bring him in."

I was hoping it to be Brantley Parker, but I guess Krupcek would be a good place to start. At least they're actually investigating now, instead of making the pieces try to fit with a suspect in mind.

I wish I could be a fly on the wall, but unfortunately we would have to make do with whatever information Bree's connection can feed us.

"And get this," she continues, "the chief himself is sitting in on the interview."

"Guess he doesn't want to chance the ire of the DA again," I observe. "Says something about the faith he has in his staff, or lack thereof. Bet that's going over well."

"From what I hear everyone's been on eggshells. Bergland was apparently suspended first thing Tuesday morning and Craig has been put on desk duty."

Good to know that asshole, Bergland, has been at least temporarily put out of commission, although I'd love to know what his angle is in this case. Why he was so quick on the trigger, especially with Willa. *How* was he so quick on the trigger? The victim was found by the railroad tracks, not that far from the shelter, but how were they so quick to focus on Willa as their main suspect? From what I hear they supposedly received an anonymous tip—Hank found that out—but what would motivate Bergland and Craig to consider that enough to take her in?

"Radar!" I call over my shoulder.

"Yeah?" He sticks his head out of the door.

"Can you get access to financial information? Bank accounts and the like?"

I know what I'm asking him, but in our line of work the boundaries are often blurry. We're not law enforcement bound by rules and protocol, but we're also not above the law. It just means we have to be very, very careful how we do it.

Radar is a wiz at sneaking in back doors, pulling information, and sneaking right back out without anyone the wiser.

"Who are we looking at?"

"Darryn Bergland," Bree answers for me.

"Ah, the good Officer Bergland," Radar mocks.

"Shouldn't be difficult."

"Look for nice chunks of money coming in. Spending patterns. Anything that looks a little fishy on a police officer's salary," I suggest. "Oh, and while you're at it, you may as well check Detective Craig too."

"Be careful, though," my brother's voice sounds behind me and I turn to see him walk in, his eyes on Radar. "You don't want to leave any trace behind."

"Sure, Boss."

"What did I miss?" Yanis asks, propping a hip on my desk. Bree fills him in on the latest and he listens attentively. "What about Parker? Do we know what's happening with him?"

"Haven't heard anything, but I'll see what I can find out," Bree says, turning to her phone.

Yanis looks at me. "I'm on my way to meet Jake at The Red Apple for that installation we missed on Monday. It shouldn't take us more than a day. In the meantime, I'd like you to work with Bree cross-referencing the main players in this shit show. Don't leave anyone out. See if you get any hits."

"Okay, I can do that."

"Who do you have on the shelter?" he wants to know.

I haven't mentioned anything specific to Willa, other than to say she'd be safe, but we called in a couple of our freelancers for security surveillance. One guy watching the shelter during work hours, and we also have someone keeping a close eye on Britt, just in case. Brad vowed to keep an eye on Willa on the inside.

It's been tapping our reserves these past few days since there's no client footing the bill, but we all agreed it was necessary.

"I've got Shep on Willa and Kai on the girl."

Shep Kirwin and Kai Olson are contract guys. Ex-military, both of them. Yanis has tried to get them to sign on permanently a few times, but they seem to prefer working on an as needed basis. It just so happens we call on them a lot.

"Good." He stands up and raps his knuckles on my desk. "Hold down the fort for me."

"Will do."

I watch him walk to the door where he stops and turns back.

"Oh, and I think it's about time I got an invite so I can properly meet that woman of yours."

"Fine. How's Saturday?"

"Sounds good to me. I'll bring food."

As soon as he disappears I turn to Bree.

"You should come too."

She laughs at me. "You just want me to come as a diversion."

"Yeah? Your point?"

"You can deal with your brother on your own. Besides, from what I've seen and heard of Willa, she can handle him."

I smile at her characterization of Willa. She's dead-on. Willa won't easily be intimidated by my brother.

It may actually be fun to see him taken down a peg or two by her sharp tongue.

Suddenly I'm looking forward to Saturday night.

WILLA

"Hey, Short Stack," I hear Dimas greet Britt as she gets in the car.

"Guess what?" is the first thing out of her mouth, and my eyes meet his, smiling.

It's been like this every day this week. Each time she gets in the car she's full of stories.

I've tried a few times to connect with my sister, to let her know her daughter is having a good time, but she's not answering my calls or my texts and it's starting to worry me a bit. Last night I resorted to calling my brother-in-law, who said she was fine and then basically blew me off.

I voiced my concern to Dimas who suggested feeling out Britt, which I'd planned to do tonight.

"What?" he asks on cue.

"Twister can roll over and play dead. She's sooo smart! She doesn't even need a leash when we walk outside. She stays right beside me."

"That's amazing."

"Yes," she emphatically agrees, which has me snicker. "And…Steve says I'm really good at training her and looking after her."

The hint is not lost on me or on Dimas, from the way his shoulders silently shake. More like a repetitive two-by-four between the eyes since she started there on Monday. The girl wants a dog. No, she wants *that* dog. The one who, according to Britt, has been at the shelter for over a year because nobody wants her. Something that admittedly does not leave me unaffected.

I have a dilemma, though; let's suppose I adopt Twister, Britt won't be able to take the dog with her when she goes home—I don't think Connie would allow it and there's no way for me to check—which would mean the mutt is mine. Plus, Britt might still be heartbroken if she had to leave Twister behind.

Also, when I occasionally had thoughts about a dog, I envisioned maybe a cute Labradoodle or an Aussie with those pretty eyes. Not a schnug. The name alone.

Although, Twister *is* kind of ugly-adorable and super sweet.

"Tell you what." Dimas breaks the loaded silence from the back seat. "Why don't I take you two out for dinner? What do you wanna eat, Britt?" he asks in an attempt to distract her. "Seafood, Italian, Thai, Greek, Mexican?"

"Tacos!" she yells from the back seat.

I reach over and give Dimas's hand a squeeze.

"Tacos it is," he responds, lacing his fingers with mine.

Britt loves the little, out-of-the-way restaurant where all they serve is tacos, Corona beer, margaritas, and a few nonalcoholic drinks. I was here before, but it's been a while.

The interior is very rustic. Somewhere between old shack and outdoor picnic. A lot of the decor is recycled wood, metal, and furniture. There's not a chair matching another and half the tables are made of old pallets. The rest are simple wooden picnic tables you'd find outside in a park. Britt chooses one of those for us to sit at.

The menu hangs on the wall, written on a chalkboard. Thirty-seven different taco-fillings, anything from shellfish salad, to roasted vegetable, to meat lovers. They all come with a side of homestyle coleslaw or guacamole.

A girl in cutoff jeans and flip-flops wearing a shirt that says Tacos Only, the name of the restaurant, brings us some water and takes our drink and food orders. While we wait, Dimas and Britt play a game of hangman on the brown paper covering the picnic table.

It's nice, uncomplicated, and relaxing, until Britt has to visit the ladies' room and Dimas grabs my hands across the table.

"You're caving, aren't you?" he says with a smirk. He doesn't have to spell out he's talking about the dog, I know.

"Agh," I groan. "It's so complicated."

"About as complicated as you make it, sweetheart." I shoot him an annoyed glare, which bounces right off him. "What's the worst that can happen?"

"She's going home at some point, Dimas. She'll

have to say goodbye to the dog."

"She'll have to say goodbye one way or another. Except if you have the dog, she can visit and see her."

"You're being reasonable and it's annoying," I grumble. I'm gonna get the dog. Not that I didn't know that already. It's just the control thing again. "How fun will it be for the dog to be home alone all day?"

"Take her with you."

I open my mouth to protest, but then I close it again. Huh. Take her with me to the shelter. That might not be a bad idea. Good dogs give affection freely, and they don't judge you by the way you look, they judge you by the person you are. They are four-legged morale boosters; they love the unlovable.

An idea starts bubbling up, but before I let that run away with me I'll have to talk to Rosie first.

By the time Britt comes back to the table, the food has arrived and we're too busy eating to talk.

I wait until we leave Tacos Only and are on our way home.

"Maybe tomorrow when we pick you up, we can have a chat with Steve," I suggest, looking at my niece over my shoulder.

I watch as her bottom lip starts wobbling and her pretty eyes fill with tears.

"For real?"

Dimas flicks a glance in his rearview mirror when he hears her weepy voice and smiles.

"For real. But, Britt, honey, when you go home,

you know the dog will have to stay with me, right?"

She nods furiously, trying to wipe her nose at the same time.

"I can still come visit her."

I side-eye Dimas, who has his eyes on the road, but is wearing an I-told-you-so smirk on his face.

"Of course you can. Let's not get ahead of ourselves yet, okay? I still need to talk to Steve."

"Okay," she easily agrees, but she can't help darting out of the truck when Dimas pulls into the driveway.

I smile at her excitement as I unbuckle my seat belt and am about to open my door, when Dimas holds me back with a hand on my arm.

"That's one happy kid, sweetheart," he says when I turn to look at him. "She's lucky to have you."

The compliment warms me from the inside out and I lean over the console to press my lips on his in a soft kiss.

"You were right," I mutter, watching the fine lines by his eyes deepen with his smile.

"It happens," he says humbly, and I'm grateful he's not rubbing it in.

"You're a good man, Dimas Mazur. The best."

I'm rewarded with a tender brush of his fingers over my lips.

"Let's see if we can get that kid to bed early," he suggests, and his implication runs like a warm tingle all the way down between my legs.

We each get out of the truck and meet at the base of

the path to the house, his hand closing around mine.

We're halfway to the front door when I feel something whizzing by me, close enough to brush my hair and followed immediately by a sharp crack.

"Down!" Dimas yells, and everything suddenly slows down.

My eyes search out Britt, who is turning around, her eyes wide, as I feel myself knocked off my feet.

"Britt! Get down!" Dimas yells again, even as he takes me down hard to the pavers and lands heavily on top, knocking the breath from my lungs.

Another crack. This time slivers of stone fly up to my face and my eyes close tight.

Shots. Someone is shooting.

CHAPTER 22

DIMAS

*H*OLY FUCK!

My body recognizes something slicing the air before my ears pick up the distinct crack of a gunshot, and I yell a fraction of a second before I tackle Willa. I yell again, this time at Britt who is standing alone and exposed by the front door.

Another shot has me cover Willa's head with my arms.

Then a sharp burning in my shoulder the moment my ears register a third.

We're sitting ducks.

"We've gotta move," I growl into Willa's hair, pushing up on my knees and bringing her with me by wrapping an arm tightly around her chest.

The fourth shot goes wide, and I glance over my shoulder to the banks of the Colorado River to see where the shots are coming from. With Willa tight against my front, I manage to shield her with the bulk of my body as I half-carry her to the small hedge under the living room window.

Another crack, but by now I'm fueled with adrenaline and a singular focus in mind—keeping Willa safe—I don't think bullets would be able to stop me.

I vaguely hear Britt whimpering.

"Stay down, baby!" Willa calls out to the girl from where I shoved her behind the hedge. Her voice is surprisingly firm.

I'm crouched beside her, trying to take stock of the situation. My gun is already in my hand, even though I have no recollection how it got there. I need to get us inside.

"Willa. Key," I snap, not taking my eyes off the copse of trees on the water's edge across the road.

The fifth shot hits the window right above my head, which shatters, raining down glass on both of us.

But I saw the flash this time, coming from the tree closest to the road, and I could've sworn I heard the bolt click in place.

"In my pocket," she says, her voice still steady despite our precarious situation.

"Got your gun?"

"It's in my purse, I dropped it on the walkway."

"Shit. Okay, shooter is in that group of trees beside the river. I need you to get up the steps, open the door, and get Britt inside while I cover you. I have a full clip."

Another shot ricochets off the concrete steps. *Fuck.*

"Ready?"

Immediately on her, "Yes," I start firing at the trees as we move to the steps. I make my body as big a target as I can and pace my shots to keep the gunman's fire suppressed, but still give Willa time to open the door. Behind me I hear the door open and Willa hustle Britt inside as I fire my last bullet.

"Dimas," she hisses, and I turn and dive in the door, just as the shooter fires.

"In the kitchen, behind the island! Now," I bark, as another shot shatters the narrow pane of glass beside the front door.

Desperation has the fucker shooting blindly.

I pull out my phone and dial Yanis, even as I hear sirens in the distance. Someone's called in the troops.

"Someone's taking shots at us from across Willa's house."

"Stay down. On my way," is all he says before ending he call.

I crawl over to where a stoic Willa and a softly crying Britt are huddled on the floor behind the kitchen island.

"Come here." I sit down with my back against the cupboard and haul both of them into my arms.

Huddled together, we listen to the sirens closing in.

"We're okay, baby," Willa whispers to her niece, whose face is pressed against her shirt. "We're gonna be okay." Then she looks at me and mouths, *"You good?"*

I nod affirmatively but she still reaches for the

kitchen towel, wads it up, and presses it to the top of my shoulder.

"You're hit," she whispers, her eyes concerned, and I notice a trail of blood running down the side of her forehead.

Where the last five minutes dragged out like a slow motion movie, the next half hour plays out on fast-forward.

I watch as an EMT closes the fortunately shallow cut close to Willa's hairline. She has Britt's head in her lap and her hand never stops stroking the girl's purple hair, but her eyes are locked on mine. So strong, this woman didn't panic once.

I can't help wincing when the second first responder cleans out the groove left in my shoulder by one of the shots fired at us. We were lucky, with only superficial wounds as a result of getting pelted with bullets.

The settling darkness had helped, as had somewhat windy conditions, making accuracy a challenge for whoever has it out for Willa. Yes, there's no doubt in my mind she was the target.

The entire street has been blocked off and cops are everywhere, among them my brother, Jake, and Bree, who showed up minutes after they did.

"They found four shell casings," Jake says as he walks up. "Looks like he may have collected the rest before he ran."

Of course the shooter had taken off before the cops pulled up outside. My guess is he was on foot and had his car parked somewhere down the road. There's a trail of sorts right along the river he probably used for access.

"Any sign of the guy?"

Jake shakes his head. "Cops are up and down the street, knocking on doors. But here's an interesting tidbit Bree just picked up; that guy Parker? Apparently the cops have been unable to locate him thus far."

"He'd be my guess," I share, as I watch Willa walk over with Britt. "Hey, sweetheart, you good?"

"Just a scratch," she says with a smile.

"Yeah, me too." I look at Britt, who glances up before her eyes slide over to the house. Still shell-shocked. "Hey, Short Stack. How about we do a sleepover at my place tonight?" Her eyes come back to me. "I've got a huge couch we all fit on and we can watch a bunch of movies."

"Okay," she says, clearly warming to the idea.

"Willa?"

She has a soft look on her face and gratitude in her eyes.

"That sounds perfect."

"How about Jake clears the way inside for you, and you guys can pack a bag?"

"We can do that." She leans forward and brushes my lips lightly with hers, before turning to Britt. "Ready?"

The moment they're out of sight, I turn to the man I noticed standing a few feet away from the ambulance. I've never met him but I know who he is.

"You're good to go." The medic gives my good

shoulder a pat and I slide down the back of the rig and walk straight up to him.

"Don't think we've ever had the pleasure," I comment, not without a dash of sarcasm. "Dimas Mazur."

The chief of police grabs my hand and shakes it.

"Chris Underwood."

He's younger than I expected, fifty at most.

"What can I do for you, Chief? I already spoke to a couple of your officers. Not sure what more I can add."

"Wanted to personally assure you and Ms. Smith we'll do whatever it takes to find this guy, but I didn't want to intrude with the girl present."

That's actually considerate of him. "I appreciate that."

"If you wouldn't mind passing it on?"

"Be glad to, and I'm sure she'll be thrilled to hear it."

I don't even bother hiding the sarcasm here. I don't care how 'involved' he is after being called out, the fact remains shit clearly was happening in his department he either turned a blind eye to, or was completely oblivious to. Neither option says good things about him.

"Right," he mumbles, reading me correctly. "I gather from your brother there is—how did he put it—'not a fat chance in hell' your team will stand down, but I'll repeat to you what I told him; it would be in our mutual interest to share any findings."

I can see why he's chief, the politics shine through in his words. Basically what he's saying is, I don't care what you do as long as you let me take the credit. That's fine. It's not like we like the limelight in our line of business.

"You bet, Chief."

I nod at him and turn toward the house, ready to collect my girls and watch some movies.

Anything to distract from the fight or flight charge still buzzing right under my skin.

WILLA

It takes me a minute to figure out where I am, when I wake up in the middle of the night.

Drool is gathering under my cheek pressed into the well-worn tan leather of Dimas's sectional. I immediately do as much damage control as I can by the faint bathroom light he left on.

Britt is still curled up asleep by my feet, covered in an old quilt he pulled out of the hallway closet. She'd been the first to fall asleep, while Dimas and I were still killing off the bottle of wine he suggested to settle the jitters. It worked. I slept when I didn't think I'd be able to.

Until now, that is.

Dimas isn't on the couch, or in the kitchen.

I carefully lift my feet over Britt's head and sit up, waiting to see if I can hear anything. It's quiet. Getting up, I head down the hallway, maybe he was uncomfortable and took to his bed, but he's not there either. Not in either of the bathrooms, or the spare bedroom.

Worried, I peek out the bedroom window, but his truck is still parked in the driveway. He can't have gone far. The alarm clock on the nightstand shows three forty-five. Fuck, that means we barely had two hours of sleep.

I walk back into the living room and peer out those windows. Nothing is moving in the sparse shine of the streetlights. Finally I head to the back doors off the kitchen.

At first I don't see anything, but then I hear a strange clacking noise over the hum of the air conditioner. Almost like teeth chattering.

The night is appropriately warm for July as I step outside, carefully closing the slider behind me. I try again to get a bead on the sound, which seems to be coming from the side of the house.

"Dimas?" I softly call out, but get no answer.

I venture down the wooden steps until my bare feet hit the grass. I stop again to listen. Yes, definitely from around the side. There's a thin cloud cover and the barely visible moon gives off a faint light. Just enough to safely find my way around the corner of the house.

I don't spot him right away, curled up with his back wedged between the AC unit and the concrete foundation. His knees are pulled up to his chest, circled by his arms, and his head hangs down. I take a few steps closer and note his entire body seems to be shaking.

"Dimas?"

I crouch in front of him and reach out, touching his arm lightly.

It's like a spring uncoils as he flings out both arms, one catching me on the jaw and knocking me back on my ass.

Shit.

I push up to see he's semi-crouched, his unseeing eyes darting around, looking for what I assume is the enemy still haunting him. I'm not sure what to do. I recognize the absence of the here and now in his face, similar to how Brad presented earlier this week, except Dimas seems further gone.

I stay where I am, but curl up tight, much like he was earlier, hoping to be less threatening this way. Then I start talking, softly.

"I'm right here. Not going anywhere."

It's a phrase I repeat again and again. The rest of the time I talk mostly nonsense, about his house, how much I like it. About the tacos we had for dinner, and Britt's stories about her beloved dog. I talk about the things I smell, the fresh cut grass from next door and a faint scent of honeysuckle. I talk about anything that comes to mind, regularly repeating how I'm right here to stay.

I have no clue how long we sit here, but my voice is hoarse and dry from talking so much. The chattering of his teeth and the shaking seem to have subsided and—knowing I'm taking a risk—I reach out once again, this time gingerly touching his knee.

"Dimas?"

His eyes blink and he takes in a deep breath like he's been holding it all this time. He sinks back on his butt.

"Willa?" The moment I hear him say my name I scoot closer, as close as I can, and press myself against him. "What…?"

"It's okay," I mumble, putting a hand on his chest. His heart is beating a staccato under my palm. "We're at your house and everyone is fine."

"Did I…? Was I…?"

"Shhh," I press a kiss to his chest and push myself to my feet, grabbing his hand and pulling him up with me. "It's still early. Let's get some sleep."

I don't look back when I lead the way up the steps and into the house, but his fingers tightly grip my own.

"Couch or bed?" I ask when he stops at the edge of the living room, looking at Britt's sleeping form.

"Couch," he answers, sitting down on the edge.

I kneel down in front of him and roll up the track pants he changed into earlier, unstrapping his prosthesis and putting it aside. I can feel his eyes on me and finally look up. They show a world of uncertainty I want to take away.

"Lie back."

His gaze is locked on me as he lowers himself slowly. I lie down, half on top of him, and kiss him softly on the mouth. He shifts slightly so we're both on our side, face-to-face. I run the tips of my fingers over the frown on his forehead and down his cheek, before pressing my face against his chest.

"Sleep, my love. I'm right here."

His arms close around me as I listen to his heart slow to a regular beat.

CHAPTER 23

DIMAS

I CAN'T STOP looking at her.

That bruise along her jaw—I did that. *Fuck.*

She's smiling, twisted in around so she can talk to Britt in the back seat. She doesn't look like it's bothering her, and she reassured me about ten times she was fine, but that doesn't negate the fact it was my fist causing the blue mark on her face.

The thought makes me sick. Had it been any harder, I could have broken her jaw.

Jesus.

"Hey," her voice is as soft as her hand stroking my arm is. I glance over and catch a glimpse of concern in her eyes. "You good?"

"Yeah."

"Are we still going to talk to Steve after?" Britt asks from the back seat.

"We will, honey, but it may not be today," Willa explains.

We're on our way to the PASS office to sign our

police statements. It had been Bree's idea. She'd been over this morning to check up on us, when I got a call from Chief Underwood. He wanted us to come to the station, but Willa didn't feel comfortable leaving her niece. Understandable after last night, but I also suspect she's not eager to head back to the police station. Her last experience hadn't exactly been a good one. Bree suggested we could come to the office so Britt could hang out with her, while we were next door in the conference room dealing with the statements. Underwood agreed to meet us there.

It seemed to be a foregone conclusion none of us would go in to work today, not with the shooter still out there. Last night, when Yanis traded vehicles with me—I'm driving his Yukon—he mentioned he'd also be putting both Shep and Kai on my house. I'm glad I didn't argue with him, not after what happened early this morning. The thought I might've left Willa and Britt unprotected eats at me.

I glance in the rearview mirror to see Kai behind me in his pickup.

"What do you do, Dimi?" Britt asks, leaning forward between the two front seats. She started using the name everyone calls me, except Willa.

"I'm a security specialist. You met my brother last night, Yanis? I work for him. We're hired to protect people or companies, either with technical support or in person."

"Like a bodyguard?"

I smile at the excitement in her voice. If only she

knew how utterly boring our line of work can be a lot of the time.

"Sometimes, yes, but we spend a lot of time behind a desk as well."

"Oh." She seems disappointed.

"And even when we are protecting a person or people, it's really not as exciting as it may sound."

"You're good at it, though." I glance over and she's looking at me with tears welling in her eyes. "You kept us safe last night."

I don't know what to say to that so I say nothing, shooting her a wink instead.

"He sure did." My eyes meet Willa's over her niece's head.

"Is he coming back?" Britt's voice wobbles when she asks the question.

She's been as tough as her aunt, waking up this morning on my couch and acting like it was a normal morning after a normal night, when it had been everything but. How ironic, the one person who's supposed to be used to getting shot at was the only one losing it.

"It doesn't matter if he does, Short Stack, I'm not gonna let anything happen to you or your aunt."

"Okay." She doesn't sound very convinced as she sits back in her seat.

When I pull around the office building to the back, I see one of the bay doors was left open and I drive right inside. Radar must have his eye on the monitor, because the moment Kai's truck clears the door, it immediately closes behind us.

I turn off the engine and get out of the SUV, opening the back door for the young girl who hops down easily.

"Britt?" She looks up and I bend closer, placing a hand on her narrow shoulder. "I promise."

Her "Okay" this time sounds a little firmer.

I introduce Kai to the girls and have to send the tall Scandinavian a warning glare when he's a little too charming with Willa.

"That was priceless," Jake says, pulling me aside when we walk into the bullpen.

"What?"

"Watched you on the monitor, brother. If looks could kill, Kai would've been down. You used to bust my balls all the time about being territorial with Rosie. I'm gonna fucking enjoy busting yours," he says with a wide grin, clapping me on the shoulder.

"Asshole," I mutter, as I watch Bree walk up to Willa and Britt, the girl still not moving very far from her aunt's side. Jake's chuckle is annoying.

"Check in with Radar, he's got something to show you."

I stick my head into Radar's office where he's glued to his three computer screens, as usual.

"You have something?"

"Yeah. Come in." I take a seat across from him and he slides two sheets of paper across the desk. "Left is Bergland's savings, right is Craig's checking account. Check Bergland's first."

Highlighted on the sheet is a fifteen thousand dollar deposit and a few days after a withdrawal of five thousand.

"What am I looking at?"

"Bergland has a pattern; when his biweekly pay comes in, he withdraws two hundred dollars in cash, nothing more until the next deposit. I've gone back six months and it's always the same. In between he seems to use his debit or credit card. Check the date on that large deposit?"

"That's the day Arthur Hicks was found."

"Exactly. Now look at the date on the large withdrawal and compare it to Craig's account. He pulls money out of his account almost daily, but he hasn't made a single cash withdrawal since that day."

Yanis sticks his head into the office.

"Underwood is here."

"Coming." I get up and grab the sheets. "Can I keep these?"

"You gonna tell him?"

"I'll take full responsibility for the hacking, but yeah. Those two are dirty as fuck."

I walk over to Willa, who is leaning a hip on Bree's desk, while Britt is on the other side, giggling at something Bree is pointing out on the computer screen. I take Willa's hand, ruffle the girl's hair, and head to the conference room where Chief Underwood is already waiting.

"I have some good news," he says, when we sit down at the big table. "State Patrol picked up

Brantley Parker earlier today near Montrose. He'll be transported back here tomorrow."

I feel a weight lift off my shoulders.

"That is good news. I have some news as well, but I'm thinking you won't be happy with this."

I slide the printouts across the table and explain what he's looking at. He studies the papers and looks to have aged a few years when he finally looks up, shaking his head.

"Do I wanna know how you got this?"

"Probably not."

He stares at me across the table, then turns his eyes on Yanis, who looks back straight-faced.

"Shit. I can't use this to call the Internal Affairs Unit in. I can't use this to get a warrant to dig into the source of that payment."

"We can," Yanis answers calmly. "We'll find you something you can use."

Underwood runs a hand through his hair and groans.

"You know you're breaking the law, right?"

"I wouldn't say that," Yanis responds casually. "In the end, we're all about getting the bad guys. This office can afford to be a little more creative with the interpretation of law than yours can. That's all."

The police chief looks from Yanis to me, and finally Willa, giving her an apologetic smile.

"I apologize for what happened to you under my command. I promise you this case will have my personal focus until we have it resolved."

Willa nods, and Underwood turns his eyes on me, shoving the papers back in my direction.

"You bring me something usable and in the meantime, I've never seen these."

WILLA

Britt darts back to the kennels the moment we walk into the animal shelter. Steve stands up from behind the front desk, grinning after her.

"Sorry she missed today."

His face turns serious when he looks at me.

"God, don't worry about it. Bree told me what happened last night. I couldn't believe it. Are you all okay?"

"We're fine," Dimas rumbles from behind me. "Everything should be back to normal after the weekend."

I twist my neck to look back at him. I sure hope what he says is true, and I'm not just talking about people taking potshots at us. Something's changed. I can't exactly put my finger on it, but from the moment we got up this morning something is off with him. I know why—that doesn't take a genius to figure out—but the few times I probed today I was either shut down in a hurry or ignored.

"Actually, I was hoping to talk to you about adopting a dog," I explain to Steve. "What would be required?"

"That's awesome. Did you have a dog in mind or

do you want to have a look first?"

"I think my niece would disown me if I even thought about adopting any other dog than Twister."

"Really?" His face breaks open in a huge smile. "Can't tell you how happy that makes me. She's been here far too long. People can't seem to look beyond her exterior to see what a great pet she'd make. I've even taken her home on occasion over the weekends. I always feel so bad when other animals come and go, but she's never chosen."

Okay, now I feel even guiltier for thinking the pup is ugly.

For the next twenty minutes he explains what the adoption entails, having me fill out forms as we go, and when my last signature is on paper, asks me if I'd like to take her home right away.

"Actually, that might have to wait until next week." I wince when I inform him. "There was some damage to my place that is getting fixed over the weekend, so we're temporarily out of a house."

"Why?" Dimas's tone is unexpectedly abrupt and directed at me. "Think I can't handle a dog?"

Whoa.

Luckily for him, Britt comes barreling through the door, or I would've given him a piece of my mind. I know he feels shaky after last night and that's fine. It's not an excuse to snap at me over words he's putting in my mouth.

Instead I smile at my niece a little too brightly before turning to Steve.

"Do you have everything we need here?" I ask. "Food? Leash? That kinda stuff?"

"Ohmygawd! We're getting her?" Britt's high pitch has me plug my ears.

"Settle the hell down," Dimas grumps behind me, and I turn my entire body to face him, giving him my most dirty look. If he starts projecting his mood on my niece, we've got big problems. He stares back with a blank expression.

"Come on, Britt," I hear Steve say behind me. "Let's find Twister a leash."

I hear the door slam shut behind me and poke my index finger in his chest.

"No. You don't talk to me, or to Britt like that. I won't have it." His eyes immediately lower to the tips of his boots, so I know he gets me. Then I push at that small sign of remorse. "I know something happened between last night and this morning, and I was going to leave it alone, but I've changed my mind. I'm not okay being a lightning rod when no one warned me there's a storm brewing."

"Sweetheart, I—"

"They have a red one!" Britt squeals, waving a leash and collar around.

"Honey, I know you're happy but you've gotta turn down the volume, I think you just pierced my eardrum."

She immediately winces and I see her eyes dart over my head.

"Sorry," she mumbles.

"Don't be, I'm glad you're so excited. Now how about you go find Twister and get her gussied up with that collar, and I'll settle up with Steve."

"No one says gussied up anymore, Auntie Will. It's blinged out." Educating me with that nugget of wisdom, she darts back to the kennels.

Ten minutes later, Twister's head is hanging over the back of the driver's seat, drool dripping on Dimas's shirt, and I'd swear that dog is smiling. Dimas is not, but he's not pushing Twister back either.

Britt—over the peak of her excitement for now—is surprisingly quiet in the back. When I turn to check on her, though, she's looking out of the side window, a big goofy smile on her face.

"Happy?" I ask, sticking my face between the headrest and the doorframe. She nods her head so hard, her hair falls in her face. "Good. Now guess who's gonna be responsible for scooping the poop from the backyard?"

I laugh out loud when her smile disappears and is replaced with a grimace of sheer disgust.

"You're kidding, right?"

"Nope. Not even a little."

"Gross!"

I straighten in my seat and glance over at Dimas and notice the corner of his mouth twitching, but he still won't look at me. That's fine; he won't be able to avoid talking to me for long.

Except when we get to his house, he opens the door and waves us inside.

"I just need a word with Kai," he says, pulling the door shut behind us.

Kai is the tall, Scandinavian guy he introduced us to at the PASS office. And when I say tall, I mean *tall*. Hell, Dimas is probably around six four, but this guy is even taller. Like, basketball player tall.

Britt and I get Twister's stuff sorted in the kitchen, getting her a bowl of water and one with kibble, while the dog runs through the house, sniffing everything her nose can reach. Including Dimas's crotch when he comes in the door.

"Down, Twister." His deep voice apparently makes an impression. The dog takes a few steps back and sits right down. "Kai is parked in the driveway," he says to me from the doorway. "I've got a few things I need to take care of, and I'll swing by PetSmart on my way home and pick her up a bed. Anything else she needs?"

"She needs toys and treats," Britt announces.

"Consider it done, Short Stack." He grins at her before facing me. "I don't know how long I'll be, but why don't you guys go ahead and order some pizza? I'll see you later."

Off he goes, without a touch or a kiss. I'm so frustrated I could scream. Rationally I know this is likely not even about me, but it's hard not to feel a little rejected.

Twister is back on her trail of discovery, sticking her nose in my purse sitting on the couch.

"Nosy dog," I observe, as my niece pulls herself

up on a stool while I fill a glass at the tap.

"Auntie Will?"

"Yeah, baby?"

"Do you think Mom's gonna call?"

I turn off the tap and swing around, leaning my butt against the counter.

"Sure she will," I tell her, trying to inject as much conviction as I can muster into my voice. "She loves you like mad. You know that, right?"

"Whatever," Britt mumbles, shrugging. "I like it better here anyway."

There's not a doubt in my mind my sister loves her kid, despite the arguments they seem to get into all the time, but it worries me she hasn't called at all. Other than her text a week ago saying she'll be in touch, I haven't heard a thing, and what's even more concerning; I haven't been able to get her on the phone.

"What's going on at home, Britt?" I ask her gently.

Her eyes fill with tears.

"They fight, Aunt Will," she sobs. "They fight all the time."

CHAPTER 24

WILLA

I GAVE UP waiting for him around eleven thirty.

It had been a long hard night, discussing a few difficult subjects with my niece. I wasn't really up to launching into another one with Dimas.

Britt talked about my sister and Jim and their more frequent loud fights these past few months. How she overheard her mother call him a cheating bastard. She was crying so hard at some point I ended up on the floor with her in my lap, Twister nudging close to complete our huddle.

Then she asked me in a shaky voice why someone was shooting at us. I'd been waiting for her to ask. She'd seemed so normal all day; I didn't want to bring anything up if she wasn't ready to talk about it. I contemplated whether to deny knowing why or giving her a condensed version of the truth. I opted for the latter and reminded her of the promise Dimas made her to keep us safe.

She wanted me to put her to bed not long after that,

and I sat up waiting for a while before letting Twister take care of business in the yard one last time.

Britt was in the spare bedroom already asleep on a mattress on the floor, so I crawled into Dimas's bed. Five minutes later, Twister started whining outside the bedroom door and the next moment I heard the front door open.

When he finally crawled into bed, I was curled up on my side but found myself hauled across the mattress. His arm around my waist pulled me into the curve of his body. I waited a long time for him to say something, but he stayed silent until I could hear him start to snore softly.

This morning he's already up by the time I drag myself out of bed. I find him in the kitchen with Britt, eating toast and cereal. My focus is on the coffeepot as I make a beeline straight for it. I feel him move up behind me and his arms slip around my waist as he presses his face in my neck.

"Come sit down, sweetheart," he mumbles there. "I'll get you coffee and toast. Please…" he adds.

I let him guide me to the stool he just occupied and sit down next to Britt.

"Morning, honey," I tell her, leaning over to give her head a kiss.

She mumbles something I can't quite make out. My niece needs a little time in the morning to get going. Normally I'm a morning person, but today I need a little extra time too. I did not sleep well.

Dimas slides a mug toward me and I almost groan

out loud at that first hit of coffee. I keep my eyes closed while waiting for the caffeine to make its way into my bloodstream. A secondary benefit is that I don't have to look Dimas in the eye.

I hear the sound of the sliding door opening and the next moment a wet tongue hits my bare feet.

"Morning, Twister," I mumble, reaching down to scratch the dog's head.

"Can I watch TV now?"

I turn to look at Britt, but she has her eyes on Dimas, showing him her empty bowl. Apparently there'd been some kind of deal made between the two I wasn't privy to.

"Sure, but use the TV in my bedroom, okay? Remote is on the dresser."

Britt slides off her stool, shuffling down the hallway to the master. I'm hoping he sent her to watch TV in the bedroom so he can talk to me. God, I want him to talk to me.

I'm not going to lie; it hurt, having him shut down and disappearing on me last night. Granted, the emotional conversation with Britt had taken its toll as well, but his silent absence had cut me.

Dimas slides a plate with toast in front of me and I finally look him in the eyes. I see none of the reservations that had shimmered there these past couple of days. No shields up this morning.

"You eat while I talk," he says, nudging the plate closer.

Despite insecurity gnawing at my stomach, I sink

my teeth into the toast.

DIMAS

I hate I put that doubt in her eyes.

These past few days, I've had some serious questions myself, but never about her.

I've been shot at before, been hurt before, but I've never felt cold fear like I did a few days ago. The episode during the night and discovering the next morning I'd hit Willa, at some point during my fugue state, left me crippled with self-loathing. That only intensified when I couldn't seem to stop myself from being an asshole. Fuck, I even snapped at poor Britt, who looked at me with suspicion this morning. I can't blame her. It's like I was trying to prove to myself through my behavior I'm not worthy of Willa.

Hell, she never gave me reason to believe that. In fact, she'd been understanding and supportive until I barked at her niece. Then she confronted me fiercely and it scared the shit out of me.

Brad met me on the trail along the river and walked beside me for hours. I talked, I listened, and there were long periods of silence where I processed. At the end of it, my head was clearer and the nausea of guilt eating at my stomach gone.

"I'm in love with you."

It's clear that's not what she was expecting me to say as I watch her eyes grow big. Fuck, it's not what I intended to start off with, but it came flying out anyway. I run an agitated hand over my beard. *Christ*, I'm already fucking this up.

"I've been an asshole and I'm sorry." That's better. "The thing that scares me most is you getting hurt, and somehow that's exactly what I've ended up doing."

"Dimas…"

Her voice is gentle as she reaches across the counter I've purposely kept between us. Already she's forgiving me, making it too easy.

"Hear me out," I plead, waiting for her nod in acknowledgement. "I struggle. Not often, but I get nightmares sometimes. On rare occasions a sharp sound or a bang can unnerve me. This…thing, it feels like existing on parallel levels in different worlds, where something as simple as a car backfiring or the slamming of a door can blur the wall between the two. I'm used to it. When it happens it's no more than a disorienting moment until I can feel my feet under me in the present." I lean my elbows on the counter and take the hand she left stretched out, in mine. "That night, that wall wasn't blurred, it was gone. I know it happens to some, but that had never happened to me. I was scared after. Even more so when I discovered I'd hurt you at some point, and I have no recollection at all."

"Honey." The endearment slips from her lips as she covers my hand with hers. "You can barely see it now. Look." She turns her face into the light and sure enough, the bruise is already fading. "I shouldn't have touched you. I know better. I'm as responsible as I would be if I got this running into a door."

I open my mouth to object but catch myself. There really is no point in arguing about this, we clearly both regret it happened. I lift our joined hands and kiss the back of hers.

"I met with Brad last night," I confess. "Talking to him helped. Even just being with someone who experiences what I experience helps. I didn't mean to shut you out, but I needed things clear in my head and—"

"You don't need to explain. I'm glad you guys have each other, I'm even happier you can talk to someone who understands where you're at. Plenty of people don't have that, so I'm grateful."

Holding onto her hands, I move around the counter as she turns to face me.

"Did I mention I'm in love with you?"

Her smile beaming up at me has a lump stick in my throat. How did I get so fucking lucky?

"I vaguely recall," she teases, snaking her arms around my waist and pressing a cheek in the middle of my chest. "I feel the same way."

I move slightly back and tilt her head back with my hands.

"Look at me and tell me."

Her eyes are warm and faintly amused when she locks eyes with me.

"I'm in love with—"

I swallow the rest of it when I cover her lips with mine. Everything I'm feeling I pour into the kiss. I feel her fingers dig into the muscles of my back, pulling me between her spread legs. My cock is already hard when she slides forward, pressing her hot core against me.

"Gross."

Visions of Willa naked on my counter evaporate at the sound of Britt's voice and my head snaps up. As she dives into the fridge for something to drink, Willa chuckles with her face buried in my shirt.

"Good," I tell the young girl. "I hope you keep thinking kissing boys is gross for another twenty years or so."

Britt surfaces with a bottle of water and glances at me, tilting her head.

"I didn't say anything about kissing boys being gross. I'm talking about old people."

"Hey!" Her aunt lifts her head. "Who are you calling old?"

Snickering, Britt disappears to the bedroom, Twister following behind.

Reluctantly I let go of Willa to grab the coffeepot for a refill.

"She seems to be in a good mood," I note.

"We had a long talk last night. I was gonna bring that up with you today. I may need your help."

"Talk about what?" I ask, studying her concerned face as I stay safely on the other side of the island. Getting caught once is enough.

"Connie and Jim, her parents. Britt says they've been fighting more and more lately. From what she tells me, it sounds like Jim's been stepping out. I'm worried, Dimas, she still hasn't answered any texts or messages I've left."

"When's the last time you heard from her?"

"Friday a week ago. The day before Mom and Dad dropped Britt off."

"And she didn't say anything?"

"Just that she'd be in touch."

I grab a pad of paper and pen I keep on top of the fridge.

"Give me their full names and phone numbers." I jot down the information, ask for their home address, as well as any contact info she might have. "What about your parents? Had any contact with them?"

She shakes her head. "No, they don't believe in cell phones. I could contact the Airbnb they usually stay at, but I really don't want to worry them for nothing."

"I'll look into it. Why don't you go grab a shower while I make some phone calls?" I suggest, leaning over the counter to kiss her forehead.

The moment she disappears into the bedroom, I grab my phone and the pad and walk out on the deck.

"Radar? Grab a pen and paper, will ya?"

I pass on the information and explain what I'd like him to look into. I have a bad feeling about this. It's one thing for her sister not to follow through on her promise to get in touch, but her daughter is here and Willa's been blowing up her phone. If I were a parent, I'd be worried something might be wrong with my kid.

Apparently Bree is in the office as well and wants to speak with me.

"Just got a call from my guy at the police station. Guess who was just brought in by the State Patrol?"

"Parker? Awesome."

"Got it in one. Apparently his lawyer was at the station already waiting for him."

"Figures. I forgot to ask Radar; he dig up some more on those financials?"

"Pretty much hit the mother lode on that. The transfer came from an account in the name of Elizabeth Woodbridge, an eighty-three-year old living in a full-care facility. She has close to three million dollars in her account, and guess who has power of attorney?"

"I give up," I immediately return.

"You're no fun," she complains. "It's her son, one Dr. Brantley Parker."

"That stuff needs to go to Underwood."

"He can't use it."

"Call it in as an anonymous tip, I don't care. He'll have to come up with justification to pull those records. He won't want Parker to walk."

"I'll give Yanis a call, see if he has any ideas."

"Fine. Krupcek talking yet?"

"Not that I've heard."

"When you're dropping anonymous tips, you might wanna suggest they let Krupcek and Parker see each other at the police station. Bet you that'll loosen tongues."

It's been a lazy day.

Willa did some laundry—she offered—and we all watched a Rockies' game this afternoon.

I just let Twister out back and I'm digging through my drawer of takeout menus, while Willa is putting the sheets back on the beds. It's close to five and I'm starting to get hungry.

The dog starts barking outside moments before the doorbell rings. Britt jumps up from the couch and runs for the door.

"Hold up, Short Stack, better let me," I call out, making my way to her.

I gently move her behind me as I peek out the small window in the door to find Yanis standing outside with an armful of brown paper bags.

Fuck. I totally forgot about dinner. Unlocking the door I move aside to let him in, when suddenly my parents step into view, big smiles on their faces.

"Surprise!" Mom yells while my father rolls his eyes behind her.

I throw a dirty glare at my brother, who seems to think this is hilarious.

"You could've warned me," I growl at him, but I'm already being hugged by our mother.

"Don't take it out on your brother. We surprised him too. He said he was coming here for dinner, so we decided to tag along."

"Good to see you, Mom." I tighten my hold on her before setting her back and accepting a hug from my father.

"Oh my, aren't you gorgeous? Who is this pretty thing?"

Fuck. For a moment I forgot about Britt and Willa. I quickly turn and wrap my arm around the girl's shoulders, pulling her to my side.

"This is Britt," is as far as I get before Mom pulls the poor girl into one of her bone-crushing hugs.

"You are too precious," she coos. "Where did you come from?"

I've always suspected Mom would've liked a girl to break up our testosterone-filled household, although she's never admitted to it.

"I came with Auntie Will."

I see the confused look on my mother's face and I quickly clarify.

"Willa. She's my—"

"Hello," I hear Willa's tentative voice behind me and turn around, reaching out to take her hand in mine.

"Mom, Dad, this is Willa, my girlfriend."

Instantly my mother starts blinking.

"Here we go," Dad grumbles, when the first tears start rolling.

Mom claps her hands over her mouth as she stares at Willa like she's Janis Joplin incarnate.

"Oh, my goddess."

CHAPTER 25

WILLA

I CAN'T KEEP my eyes off their mother.

She's a sight to behold, with full gray waves falling down to the middle of her back, a Rastafarian beanie perched on top of her head, an embroidered boho tunic, and ripped jeans covering her rotund body. She looks like a throwback from the sixties.

Her husband is tall like his sons, but lanky and a little stooped with age. He's completely bald with the longest goatee I've ever seen.

Ana and Max.

Judging from Ana's reaction I may well have been the first woman Dimas has ever introduced to his parents. At first I thought she was calling *me* a goddess when she mumbled it over and over again, while squeezing the air from my lungs with her stranglehold, but then I discovered she was calling out to some divine deity.

Max was far more laid back, with a dry wit—often at the expense of his overexuberant wife—that had me chuckle quite a few times during dinner. He may have pretended to be annoyed with her, but I'd caught him looking at her more than once like she hung the moon.

Although entirely unexpected from what I gather, their visit provides a welcome distraction.

We're camped out on the back deck—Twister moving between bodies, lapping up as much attention as she can—digesting the Indian food Yanis had picked up on the way.

"More coffee?" Dimas asks, as he gets up.

"Half for me, please. I don't wanna be up all night." I hand him my mug and watch him walk inside.

"I've got just the remedy for that," Max says, pulling a Ziploc baggie from his shirt pocket, containing a handful of carefully rolled blunts.

"Dad, not here," Yanis warns.

"Why? It's completely natural."

"Not with a kid present."

"I don't see why not? We didn't hide anything from you guys and you grew up just fine." He opens the baggie and takes a deep sniff. "Best stuff too. Wouldn't hurt for you to mellow out a little too, Son."

"Dad, put that shit away," Dimas grumbles, walking out holding two mugs and handing one to me."

"Put it away, Max, baby," Ana urges in a soft voice, putting her hand on her husband's.

"But I need it. You know how messed up my bowels get by the morning if I don't get my nightly hit."

"We can light one up in the parking lot of the motel," Ana soothes. "It's probably better to be close to our own bathroom anyway. That new stuff is like inhaled polyethylene glycol. It shoots through you like a bullet."

Identical groans go up from both brothers and I struggle to keep a straight face. Britt, who was listening closely before, seems to have lost interest in the conversation and skips down to the grass to play with the dog.

"How long will you be staying?" I ask, trying to divert the conversation into a different direction before one or both brothers stroke out.

"We're leaving tomorrow after lunch. We're heading down to Havens Hot Springs for a week. It's beautiful there; hot springs, views of the mountains. We go every year," Ana informs me.

"Sounds absolutely wonderful."

"Oh, it is. We always look forward to it. You should come; the springs and the mountain air do wonders for your body and soul."

"I don't think now is a good time, but perhaps when the timing is a little better."

Apparently something I said is funny, because Yanis bursts out laughing.

"Sweetheart," Dimas mumbles in my ear. "Havens is a nudist camp."

Conversation veers into safer waters and at around ten I go in to check on Britt, who went to watch some

TV inside. She doesn't object too much when told she should say her goodbyes and head to bed.

Ana, Max, and Yanis don't stay long after that. With promises to be by in a week on their way back from the springs, we wave the guys' parents off from the front step.

Yanis bends down to kiss my cheek.

"Thanks for being a good sport, Willa."

"You owe me one, man," Dimas comments. "Better watch your back."

Yanis laughs all the way to his vehicle as Dimas pulls me inside.

"Your parents are...fascinating," I volunteer when he closes and locks the front door.

"To put it mildly," he scoffs. "How many people you know can boast their parents' pension is derived from an illegal pot grow-up?"

"Are you serious?"

I follow him into the kitchen where he starts to hand-wash the few dishes left. I grab a towel and dry.

"As a heart attack," he says. "Wyoming laws on pot are among the strictest in the country."

"Jesus, have they ever been caught?"

"Dad spent some time in jail on a trafficking charge twenty years ago." Dimas shakes his head. "He'd taken some produce to the local farmers market and thought it was a good idea to try and sell some small plants. In case you haven't noticed, my parents live in an alternate universe."

"They're certainly colorful," I concede carefully,

taking another mug from the dish rack.

"Anyway," he continues. "He's gotten a bit more clever. They only supply people they know and all transactions are cash. He even has the local sheriff as one of his best customers."

I laugh at that. It sounds like something out of a sitcom.

"They seem like good people."

"They are. A bit misguided, perhaps. As you may have guessed Mom practices Wicca. She's apparently very convincing since she managed to start a coven with a dozen or so faithful members out of the four hundred and fifty or so area residents. It still boggles my mind. She worships a goddess, and Dad worships her, and that's all I care to know about it."

"Hard to believe you and your brother come from that nest," I observe, setting the last of the mugs back in the cupboard.

"Wasn't easy growing up, let me tell you. As loving as they were, our childhood was far from normal. I don't think they were cut out for parenthood. Yanis and I both craved structure." He drains the sink, wipes his hands on the towel I'm still holding, before tossing it on the counter, and pulling me in his arms. "I love them, but I'm glad to have found my own path."

I wind my arms around him and press my lips against the hollow between his collarbones where I can feel the slow steady beat of his heart.

"Funny," I mumble against his skin. "We're both rebels of sorts, but my rebellion was because of certain expectations, and yours was the result of a lack thereof." I tilt back my head and look in his eyes. "Maybe that's why we seem to fit so well."

The corner of his mouth twitches and the green in his eyes darkens.

"Wanna see how well we fit?"

DIMAS

"I was thinking," Willa says, stroking Twister's unruly fur.

In two days the dog has made herself at home, not only at night on Britt's mattress, but during the day on my couch. The first time the pooch looked at me slyly, her moves tentative, but now she just jumps up without even acknowledging me.

All the females in this family seem to feel quite at home here. I don't really mind. Willa's windows were replaced yesterday, and my brother had taken it upon himself to install a good security system. I haven't mentioned that to Willa yet, but did get her to agree to stay here until we can be sure she is safe.

I'd much rather have them here period.

"About?" I prompt her.

"Twister. Or rather, dogs like her. Older dogs nobody wants. What if we took one on at the shelter? Maybe two? They could provide some comfort and companionship to our residents." She looks at me with eager curiosity. "What do you think? Is that a crazy idea?"

"Not crazy at all," I tell her honestly. "More and more veterans with PTSD use service dogs."

"Yeah, but these wouldn't exactly be trained service dogs, just friendly dogs who are basically as homeless as the guys at the shelter are."

"I don't think it matters much. There are a few considerations, though. The biggest one being that animals cost money. There's food and veterinary care to take into account. Having animals at the shelter may even have an impact on insurance premiums. Those are things you want to check into."

"Yeah."

"Why don't you broach it with Rosie?"

"Maybe I will. Tomorrow."

Tomorrow's Monday and Willa is adamant about being back at the shelter, even though I don't feel comfortable letting her out of my sight yet.

"Willa…"

"Don't Willa me, Dimas. It's my job. People are counting on me, these men are counting on me."

I run a frustrated hand over my beard.

"I'll make you a deal. You put another pot of coffee on and I'll see if I can get any more information."

Willa can't cook worth shit, but she makes an awesome pot of coffee.

After breakfast Britt had gone back to her room to read a book—I seriously love a kid who picks a book over social media—and we've been hanging around in the living room, since it's raining outside. I've been waiting for a call from Yanis, who was supposed to touch base with Underwood to see if anything came out of his talk with Parker. At the very least, I'd like confirmed he remains in custody before I'll even consider letting Willa go to work tomorrow. Even with someone covering her.

I step out on the deck and pull out my phone, dialing my brother.

"I was just about to call you."

"What've you got?"

"Got off the phone with Underwood not five minutes ago. Apparently Parker was only delivered by State Patrol this morning and minutes later Parker's lawyer arrived. Half an hour after that, two pissed-off FBI agents came in the back door."

"FBI?"

"That's what I said. Made clear to Underwood he was stepping into an eight-month-long, multi-state federal investigation. Told the chief to delay questioning the good doctor and hold him for the full seventy-two hours before charges have to be filed. They want a chance to tie up as many loose ends as possible and took off with any evidence."

"Holy shit."

"Yeah, Parker is a significant player, but the Feds want to try and bring the entire organization down at once. If they jump all over Parker now, likelihood is all the other players go underground."

Two guys got killed on their watch, and we've been used for target practice without as much as a beep from them. Makes you wonder what the Feds are willing to risk—or even sacrifice—to roll up this fight ring. They must've known Bergland was on Parker's payroll, but didn't step in when Brad or Willa were being falsely accused. I'm not about to trust them to keep Willa safe, and that's all I care about.

"I'll cover Shep and Kai's pay, but I don't feel good about taking them off Willa yet."

"We can worry about that later. We'll keep them on for now."

"Thanks, Brother." I catch Willa looking out the sliding doors and mouth, *"Be right there,"* at her before turning my back. "Did Radar have any luck with the info I gave him on Willa's sister?"

"Shit, Dimi. That doesn't look like a good situation. Radar found out she walked into County Memorial in Delta last Monday, and was treated for two broken ribs she claimed were the result of a fall down the stairs."

I restrain myself, knowing Willa could still be watching.

"That fucking son of a bitch," I grind out between clenched teeth.

"Yeah," Yanis agrees. "Apparently when they called in a social worker to talk to her she'd disappeared. No sign from her since. Her phone hasn't been used since the weekend. Radar's following up on the numbers she called to see if that'll give him some direction."

"Good. I'll buy him those disgusting Hawaiian pizzas he likes for a year if he can find her."

"You're in deep." He sounds smug, but I don't

give a fuck. Let him laugh. One of these days it'll be me yanking his chain.

"I'm in all the way, Brother," I confirm.

"You telling her about her sister?"

"When there's something to tell."

I'm not about to let her worry when we don't know for sure there's something to worry about. That changes when Radar finds Connie, because I have a feeling the woman will need all the support she can get. She doesn't even realize yet how lucky she is to have someone like Willa in her corner.

"Everything okay?" she asks, the moment I step through the sliding door.

I keep walking until I have her backed against the counter. Her hands come up to rest on my chest.

"Kiss me and I'll tell you."

She rolls her eyes but still slides her hands up and around my neck.

"Oh, all right," she grumbles, even as she lifts her mouth to mine.

CHAPTER 26

WILLA

"WHY CAN'T TWISTER come with me? Now she has to be all alone at home."

I take a deep breath. For some reason, Britt decided today was a good day to be obstinate. I adore my niece, but I recognize the stubborn streak she probably inherited from me.

This discussion started over breakfast when she announced she'd be taking the dog to the animal shelter. I tried to explain why that wasn't a good idea, but she got it in her head Twister would be lonely if we left her by herself. Dimas tried to talk to her, but my niece seems determined.

I'm not sure whether this is just stubbornness, separation anxiety—she's had the dog as her shadow the entire weekend—or a reaction to all the uncertainties in her life. I suspect probably a bit of all the above.

Dimas is already waiting outside, but Britt is holding us up. Trying to rein in my impatience, I put my hands on her shoulders.

"Listen to me; Twister is perfectly fine staying here for a few hours. I'm sure she won't mind catching up on some sleep."

I almost laugh at the determined pout on the twelve-year-old's face, it hasn't changed much over the years.

"But—"

"Britt. Enough. Think about it this way. If you bring Twister to the shelter, she might think you're going to leave her there again."

Something seems to work behind that stubborn mask and finally she drops it.

"But I'd never do that."

"I know that, but how is she supposed to know? She's a dog."

When we get into the truck, Dimas raises a questioning eyebrow and I respond with a silent roll of my eyes. By the time we reach the Humane Society, Britt's mood seems to have lifted and she's eager to get inside.

"I'll check in with you later," Dimas says when we stop outside the shelter, pulling me partway over the console to plant a hard kiss on me. "Shep's gonna keep an eye out." He points at the man sitting behind the wheel of an old pickup in the parking lot.

"Fine," I grumble. I don't really see the need when Brantley Parker is still in police custody and apparently the FBI is on the case, but we've already had one tantrum this morning, so I'm not about to add another one.

Dimas mentioned earlier he was going to swing by my place sometime today. He wants to make sure the repairs have been taken care of. Part of me wondered whether that was his way of saying he wants to make sure we can move back home again.

I turn and wave before walking into the shelter, thinking how I'm not all that eager to go back home. The memories of that night still a little too fresh, I guess, but another part is I like sharing space with Dimas, which is a bit of a surprise. I'm sure it would be fine back home, as long as Britt is with me, but it'll be quiet when it's just Twister and me.

I duck my head into the dining room and spot Brad sitting by the window, reading the newspaper. Grabbing a coffee, I make my way over to his table.

"Care for some company?"

"Sure." He folds the newspaper to make room. "To be honest, I didn't expect you in."

"How come?"

I pull out a chair and sit across from him.

"I didn't think Dimas would be ready to let you go."

I'd almost forgotten Dimas had sought Brad out Friday night when he disappeared.

"I'm not sure he is," I admit, grinning. "Today's detail is in a truck outside in the parking lot." Brad grins as well until I put a hand on his arm. "I came over to thank you for looking after him Friday night."

"He told you?" Brad seems surprised.

"Enough for me to know you were there for him when he wasn't ready to talk to me."

"Goes both ways," he mumbles, clearly a bit uncomfortable.

"And I'm grateful for that too. I don't think I've ever fully appreciated how important talking to someone with the same or similar experiences can be. I don't mean this to sound flippant or dismissive or unfeeling, but I'm so glad you and he have that. Which brings me to the next reason I wanted to touch base with you."

After pitching my shelter dog idea to Dimas, I spent a lot of time thinking about what he said. Things I need to discuss with Rosie. But something else that has become obvious is the need for someone willing to take on the day-to-day responsibility for the animals. Making sure they're fed, taken out, well-treated, healthy, etcetera.

"How are you with dogs?" I ask Brad.

"Love dogs. It's just not easy to keep one when you're on the street or don't have your own place."

"What would you think…" I give Brad my spiel, explaining the idea is still in its infancy, but I wanted to see if he'd be interested in helping with it.

By the time I walk into Rosie's office—fueled by Brad's enthusiasm—I'm convinced I can make this work. She was all ears as well, and suggested I check at the nursing facility where her mother resides. Apparently they have a similar program where dogs are brought in for their patients to interact with.

According to Rosie, it's having a positive impact on her mom and other patients.

I come out of her office with a notebook already half-filled with my scribbles, a head full of ideas, and a smile on my face.

The day flies by with a productive group session with Brad attending, catching up on things I missed last week, and putting a work-slash-business plan and budget in place for my shelter dog idea.

Before I know it, the clock shows close to four. I'm surprised Dimas hasn't shown up yet. We texted back and forth a few times during the morning, but now that I think about it, I haven't heard from him since the group session.

I try calling, but am directed straight to voicemail, so I send a text instead.

Me: You picking me up?

His response is almost immediate.

Dimas: I'll be tied up a bit longer. I'll pick up Britt first. You hang tight there. Everything good?

Me: Yeah, fine. xo

Not sure what he's tied up with, but I don't want to waste his time asking. I'm sure he'll tell me later.

I turn my attention back to the notes I was writing on our newest resident's file. I was pleased he showed up for group this afternoon and actually shared a little of how he ended up on the streets. It usually takes these guys a lot longer than that. He did mention Brad had suggested he show his face, so perhaps I have him to thank for it.

"Aren't you usually on your way out the door by now?"

I look up to find Ron leaning against the doorpost.

"My ride is a bit delayed," I share. "Besides…" I smile at him, indicating the file I'm working on. "I still have some notes to finish."

The smile drops instantly and I freeze when I see a figure I haven't seen in weeks pass down the hallway behind Ron.

"What's wrong?"

I motion for him to step inside and close the door.

"Dave Williams. Since when is he back? I haven't seen him around for a while."

"Dave? He came in Friday. Said he'd hit a rough spot but wanted to get back on track. Why? You look freaked."

"That's because he freaks me out a little. I just don't like the way he looks at me. So intense."

"He's definitely a bit of an oddball," Ron agrees, as he moves toward the window behind me. "Maybe he's taken a shine to you? It's possible." He seems to be mumbling more to himself than to me, I turn to find him looking outside through the blinds. "Maybe he's a little obsessed, got carried away when you rejected him."

There's something about his words that me make
sit up in my chair.

"Ron, what are you talking about?"

"He even looks menacing," he continues, as if he
never heard me, his eyes focused outside. "Wouldn't
be a stretch to imagine him shooting at you, jealous
when he sees you coming home with your bodyguard."

Okay, now I'm really uneasy. Something's
definitely wrong.

I slowly get up out of my chair, keeping my eyes
on him as I sidestep to the edge of my desk, hoping to
get to the other side of it for a bit of a barrier.

"He could've killed Rupert too," he continues
to mumble, and I manage to slip around my desk
undetected.

Or so I thought until he suddenly swings around.

"Where are you going?"

"I just need to…"

I draw a blank. The only thing on my mind is
getting away from him. I can't even begin to process
what he's saying; I just know it's not good.

He takes one step toward me and I panic, swinging
around throwing myself at the door, only to find he
must've locked it when I told him to close it.

All I hear is the thundering of my heart and blood
rushing through my veins as my shaking hand slips
off the lock. Before I can firm my grip on the small
tab, my head is snapped back and an arm wrapped
around my neck is cutting off my air.

I dig my nails into the forearm pressing on my

throat and kick out my legs, struggling against his hold. I need to make noise. There are people right outside this door, but everyone knows when the door is closed not to disturb. I try to scream but only a pathetic rasp comes out.

He pulls me away from the door and I kick out again, this time hitting something—a chair—toppling it over. My vision starts to blur as I feel my strength wane.

The last thing I hear is a loud crash.

DIMAS

I had the morning to catch up on things. Amazing how quickly you feel out of the loop after only a few days away from the office.

Yanis asked me to meet with the developer of the new mall they're building northwest of the city. I had a hard time concentrating on the drawings the project coordinator showed me. With what I hope is a general idea of what they're looking at in terms of a security setup, I walk out of the construction trailer with a copy of the plans and a thick book of specs under my arm.

Back in my truck, I give my brother a quick rundown of the scope of this project.

"This is not a job we'll be able to do on our own. It's big. The construction schedule is pretty tight and we don't have a lot of time to put together a proposal."

"I'll give Brandon Electrical a call. Get them on board," he suggests.

"Probably a good idea. Do you need the package they handed me now, or can it wait 'til tomorrow? I'd hoped to run by Willa's place before I go to pick her up."

"Did you grab the keys and code I left on your desk?"

"Yeah, I did. So, do you need me to swing by the plans?"

"No, don't need them now."

"Okay. Then I'll see you tomorrow."

It takes me fifteen minutes to get to her place and I pull into her driveway, noting the new motion lights Yanis installed. I also spot a camera at the corner of the garage, aimed at the driveway. As I walk up to the front door, I see a second one installed in the soffit over the front steps. Knowing how thorough my brother is, I'm sure he has at least one on the back of the house as well.

I slide the key in the lock, open the door, and quickly punch in the code on the new number pad on the wall in the entryway.

The windows have clearly been replaced and there'd been a hole in the wall, where one bullet lodged, I can't even find. They did a good job.

Before I lock everything and pick Willa up, I want to check the contents of the fridge. There's nothing worse than coming home to spoiling food in the fridge. I don't want there to be any negative reminders for Willa or Britt.

I'm just opening the fridge door when I hear the

front door open and a voice call out, "Willa?"

I have my gun in hand when a disheveled-looking woman walks into the living room, with a large tote bag tossed over her shoulder.

"Who are you?" she asks, and before I can answer her eyes dart around the room. "Where's my sister? Where's Brittany?"

I immediately tuck my gun in my pocket; I don't think she even noticed it in my hand. Shit. This is Willa's sister.

"My name is Dimas Mazur. I'm Willa's boyfriend."

I start moving toward her but she takes a step back, so I stop.

"My sister doesn't have a boyfriend."

"She didn't, but now she does."

Just then my phone vibrates in my pocket and I fish it out, keeping an eye on her while glancing at my screen.

Willa: You picking me up?

Me: I'll be tied up a bit longer. I'll pick up Britt first. You hang tight there. Everything good?

Willa: Yeah, fine. Xo

"That's your sister," I tell the woman. "Here, have a look."

I hold out my phone and take a few steps toward her. She squints to read the messages on the screen.

I notice the dark circles under her eyes and strain on her face.

"She's been worried about you. You weren't answering your phone."

She looks down to the floor at her feet.

"My phone is broken," she mumbles.

"Britt's been waiting for your call as well."

That has her eyes come up. "You're picking up my daughter?"

"Yeah. She's a great girl." I try smiling at her, but she still looks a little freaked.

"Where are they? Willa's SUV is in the driveway. When will they be home?"

"I'm about to go pick them up. Why—"

I was about to invite her to come along when my phone rings. It's Brad.

"Can I call you right—"

"Shit, brother," I can tell from his voice something's not right. "It's Willa, you need to get your ass over here."

CHAPTER 27

DIMAS

"STAY IN THE truck," I order Connie.

Shots fired. That's what Brad told me when I started running for the door. She'd heard enough of my side of the conversation to know something happened to her sister, and shy of using brute force on her—not to mention wasting valuable time—I couldn't get her to stay behind.

On the way to the shelter I called the office and got Radar, who would send Bree to pick up Britt from the Humane Society. The little girl had been the only other thought I had aside from getting to Willa.

I made it to the shelter in less than five minutes and two police cruisers are pulling in right behind me. Slamming the truck in park, I launch myself out, and hit the ground at a dead run for the door.

The lobby is empty but in the hallway to the offices a small crowd is standing outside Willa's office. I blindly shove bodies aside to get through and vaguely notice the splintered doorpost. My attention is focused on the body of a man lying on the floor, a sizable hole in his forehead.

"Where's Willa?" I ask the older black guy, talking on a cell phone. He looks somewhat familiar. He covers the phone with his hand.

"Office across the hall."

I make note of the gun on the corner of Willa's desk, and the badge clipped to the guy's waistband, before I turn and walk out.

The door is closed but I barge in without knocking to find Shep and Brad hovering over Willa's prone body on the small couch. She's covered in blood. I must've made a sound when Shep swings around.

"Not hers, brother," he quickly clarifies. "She's okay."

"Dimas?" Her voice is rough as she struggles to sit up.

Brad steps out of the way as I move forward and sit by her side.

"Stay put," I order gruffly, my hands and eyes scanning her body for holes.

"I'm fine," she assures me, her whole body shaking.

I carefully lift her to my lap, my own body doing its own share of trembling. I take a moment just to feel her breathing against me before I focus my eyes on Shep.

"What the fuck happened?"

He opens his mouth to answer when I hear a commotion in the hallway.

"Willa!"

Fucking Connie.

"Hold on, Dimi."

Shep grabs me from behind, pinning my arms against my body.

"This fucker stood by and put her in danger," I grind out between clenched teeth, straining against Shep's hold as my brother steps in front of me, blocking my view of that FBI bastard.

"Check it, Dimas," he orders, his face inches from mine. "If you don't, I'll have Shep lock you down in Rosie's office."

We're in the parking lot of the shelter, where paramedics are checking Willa out in the back of the ambulance. Connie is with her. At least a dozen officers, FBI agents, and crime scene techs are milling about, while the PASS crew, the chief of police, and fucking Dave Williams are watching Shep and Yanis hold me back.

"For what it's worth," the bastard says over my brother's shoulder. "I kept as close an eye on her as I could. Warned her as soon as I realized she was a little too curious."

"You fucking shot at her."

"I shot at him," he corrects me.

"You could've killed her," I persist.

"Not a chance in hell," he returns calmly. "I can shoot the testicles off a field mouse at a hundred and fifty yards. Wouldn't have pulled the trigger if she wasn't already limp in his arms. I had a clear shot."

All that anger, fueled by the adrenaline still surging through my blood, slowly drains. Shep's hold loosens and I try to shake out the tension in my muscles as Williams continues his explanation—unfazed by my outburst.

From what I gather, he's been undercover living both on the street and in the shelter these past two months, since Arthur Hicks' body was discovered. The FBI investigation in the fight ring extends back further than that, but the man's death had been confirmation veterans—preferably homeless ones—were a group of particular interest.

It makes sense in a way; men who have seen action but have trouble adjusting in mainstream society would make for easy targets. Unfortunately, those destitute enough to do anything for a buck. What makes me sick are not the guys to step into the cage, but the men behind it, orchestrating and capitalizing on the suffering of others.

Especially those who are supposed to be supporting them. Like Dr. Brantley Parker, and the dead man in Willa's office, Ron Midwood, a goddamn social worker.

Carefully attuned to any movement from the back of the ambulance, I notice Willa's sister climbing down.

"Fill me in later," I whisper at Yanis before moving toward the back of the rig, just as Willa appears in the opening.

The two women are as different as night and day. Willa dark, her coloring and stature much like her father, whereas Connie is much lighter and shorter like their mom. They're both quite curvy, but with her height, Willa carries it better. Or maybe I'm biased. Quite likely.

I'm just in time to lift her down the last step and am tempted to simply carry her to my truck and take her straight home.

Too many fucking thoughts and emotions chaotically tumble around my head, and I desperately need a moment to find my bearings.

Willa first.

"You okay?" I bend down so my eyes can catch hers.

"I'm good," she croaks, still hoarse.

"She should be fine," the medic, sticking his head outside assures me before turning to Willa. "Not too much talking until your throat has had a chance to heal."

"Good. Then I'm taking you home."

"What about Britt?"

"No talking," I admonish her. "Bree went to pick her up and they should be at home already."

I look over at Connie, who looks like she needs some medical attention herself: big eyes, pale face, and nervously biting her lip. She must think she landed from the fat into the fire. I can't help but feel for her.

With one arm tucking Willa to my side, I gently put the other around Connie's hunched shoulders.

"Come on, both of you. Let's find some peace and quiet at home."

As I'm walking them to my truck, I hear my name called.

"We need to ask Ms. Smith some questions," Williams calls out.

I spear him with a scathing look before yelling back, "Too fucking bad. She's not allowed to speak—medical orders."

WILLA

I can't stop looking at Connie, who's sitting beside me, there's something different about her.

Things were so chaotic at the shelter, the fact she showed up out of the blue kind of blended with all the other mad stuff going on.

Dave Williams, who I thought was a homeless veteran, turns out to be an undercover FBI agent. Ron Midwood, who I worked with and thought was a trusted colleague, ends up being a criminal. Add to that being choked near unconsciousness, then covered in blood and God knows what else, and my sister's sudden appearance was barely a blip on my radar.

Now, though, I am curious. Of course, with Britt talking a mile a minute as she tells her mom about every single animal at the shelter, I don't have a chance to ask. It'll have to wait until Britt is in bed.

I glance out the kitchen doors at Dimas, out on the back deck talking with Bree and Radar, who showed up about ten minutes after we got home. I'm sure Dimas will share whatever is being talked about later when there are no little ears around.

"Mom, where's Dad?"

My head swings around. Connie looks like a deer caught in the headlights at Britt's question.

"Home, I'm sure," she finally says, but is not very convincing.

Britt catches it too and seems to check her mother over closely.

"And where did you get those clothes?" my clever niece asks, looking at the unconventional clothes my sister is wearing. A pair of ill-fitting jeans, plain white tennis shoes, and what looks like a man's dress shirt. Very unusual for my sister to be found in anything but feminine, well-tailored clothes, and she never, ever wears flats. All her shoes have at least a two-inch heel to add to her short stature.

"These? I've had them forever," Connie lies, and she knows we know it.

Britt opens her mouth, I assume to call her mother out on it, but the sound of the sliding door opening stops her. Dimas walks inside with Bree and Radar following behind.

"Connie, Radar is going to go with you to pick up your things at your sister's place and anything else you might need."

"Oh, that's okay, I can…" Her voice trails off and

her eyes lock on mine, desolation swimming in the tears gathering.

I grab hold of her hand and squeeze it.

"Go with him. We'll talk after," I tell her softly, my voice still no more than a rasp. Reluctantly she gets to her feet, a watery smile for her daughter before she turns to Radar.

"Lead the way."

I watch as he almost grabs her elbow but thinks better of it at the last minute, instead gesturing for her to go ahead.

"Ladies first."

"Yo, Britt," Bree pipes up when they disappear out the front door. "While they do that, why don't you and I run out to pick up some dinner? You can help me choose."

I'm sure my niece knows she's being manipulated, but she still gets up and follows Bree out of the house, leaving Dimas and me alone.

"What's going on?" I want to know, looking at him questioningly.

"Shhh. You're not supposed to talk," he says, sitting down in the spot my sister just vacated and pulling me close. His lips brush mine lightly. "I love you."

My hands lift to his face and this time I kiss him. Then I mouth the same message back to him.

"Good, because you may get pissed at me. I asked Radar to find your sister. A few days ago, he discovered your sister had been treated in the ER at the hospital in Delta for a couple of broken ribs. She said she'd fallen down the stairs."

Realization comes hard and fast.

"Bullshit. They live in a one-level ranch, they don't even have a basement, just a crawlspace."

"Stop talking," Dimas orders, pressing his fingers to my lips. "Radar found that out too. He's going to talk to your sister to find out if she's in any danger." He shakes his head when he sees me gear up to object. "There are reasons why it may be easier for her to talk to someone who doesn't know her. Surely you know that."

I hate that he's right. Connie and I may not be close, but she's still my sister and I'd do anything for her.

Like drop-kick that son of a bitch, Jim, if he dares show his face.

"Whatever you're thinking right now better not be about me," Dimas warns, squinting his eyes at me. "I have a feeling my nuts wouldn't survive."

"Your nuts are safe," I snap, and he immediately presses his fingers on my lips, but I bat them away.

"Easy, tiger," he teases. "No bodily harm until we have some information on what went down and assess the kind of risk Jim represents. Radar will try to find out what he can from your sister, but until we get a bead on that situation, everyone is staying here."

"Where?"

"Radar is picking up the twin mattress from your spare room for your sister to sleep on. We can fit her in with Britt. I have a feeling those two have some talking to do anyway."

He's not lying. There's a whole lot going on between mother and daughter, has been since Britt started developing a will of her own. Add to that a broken marriage—at least I fucking hope so—I can see my niece giving Connie a hard time. That's where I hopefully can make a difference.

"Also," Dimas continues, tucking a strand of my hair behind my ear, his fingertips ghosting along my jaw. "Bree warns the FBI will likely show on our doorstep tomorrow with questions. She suggests to get it over with."

"Fine by me, but what about the shelter? Rosie's gonna need me."

"Jake is there, Brad is helping. Rosie's calling in some of the weekend staff as necessary. They'll survive." I release a deep sigh. "Come on, sweetheart," Dimas pleads, lying back on the couch and pulling me with him so I'm half draped over him, my head resting on his chest. "Let's focus on getting these current crises resolved, so I can have a taste of a normal life with you before the next one hits."

I prop my chin on his chest and catch his eyes looking down at me.

"A normal life with me?"

"Yeah." He brushes his fingers over my cheek before cupping that side of my face in his big palm. "That's what I want, Willa. When all the dust settles, that's exactly what I want. I'm not trying to rush anything—heck, I figure you'll want to go back to your place at least until your sister's shit is sorted—but I wanna be clear where I stand. I'll give you some time, and I don't fucking care whose roof we'll be under, as long as you and I end up under the same one."

I take in a deep shaky breath. I'm so damn glad my upbringing had me shy away from any real relationships all these years, otherwise, I might've missed the promise of a future with this man.

"Here," I whisper. "I want this roof over our heads. I feel at home here, with you. Even Twister likes it here."

Both of us look at the dog sprawled out on the hardwood floor, not a care in the world. Then our eyes meet again.

"Yeah?" The smug smile reaches his eyes. "You'd risk giving up your house to be with me?"

I reach up and run my fingers over the bristly hair of his beard.

"Yeah. I love you, Dimas. I've never felt like this before, and I'd risk life and limb for you."

CHAPTER 28

DIMAS

"WANT ANOTHER PANCAKE?"

It's clear Connie is used to taking care of everyone. She was up first, had coffee brewed, and batter ready to go by the time I sauntered into the kitchen, and that was at six. She'd even let the dog out, and I caught her petting Twister when she thought no one was looking.

Willa got up shortly after, mumbling a distracted, "Morning," as she padded into the kitchen, making a beeline for the coffeepot. Her sister insisted on cooking breakfast, despite our assurances there is plenty of cereal or toast.

"I'm full, Connie, thanks."

"Willa?"

"Not for me either. Was really good though, thanks. Lucky Mom's skills rubbed off on one of us," she says, grinning at Connie. It's amazing what a difference one cup of coffee makes on Willa's mood.

"You didn't even try," Connie reacts with an edge to her tone.

"You're right, I didn't."

"Why?"

Connie's question hangs suspended and I can feel Willa tense up beside me. I guess this is sensitive territory. I put my hand on Willa's knee in an offering of silent support, even though I don't really have a clue what the tension is about.

"Seriously, Willa, I want to know."

"What does it matter? I didn't...I still don't cook— as Dimas can attest to—and although there are times I regret it, it simply isn't a priority for me and I'm okay with that."

"What is a priority for you, Willa?"

The sharpness is gone from Connie's voice, replaced by an almost desperate tone, a hint of tears. A genuine need to know—to understand. Willa seems to hear it too, I can feel the tension releasing from her body.

From what I understand so far, Connie has blown off any talk about why she's here with only some toiletries and a single change of clothes in that large tote of hers. Not even Britt's glares and pointed comments directed at her mom have elicited any explanation.

"Connie..." Willa starts, her voice soft and empathetic. "I've always just wanted to be happy, like most people. Make a good life for myself. Feel meaningful. Same thing everyone else is looking for. But I wanted that on my own terms. By my own definition. Not through the approval of others."

"Not like me," Connie says, sniffling.

"For the most part you wanted the same things, though, honey. We may have gone about it in different ways, but I believe at the core of it we were aiming for the same outcome."

Her sister huffs before saying, bitterly, "Only one of us was successful."

"That was luck. I've avoided relationships all my life, thinking that was the answer. It wasn't. Sure, I had a life with no one to answer to, and I made myself believe that's exactly how I wanted it. Then I met Dimas and he scared the shit out of me. He unbalanced me." I give her leg a quick squeeze. "I fought it thinking I would have to conform to some kind of ideal if I wanted a relationship with him, but the only expectation he has is for me to be me. Nothing more, nothing less. What I do or don't do doesn't even hit on the radar, the only thing that matters to him is who I am."

Connie's eyes fill with tears. Almost annoyed, she pulls some paper towel off the roll and dabs at them.

"It wasn't like this before," she starts, staring at nothing. "I thought I had it all, you know? Handsome man who wanted me. Mom and Dad's approval. I felt good in the role I took on. Then Britt came along and I honestly thought life couldn't get any better, until it got worse. Small things at first. The baby weight didn't come off as easily as he would've liked, so he'd comment on what I ate and got me a membership at a gym. Next he started comparing me to other women, pointing out how great his buddys' wives looked after kids."

"He's a fucking idiot," I can't stop myself from saying. "I'm sorry, Connie, but every guy worth his salt should be worshiping you on his goddamn knees for making him a father. Every stretch mark, every added curve to your body after carrying his child should be treated with as much love as the child it produced."

"He's right," Willa adds, sliding off her stool and rounding the island to take her sister in her arms.

I don't know this guy but I already want to bash in his fucking brains. This broken woman is not who Willa portrayed when she described her sister. He did this.

It's like a dam broke, and Willa can barely hold the sobbing woman up. Britt could be up any minute and I don't want her to walk in on her mother breaking down, so I get up and move behind Willa.

"Our bedroom," I whisper and she nods. Taking Connie between us, we get her into bed and Willa crawls in with her, wrapping her tight. I kiss the top of Willa's head. "You worry about your sister, I've got Britt."

A barely-there nod confirms she's heard me and I back out of the room, closing the door on them. A sleepy-looking Britt is standing in the hallway when I turn.

"What's going on?"

"What's going on is your mom and Aunt Willa are

having a heart-to-heart, and you and I are going to kill off those pancakes your mother made earlier," I announce, throwing an arm over her shoulders and firmly guiding her to the kitchen.

"Mom's pancakes are the best."

"They are. Maybe later you can tell her that."

We've eaten, cleaned up, walked the dog, and are just putting groceries away from a quick run to the store when the bedroom door opens and Willa walks out, straight into my arms. Britt watches us curiously as her aunt buries her face against my chest.

"Thank you," Willa mumbles, before tilting her head back and looking up at me. I can tell she's been crying even though she isn't anymore.

"What's going on, Aunt Willa? Where's Mom?"

She turns to Britt with a reassuring smile.

"Your mom is freshening up in our bathroom. She's had a tough time of it, Britt. Maybe you can go give her some love? I bet she'd like that."

The girl looks at me and then back at Willa, concern lining her face, before heading down the hallway.

"Are you sure Connie is ready for her?" I ask when Willa beams her smile at me.

"Positive. A reminder of the one good thing that bastard left her."

"I gather you got the story?"

"Some of it. She has no identity left," she says, stepping back from my hold to put the new cereal I bought in the cupboard. I guess she needs her hands busy. "The bastard eroded it. He made her feel small and inadequate, and then went out to fuck other women. Been doing it since Britt was born, apparently. That weekend when Brad was first in trouble, called me, and I tore out of my parents' house to get back to Grand Junction was apparently a wake-up call for my sister. She finally stood up to him and told him she was done, which he didn't take lightly. He'd never been physical with her before, it was something she never expected of him."

"Fucking pussy, hitting a woman."

If anything infuriates me it's that. Hell, I almost messed things up with Willa because I'd inadvertently hit her.

"That's what I told her; hurting someone is a sign of weakness, not strength."

"How'd she get away?"

"From the hospital she went straight to a women's shelter, healed up a little, talked to someone there, and got money for a bus ticket here."

"And him?"

"She doesn't know. She ditched her phone and never went back to the house. She just wanted to be close to Britt."

"I'm guessing your parents don't know?"

"You know what? I don't know. I'm not even sure if knowing would've kept my father from his golf game, or my mother from following behind him without questioning anything. How sad is that?"

"Your parents may have limited vision, but I can't see them being okay their daughter was used as a punching bag."

"Maybe," she cautiously concedes.

WILLA

"Ms. Smith, we have a few questions for you."

Of course.

Dimas just took Britt and my sister to my place. It had been his careful suggestion—first to me—perhaps it would be a good idea for those two to have some time on their own. When he suggested they stay at my place, my heart did a little leap. I know the plan was for me to end up here eventually, but to be honest, the thought of spending any time away from Dimas—waking up without him—wasn't something I looked forward to.

Having Britt spend time with her mom without me as a distraction is probably better. Last thing Connie needs now is feeling even more unsure of her place in the world. There's some work to be done on her relationship with Britt, which she does not need me around for. Besides, I'm not even ten minutes away if they need me for anything.

"Come in," I tell FBI Agent Dave Williams and a colleague of his. "But you can call me Willa, like you did when you were just Dave to me. That is your real name?"

I can tell I made him uncomfortable, which gives me a bit of satisfaction. I get the man had a job to do, but I have a hard time getting over the fact he stood by when Brad and I were arrested for murders he knew we had nothing to do with.

"It is, *Willa*," he says pointedly as he steps inside, the other man following. "This is my partner, Agent Ken Dryden."

"Ma'am."

"Please—Willa. You're making me feel old," I tell the tall lanky guy. "Have a seat."

I don't offer to get them coffee, call it petty, but the betrayal still stings. Trust is big with me.

"What can I do for you?" I finally ask when they take a seat and the silence stretches a bit too long to be comfortable.

"How do you know Ron Midwood?" Williams wants to know.

"I work with him. Well, *worked* with him, I guess." I grimace at the memory of his blood all over me.

"Were you aware of his relationship with Brantley Parker?"

"I wasn't even aware they knew each other," I volunteer.

"I thought you took part in hiring him?"

I'm not sure why he's pushing the issue and get a bit annoyed.

"I did. Rosie asked me to sit in for part of the interview. What is it you're trying to say?"

"All I'm doing is trying to get any loose ends wrapped up, Willa."

"Okay, so yes, I took part in his interview, and no, I did not know those two knew each other. Not that it surprises me in hindsight."

"Why do you say that?"

I look at him incredulously. "Well, for one thing, neither of them were who I thought they were, and for another, both—at some point—tried to get me to go out with them."

"Did you?" he persists.

"Never. I never much cared for Parker, so that was a nonissue, and although I like…I mean liked Ron, not in a way I'd risk dating a coworker. What is it you're looking for?" I ask straight out.

He looks at his partner, who shrugs before turning back to me.

"Midwood and Parker were cousins. We were interviewing the doctor when he discovered Midwood was dead. He lost it and talked. A lot. He claims he got Ron the job at the shelter."

"What? But how…" I let my voice trail off, trying to make sense of it. Brantley had been rather pissed when I left to work at the shelter, why would he have put forward his cousin to work there? I'm so confused. Was it because of me? "You should talk to Rosie, she must've spoken to Parker, because he didn't speak to me about hiring Ron. I honestly didn't know."

"We plan to talk to Mrs. Hutchinson later this afternoon. Not that I don't believe you," he quickly adds. "Like I said, we're just tying up loose ends. We already know Midwood and Parker operated Raw Vice here in Grand Junction. We also know they had a few local officers from the GJPD on their books."

I'm sure I know which ones he's talking about. "What we weren't sure of was whether there were others involved."

"Like me?"

Williams shrugs. "It wouldn't be all that unimaginable. You have the trust of the patients at the hospital and the residents at the shelter. You'd have made a great addition to their ranks. Midwood baiting and you setting the hook."

"And here I thought I was irresistible," I lamely joke, just as Dimas walks in the front door and walks right over to me, kissing me square on the lips despite our audience.

"You are incredibly irresistible," he mumbles there before straightening up. "Gentlemen. Your timing sucks."

To his credit, Dave Williams chuckles at Dimas.

"Mazur."

"Williams. And?" Dimas prompts and introductions are made. "What did I miss?"

"Not much," I volunteer before adding sarcastically, "You just missed the waterboarding part of the program."

"Hardly," Williams disagrees a tad self-consciously. "Like I mentioned; simply a few lingering questions we were looking to get answered."

"Did you?" Dimas asks with an edge.

"I believe we have what we need for now," Agent Dryden quickly answers, reading the sudden tension coming off my guy.

"Awesome." Dimas then turns back to Williams. "You took a chance coming here to my house. I'm sure you can imagine how fucking much I want to plant a fist in your face. Not only for leaving my woman to dangle for something you knew she had nothing to do with, but for showing up at my door the day after she was brutally attacked. The only thing stopping me is—"

"He's an FBI agent?" Dryden deadpans.

"Not even close, but your partner did shoot the fucker in the head, and although it doesn't make me happy his brains were splattered all over Willa..." Okay, I was pretty cool so far, but I'm afraid I'm gonna lose my cookies now. "...He did manage to save me from landing in jail for murder, because I would've hunted him down and filleted him."

"Alrighty then," I mutter, sick to my stomach with all the visuals I'm getting. "Now that we have that cleared up. Good talk."

Now it's Dryden's turn to chuckle.

"We'll get out of your hair. If there's anything more we need we'll be back."

"Dave?"

Williams turns to look at me.

"What you said on your intake form and in group, were those all lies?"

He seems to be thinking for a moment.

"No lies. Not a single one," he says, his conviction firm in his one functioning eye.

Wow. I did not expect that.

"Thank you for the trust."

CHAPTER 29

DIMAS

"DID YOU HEAR that?"

Fuck no.

An explosion could go off in the room and I wouldn't hear a damn thing with Willa's hot and hungry mouth on my dick.

Best way to wake up, bar none. Best part of having the house to ourselves these past couple of days. Don't get me wrong, I loved having Britt around, she's a fun kid, smart as a whip too, but I like having the run of the house again.

Until now apparently.

With my wet dick catching a cold, it's easier to hear rustling in the kitchen. I shoot upright, almost knocking Willa off the bed, when I hear footsteps coming down the hall.

"Ana!" I hear my dad's voice calling out. *"Don't you dare go in there."*

"I gave birth to the boy, Max. Nothing I haven't seen before."

"Hardly a boy anymore, Ana. Besides if he's in bed at this hour, he's probably not alone."

I groan trying to pull the sheet up to cover my junk. Willa starts snickering, even as she steals it to cover herself and grabs my shirt off the ground to put on.

"Hey, what about me?" I complain when she leaves me buck naked in bed.

"What? Nothing she hasn't seen before."

"Mom! Give us a minute, okay? We'll be right there."

Willa is kind enough to toss me a pair of boxer briefs from the dresser as she pulls on a pair of yoga pants.

"Fine. I'll make a pot of mushroom coffee to go with the hemp muffins I brought. That sweet child still here?"

"No, Mom, she's not here, and even if she were, you'd have scared her off with your hemp muffins and mushroom coffee by now!"

Now Willa has a hand clamped to her mouth to hold back the laugh shaking her shoulders. I drop my head, grinning, as I fit my prosthesis on my stump and quickly get dressed in sweats. I grab a shirt out of my laundry basket, sniffing it first for offensiveness before I pull it on.

"Let's go," I tell Willa, pressing a quick kiss to her lips. "Word of warning, though, sip only. Mom's coffee is vile."

She's still snickering beside me when we walk into the kitchen, where Mom's made herself at home and my dad is sitting at the counter, shaking his head and grumbling. I kiss his cheek before walking to my mom and wrapping her in a hug.

"To what do I owe this honor?" I ask her. "Yanis not home?"

"We surprised him last weekend. Today we surprise you." She pats my cheek before she shoves me aside. "Come here, precious. Good goddess, you're even beautiful straight out of bed. Isn't she beautiful, Max?" she asks my dad, as she's already pulling Willa in her arms.

"Just lovely," Dad replies, without taking his eyes off the newspaper he must've brought inside.

"How was your trip?" Willa asks, throwing me a sharp glance when I inadvertently groan.

"Let me get you some coffee. We can sit outside and I'll tell you all about it."

That's what I was afraid of.

I have to admit, the hemp muffins aren't bad, but the mushroom coffee still makes me want to hurl. I drink it anyway, because Mom swears by the stuff. It's supposed to be healthier for you than regular beans and I'm not about to argue with her on that.

For the next twenty minutes, I have to listen to more details than I ever wanted to hear about my parents' vacation activities. There's just something about visualizing your folks playing badminton or practicing yoga in the buff that simply isn't right.

Willa seems to be in a perpetual state of amusement, her twinkling eyes occasionally darting my way. The fact she doesn't seem put off or is downright mortified by Mom's detailed descriptions of certain fellow nudists' attributes only makes me love her more.

It's clear my mother is already halfway gone for Willa as well, and I even notice Dad is eyeing her with a smile occasionally. As much as my parents exacerbate me, it means a lot they seem to take to her so well, and vice versa.

After we're done with what was supposed to pass for breakfast, and Mom starts pelting Willa with questions about her family and her work, I slip inside heading for the bathroom to get cleaned up. I can hear them laughing as I'm brushing my teeth, and I realize I've never felt this at ease around my own parents. The difference is Willa.

"What are your plans?" I ask, walking out on the back deck.

"Us?" Mom answers. "We don't have any. Thought we'd stick around until tomorrow before heading back home."

Disturbing thoughts of my parents sleeping in the spare bedroom, down the hall from where I share a bed with Willa, must've shown on my face because Mom starts giggling.

"Chill out, Son," Dad intervenes. "We're going to crash at Yanis'."

"Does he know?"

"What's the fun in that?" my mother shares. "You know I love to surprise people."

Yes. Yes, I do. I also know Yanis is going to have

not one cow, but a herd of them, when he finds out.

Let's just say my parents have an active sex life. Believe me, I wish I didn't know that, but they've stayed with me before. As if childhood hadn't scarred me enough, listening to them go at it down the hall left me with some fresh reminders. I'd rather have my balls removed with dental floss than have to listen to that again.

Yanis is fucked. Normally I would've given him a heads-up, but seeing as he didn't do me that favor last week when they showed up, I'll let Mom 'surprise' him.

"Thank you for breakfast," Willa says, as she gets up and collects the dishes. "We'll do the dishes, and I'll make the next pot of coffee. You guys sit and relax for a bit."

To my surprise, Mom doesn't object and Willa motions for me to follow her inside. I make sure to close the sliding door behind me.

"I love your parents," Willa stage-whispers as she drops the dishes in the sink before she turns to face me. "They're warm and funny. God, you're so lucky to have them."

I pull her into the circle of my arms and she plants her hands on my chest, smiling up at me.

"They're also weird, invasive, and horribly inappropriate," I counter, but Willa is not deterred.

"And loving," she adds. "I'd much rather have that than traditional, authoritarian, painstakingly appropriate, and cold."

She makes a good point.

"I love how easy you are with them," I admit. "It makes me easy too."

She slides her hands up and around my neck, pulling my head down. I read and welcome the invitation, kissing her lush lips as my hands sink down to the swell of her ass. Easily lost in the combination of her taste and the feel of her body pressed against me, I barely hear the first knock.

I don't miss the second, though.

"Shit," I mumble against her lips. "Who are these people who think it's a good idea to show up unannounced on a fucking Sunday morning?"

WILLA

"Hey, Auntie Will," Britt chirps when I open the door.

I don't even have a chance to formulate a greeting when I spot my sister, father, and mother standing behind her.

Connie looks tortured and mouths, "Sorry," at me.

"Guess who showed up at your house?" Britt says, walking past me inside, followed by a demure Connie.

"Morning, dear," Mom says, stepping over the threshold and I bend to give her a kiss on the cheek.

"Mom," I manage.

My father just nods as he steps inside, instantly roaming the place with critical eyes.

"Dad."

In my head I can already see the disaster ahead.

Like watching a movie scene unfold with the privilege of knowing all the players in advance.

It's Sunday—the day of reckoning.

Numb, I hear Mom saying hello to Dimas, his deep voice rumbling a greeting as I close the door and lean my forehead against it. I'm not the praying kind, but I'm willing to sink down on my knees and plead to any being with higher powers to send a swarm of locusts, or a big flood, to distract from what I'm sure will be a catastrophe of epic proportions unfolding behind me.

"Oh my goddess! What a surprise!"

And there it is.

I can only imagine my prim and proper mother's reaction when she encounters the eccentric and free-spirited Ana. I'm sure she thinks people like that only exist in movies. Certainly not in any circles she's ever moved in. And my dad…oh God, I think I'm going to be sick.

"Breathe, sweetheart."

His voice is soft in my ear as he pulls my body into his and I lean back, letting him take my weight. Even if only for a moment.

A short bubble of reprieve, even as the sound of Twister's barked greetings and Britt's excited introductions filter through.

"I'm okay," I finally whisper, feeling the brush of his lips over the skin at the base of my neck.

I turn in his arms and look up into his smiling green eyes.

"Thrown in the deep end," he states fittingly,

letting me go but taking my hand, entwining our fingers. "Let's swim."

With help of a smiling Britt, Ana is handing out hemp muffins—I now secretly hope she laced with pot—to everyone. A little mellowing wouldn't be misplaced in this room. Max, who has come inside and is leaning against the door, seems to do his casual observing from the sidelines, while my parents appear transfixed, struggling to keep their careful composure. They probably think they've landed on Mars. Connie's wide eyes bump around the room, trying to take in this strange dichotomous tableau.

The only ones unaffected by the weirdness in the room are Britt and Ana.

"I didn't know your parents were coming," Ana titters. "I would've brought more mushroom coffee."

Dimas chuckles behind me at the look of shock on my mother's face, while I thank the gods for small blessings.

"I'll get a pot of regular going," I offer, rushing to the coffeepot. That's something I can do.

"Chuck," I hear Dimas behind me. "How about you, Dad, and I go pull some folding chairs out of the garage? It's a nice day, we shouldn't spend it inside."

Have I mentioned I love that man? I watch him open the door and head outside, followed closely by the dog and our fathers.

"What is in these?" Connie asks Ana, and my heart stops for a moment.

Please don't say marijuana or any other cannabis

related product.

"Well, hemp and sunflower seeds. Almond flour, overripe bananas, ground cardamom, and cinnamon. Oh, and coconut oil."

Thank God.

"No eggs?" my mother wants to know.

"Completely gluten-free, dairy-free, sugar-free, and organic," Ana confirms proudly. "They're good, aren't they?"

"Surprisingly, yes," Mom confirms, and I finally allow myself to breathe normally again.

Not for long.

"You should try my hash brownies."

Bless her heart, but right now I want to stab Ana with my coffee scoop.

"Oh look," I say in desperation. "More chairs. Why don't you guys head on out while I get coffee ready?"

"I can help," Mom immediately says, but I can feel a passive aggressive parental chat coming on and that would tip me over the edge.

"Nope. Absolutely not. Connie will help, right, Connie? You go right on out and relax."

"Hash brownies?" my sister hisses behind me when the door closes behind the others.

I turn to face her with my eyes bulging out of their sockets.

"They grow pot. They grow it, they smoke it, and apparently they eat it. And Connie? They're the nicest people ever."

"This is going to be a disaster," she echoes my

thoughts and I give an affirmatory nod.

"Without a doubt. Now help me get coffee ready for everyone."

Right before we walk out with everything we'll need, Connie holds me back.

"Hey, do you think they brought extra?"

"Muffins?"

"No, pot."

⸻

"That went well."

Dimas climbs into bed behind me, immediately hauling me into his body I discover is blissfully naked.

He's right. That disaster I'd been waiting for never really happened.

As it turns out Max and my dad have an appreciation for vintage cars in common, something they discovered when pulling chairs out of the garage, where apparently Dimas has a vintage 1964 Mustang hiding under a tarp. I had no idea.

Britt hung mostly with the guys while they spent most of the day tinkering around with the car, since it's apparently still a work in progress. Bummer. I was looking forward to taking it for a spin.

Ana and my mom bonded over food, albeit from completely different directions. All was well until Ana asked Connie if she was perhaps sick. Said she read a darkness in my sister's aura. That drew my mother's attention and brought up Connie's asshole husband.

Apparently, Connie had to explain how she came to be staying at my house without me, and bit the bullet even before they showed up here this morning. It had not gone well, judging by Mom's pleas for my sister to reconsider what she might have done differently to avoid this outcome. That had me jump to Connie's defense. I told Mom, even if years of verbal abuse were in any way excusable—which they aren't— beating and kicking Connie so violently she had to go to the ER certainly wouldn't be.

"Other than a few little hiccups, I'd have to agree."

"Will your sister be okay?"

My parents insisted she come and stay with them, but I told her she could stay at my place as long as she wanted. The old Connie and the new Connie seemed to struggle over that, but she ended up making the correct decision and staying right here in Grand Junction. Even if it's only temporary.

"She will be. I think she's made of sterner stuff than she even realized."

Dimas presses a kiss on my shoulder.

"Just like her sister," he mumbles, his hand tugging up on my nightshirt.

"What are you doing?" I twist my head to catch his eyes as his fingers find me naked underneath. His hand clenches on my hip as I hear him curse under his breath. Then he slips a few digits between my legs, finding me wet for him already.

"Finishing what you started this morning," he answers hoarsely.

"I'm on board with that."

I moan when he dips a finger inside and wantonly open my legs for him.

"God, you're so perfect," he growls, rolling me on my back and settling his hips in the cradle of mine.

"You're blinded by love." I look into his eyes and see right down to the soul of him.

"I'm fucking helpless with love for you," he whispers, and my eyes fill with tears.

"Ditto," I manage before his mouth descends on mine, kissing me with such conviction, it leaves no question to his feelings for me.

Then he gently slides inside me, filling me body and soul.

CHAPTER 30

DIMAS

"YOU SURE YOU'LL be okay?"

We're parked out front of the shelter with Twister, who was supposed to be on the back seat, with her paws on the console in between us, tongue lolling.

"I'm fine. My throat is fine; the dog is fine. We'll be fine," she says rolling her eyes. "You're overprotective."

"I'm cautious with very precious cargo," I fire back. "Sue me."

The corner of her mouth twitches and she finally gives in to the smile. Then she reaches over and puts a hand on mine.

"Honey…I promise I'll be careful, but you have to promise to let up a little. Driving me to work every day is not an option. You have work to get to and so do I."

I wasn't happy she was ready to go back to the shelter today, but she conceded I could drive her and pick her up. Apparently only today.

"You let Connie use your vehicle, though."

"And she can keep it. I'm signing it over to her; she needs wheels. I've got some money saved up and I've had my eye on a cute Kia Soul. I'm thinking lime green. Maybe Rosie wants to go shopping with me."

I twist in my seat and look at her with disbelief.

"Kia Soul? Hell no. First of all, those things are cookie tins; one tiny bump and it'll crumple into origami artwork. Secondly, you're not taking Rosie. I'm car shopping with you and we focus on safety, fuck color and fuck cute. We go tonight."

"Okay."

Wait. That capitulation was far too easy and she looks much too pleased with herself. Have I just been had? I would've been happy with the status quo, driving her wherever she needs to go, but suddenly I find myself insisting on taking her car shopping. Tonight, no less.

I reach over and tag her behind her neck, pulling her toward me. Twister takes immediate advantage of the proximity of our faces and we're both rewarded with excited licks and a hefty whiff of dog breath. I nudge her back a bit so I can touch the tip of my nose to Willa's, staring her down

"You just manipulated me," I accuse her.

Her loud peal of laughter, as she tilts her head back, rolls over me like the warm sun on the first day of spring.

"That was easier than I thought." She grins smugly, her dancing brown eyes fixed on mine.

Only one thing to do. I tilt my head and kiss that smirk off her face until I can feel her whimper in my mouth.

"Fuck, but I love you."

Her hand comes up and strokes along my jaw and down my beard.

"Love you too, Dimas."

We clearly wore out the dog's patience and she starts whining, nudging her face between ours.

"What time do you want me to pick you up?" I ask her, scratching Twister's head absentmindedly.

"Probably five. I'll have a little catching up to do."

"Five it is."

She leans closer to give me a peck on the lips before hopping out of the truck, taking Twister with her. I don't drive off until I see both of them disappear into the building.

I spend the fifteen minutes it takes me to get to the office thinking about all the ways my life has changed in the relatively short time I've known Willa. How I can no longer imagine waking up every morning without feeling her warm body snuggled against me, her long hair tickling my face, the soft puffs of air escaping between her luscious lips. How we seem to easily move in each other's space, without it feeling crowded or oppressive. How content and relaxed she makes me feel, even as we deal with a house full of our collective, somewhat dysfunctional families.

She moves through life with an ease, a calm confidence, that seems to rub off on me in the best of ways. Her sharp mind, her generous heart, her sexy as fuck body. I've never felt so perfectly connected to another human being. It's both exhilarating and terrifying. I used to scoff at the concept of needing someone else to feel complete, but not anymore.

With Willa I feel like a better version of myself. A more rounded version. Life is less black and white, less rigid angles and hard edges. She smoothes and softens those.

My instinct is to shield her from the world, keep her safely tucked away under my control for fear of losing her, but the truth is; her independence, her fearlessness, her capacity for trust, are what made me fall in love with her.

"Good morning, Lena."

Our assistant slash office manager lifts her head in surprise.

"Have you been drinking already?"

I grin at her. I'm not known around the office for my particularly sunny disposition in the morning.

"Just high on life, Lena, just high on life."

"Well, you tell her thanks for me, will ya?"

I'm still smiling when I walk into our office space, Jake and Bree already at their desks looking up at me. I spot Radar through the large window into his office, his shoulders hunched as he's working on his computers.

"What did I miss?"

Bree is the first to answer.

"Your brother has Chief Underwood in his office."

"What's he doing here?" I pull out my chair and sit down.

"Not sure," Bree answers just as the door to Yanis' office opens and both men walk out.

Underwood nods, mumbling, "Morning," as he heads toward the reception area, my brother behind him.

All three of us crane our necks to see them shaking hands at the end of the hallway, Yanis watching the other man leave before he turns around and heads back this way.

"What was that all about?" Jake is the first to ask.

"Hang on," Yanis says, walking toward Radar's door and opening it. "Got a minute?"

"Sure," I hear him mumble.

Yanis takes a corner of Jake's desk to perch on, while Radar opts to stay standing, leaning with his back against the wall.

"Chief Underwood just found out last night the entire Grand Junction Police Department is under investigation by the FBI. Apparently, in addition to Bergland and Cairns, there are at least two other officers and one more detective who were implicated in interviews the FBI conducted with Brantley Parker. Aside from taking responsibility for Arthur Hicks' death as a result of a fight he arranged, and ordering the hit on Willa Smith, the doctor is hoping to make a deal by throwing everyone else under the bus."

"Holy shit," Bree hisses.

"What about the other dead guy?" I want to know.

"The one Willa was suspected for?"

"Parker claims that was his cousin, Ron Midwood, who was caught by the old man while riffling through Willa's office."

"Conveniently blaming the murder on the dead suspect," Jake observes dryly.

"Exactly. No way to know what actually happened there," Yanis agrees. "Still, good news in terms of the investigation into the fight ring; they've been able to pick up most of the major players and have apparently disabled the organization, but the tying up of loose ends will likely be months yet. The news is not so good for the GJPD."

"I'd say that's debatable," I suggest. "If it means weeding out the bad seeds, it may end up being a positive thing."

"He's got a point," Radar agrees.

"As true as that may be, it stands to be a long fucking process, and Underwood wants to do an internal cleanup as quickly as possible before the morale of the department erodes altogether."

"And he wants our help for that?" Bree asks. "Isn't that highly irregular?"

"Yes, it is," Yanis confirms. "However, we've just been officially hired as security consultants to the GJPD, with the blessing of the Feds. Just had Williams on a conference call in my office. The caveat is that any and all findings are promptly reported to him. He's as eager to bring this case, along with the resulting investigation into the GJPD, to as fast as possible conclusion."

"Wow. That's a new one," Jake comments. "Sounds like a fuck load of work."

"It is. Which isn't a bad thing. I'd like to see if we can convince Shep and Kai to sign on at least for a contract term, if not permanently. I have a feeling this is gonna raise our profile in the marketplace once all is said and done."

He's right; this could be very good for us. Maybe we won't have to take on shitty protection details like Mercedes Rockton or her daddy to pay the bills again.

Life is looking up.

WILLA

"How is she doing?" Rosie asks, indicating Twister when we pass her office after the group session.

I let Twister roam free in the meeting room, and she seemed to sense which of the men needed a little affection during the difficult session. The events of the past couple of months had taken their toll on the shelter residents. The erosion of trust, fear, the sense of betrayal discovering FBI Agent Dave Williams had infiltrated what they'd come to think of as a safe haven.

It's going to take months to rebuild what was destroyed, but I have a feeling Twister—and maybe a few other dogs like her—could really help with this.

"She did great. Dogs are so incredibly perceptive and attuned to emotion and energy, she seemed to catch on to any distress before I could."

As if knowing she's the topic of conversation, Twister slips around the desk, putting her head on Rosie's lap and gently sniffs her baby bump.

"Good. I know we were going to move slowly on this, but I wonder if, with the current unrest in the house, adopting one or two dogs now might actually help to create some stability for the guys?"

I take a chair across from her.

"Yeah, I can see that. Let me talk to Brad, see if he's ready to take this on. Maybe it's a good idea to take him with me to the Humane Society tomorrow."

"Makes sense, and I'll see what I can do about raising some funds for their care."

"Actually, I have some ideas for that. My sister is in town for a while and she used to organize fundraisers for her daughter's school. Let me see if she has some ideas," I suggest.

I was thinking about this over the weekend, wondering whether my sister could be convinced to stick around town. It would mean finding a new school for Britt, but she was going into high school anyway. Of course we haven't heard a thing from Jim, and Connie isn't ready to tackle that mountain yet, but this fundraiser may at least give her back the sense of purpose she seems to have lost somewhere along the line.

"If she wants to take it on, I'm all for it," Rosie concedes with a smile. "Which brings me to our last dilemma; we need someone to replace Ron. We're spread thin as we are, with a lot of responsibility on your back, which is only gonna get worse when this baby gets here. I hope to stay healthy and keep working until then, but you never know what those last weeks bring. Plus, I plan to take at least six months of maternity leave."

"You should. Take time to enjoy her. We'll sort things out here."

"I'd feel better if we have something already in place. Now, I have an idea, but I want to pass it by you first. My friend, Hillary, is an RN who has lots of experience working with Alzheimer's patients. I know we wanted someone with a psychology degree, but I thought—"

"That's perfect," I interrupt. "I mean, it would actually be better to have someone who could also assess physical health. Is she looking for something?"

"She hasn't said anything, but I know she's not happy where she is so could maybe be convinced."

I snicker at the fake-as-hell innocent look on Rosie's face. I see I'm not the only one plotting here.

The moment I get back to my office, I put in a call to Steve at the Humane Society to see if they currently have any dogs that might fit the profile of what we'd be looking at for the shelter. After that I go in search of Brad, finding him in his usual spot between meals in the dining room.

"What is a good time for you to go look at a few dogs with me tomorrow?" I ask, trying not to give him the option of refusing. I truly believe this may do wonders for him and I really like Brad. I want him to thrive.

"Tomorrow?"

"Yeah. Had a tough group session today, my friend. This shit show has left some damage in its wake, and I really think pursuing this idea of companion dogs will be good for everyone."

It's shameless manipulation and I'm not one bit sorry for it. I'm afraid the man won't make decisions based on what might be good for him, but there's not a doubt in my mind he'd do anything to make the life of others the best it can be. That's why I'm not surprised when he gives me a time after lunch.

All in all I've had a good day when Dimas picks me up at five and drives me straight to a Subaru dealership.

"Who says I want a Subaru?"

He throws me a side-glance as he pulls his truck into a parking space.

"The Outback is high enough to give you better visibility, it's one of the 2020 top safety picks, it retains its value well, it doesn't come in ridiculous colors, and it has extra headroom in the front," he rattles off.

I have to chuckle at the color remark, I guess he didn't feel so hot about the lime green. It's clear he's done his homework, though, and I decide not to tell him the Outback was one of my top picks. Let him think it's been all his idea.

"Why does it need extra headroom in the front?"

He turns off the engine and twists in his seat.

"For when I'm driving."

My eyebrows shoot up.

"Why would you be driving my vehicle?"

He raises one of his in response.

"When we're both in it, I'll be behind the wheel."

"Why?" I push him a little. I don't really mind. It's a small sacrifice if it makes him feel better, but I can't resist teasing him a little.

He reaches over the console and cups my face in his large hands.

"Because I would risk life and limb to keep you safe."

EPILOGUE

WILLA

"OH MY GODDESS, look at my precious baby."

I'm not sure whether Ana is referring to Jake and Rosie's daughter, Tessa, or Dimas, who is holding her in his big palms, his face as soft as I've ever seen it. Both are equally adorable.

Rosie had Tessa by C-section two days ago. These last few months were tough on her physically. Having a baby at any age is no cakewalk, but apparently even more so when you're over forty.

She'd been exhausted and eventually her doctor put her on bed rest. I'm sure it had as much if not more to do with everything that's happened since opening the shelter. It hasn't exactly been a calm and peaceful time.

Rosie doesn't seem to be the worse for wear, though. Her smile beams and her energy appears to have returned in spades. But she just had major surgery and is not a spring chicken, so Ana—who has been a mother to Jake most of his life, apparently—

drove down to help out for a few weeks.

"Enough hogging, Son," she chastises him, making a grab for the baby.

"Hey, I'm her godfather," he complains.

"And I'm her grandmother. You go have some babies of your own," Ana fires back, having a hold of Tessa and settling back in the couch, the baby nestled on her shoulder in a picture of perfection.

Yanis and Bree already came and went. Well, technically when Yanis came, Bree went, but they're both gone now. We should probably head home soon as well; give the new family some rest.

Home. That's what Dimas's house now represents. Our home.

My sister and niece found theirs at my place. Conveniently close to a great high school for Britt, and not too far from Connie's new job. She still hasn't heard from Jim—not that she's been trying to get in touch with him either—and Britt refuses to have anything to do with her father. I'd hoped Connie would press charges on him, but she was more concerned with getting her feet back under her than to drag out a past she'd rather forget. I have to respect that.

I knew my sister had a spine of steel under there somewhere. Her life as she knew it had been crudely destroyed, and yet, she didn't lick her wounds for long. Dimas arranged for Hank's firm to tackle her divorce and because Connie is too proud to take handouts, she'd offered to work off any lawyer's fees. Since Hank's receptionist was retiring and he'd been looking for someone new, they were able to come to an arrangement that benefited everyone.

Connie and I have an ongoing argument over the rent she feels she should be paying me, but as I've tried to make clear to her, I won't accept a dime until she is well and clear of that bastard.

I'm proud of her. Proud of the way she holds her own with our parents. Especially Mom, who still occasionally tries to convince her perhaps going back to Jim is the better option. I'm pretty sure it's because Mom wouldn't have the strength it takes to reinvent herself, the way Connie is. I think she forgets my sister is also a part of our father, who is all steel.

As far as I know, Jim has not been in touch with our parents either, and something tells me he's wise not to go there. At least when it comes to my father, judging by the barely contained rage in his eyes when Jim's name comes up. Dad may not be warm and loving with his daughters, but that clearly doesn't mean he'll sit by and let a man use his fists on them.

Good to know.

"We should probably head out," Dimas says, drawing me from my thoughts.

"Yeah."

I glance over at Jake, who can't seem to keep his eyes off his wife, looking at her with such reverence; it brings tears to my eyes. She's lucky, and so am I.

I look up at Dimas, standing beside my chair.

My God. His gaze on me is a carbon copy. Both tender and hot, opening a view right into his soul. For me. My emotions run so deep, they spill over onto my cheeks.

He smiles softly, brushing the tears from my eyes.

"Come on, sweetheart. Let me take you home."

After hugs and goodbyes, plus a quick kiss for Tessa with a sniff of that uniquely delicious baby smell, we walk to my SUV.

Dimas opens the door for me and waits until I'm seated before he leans in, dropping a kiss on my lips. Then he rounds the hood and I wait until he gets in behind the wheel.

"Honey?"

"Mmm."

"I'm almost forty."

"End of the month, I know," he confirms, throwing a smile my way.

"Forty is old."

He turns to me struggling to contain laughter I can see in his eyes.

"Thanks, sweetheart. I'm forty-one, I know how old it is," he says, suddenly reaching over and sliding a hand along the side of my face. I instinctively lean into it.

"I just thought, maybe..." I let my voice trail off.

I don't have the guts to ask after all. Shit, we've been together for four months, inseparable almost from the start, and somehow the subject has never come up. I'm terrified what his answer will be if I finish the question.

His second hand comes up to frame my face.

"Willa, sweetheart, if you're trying to ask me if I'm ready for a baby, the answer is easy. Fuck yeah."

THE END

ABOUT THE AUTHOR

USA Today bestselling author Freya Barker loves writing about ordinary people with extraordinary stories.

Driven to make her books about 'real' people; she creates characters who are perhaps less than perfect, each struggling to find their own slice of happy, but just as deserving of romance, thrills and chills in their lives.

Recipient of the ReadFREE.ly 2019 Best Book We've Read All Year Award for "Covering Ollie, the 2015 RomCon "Reader's Choice" Award for Best First Book, "Slim To None", and Finalist for the 2017 Kindle Book Award with "From Dust", Freya continues to add to her rapidly growing collection of published novels as she spins story after story with an endless supply of bruised and dented characters, vying for attention!

freyabarker.com

If you'd like to stay up to date on the latest news and upcoming new releases, sign up for my newsletter: subscribepage.com/Freya_Newsletter